DEAR THIEF

Samantha Harvey

Dear Thief

JONATHAN CAPE
LONDON

Published by Jonathan Cape 2014

2 4 6 8 10 9 7 5 3 1

First published in Great Britain in 2014 by
Jonathan Cape
Random House, 20 Vauxhall Bridge Road,
London SW1V 2SA

Supported using public funding by the Arts Council England

www.vintage-books.co.uk

Addresses for companies within The Random House Group Limited
can be found at:
www.randomhouse.co.uk/offices.htm

The Random House Group Limited Reg. No. 954009

A CIP catalogue record for this book
is available from the British Library

ISBN 9780224101721

Typeset in Adobe Jenson MM by Palimpsest Book Production Limited,
Falkirk, Stirlingshire
Printed and bound in Great Britain by
CPI Group (UK) Ltd, Croydon CR0 4YY

'I'll write to you. A super-long letter, like in an old-fashioned novel.'

Haruki Murakami, *After Dark*

December 2001

I n answer to a question you asked a long time ago, I have, yes, seen through what you called the gauze of this life. But to tell you about it I will have to share with you a brief story.

One night in the hot summer of '76 I was staying with my grandmother, who was dying, and I was reading a book of Buddhist stories. My grandmother was asleep in the rocking chair, inhaling with feathered breaths. Her exhales were smooth and liquid, which seems to me now the surest sign of a life's exit – when the act of giving away air is easier than that of accepting it. In fact I knew she might be facing her last night but I didn't do much to cling to those moments. I was sitting on the sofa in my underwear with my legs drawn to the side, watching her for minutes at a time while the breaths fluttered in through the dignified gap between her lips. She was sweating around her brows, and at the base of her throat. I remember vividly her sapphire pendant in the dip there where the skin was moist.

My grandmother had gone beyond the point of caring about death. She'd phoned me the previous night to say she was on her way to the ever-after and could do with somebody to feed the dog; I never did know what she thought would happen to the dog after she was gone, though maybe she had no concept of after, or no stomach for it. When I had spoken to her I called my parents at their hotel in Kerala in India and told my father that his mother was dying; I packed a small number of things, including the book of Buddhist stories on my parents' bookshelves, and made the journey to London the next morning.

It had meant walking at first light from Morda to Oswestry, to catch a bus to Shrewsbury, to catch a train to London. I went along the lane that you and I had walked so many times, from my house to Morda village, one-and-a-half wingspans wide and hedges of six feet, crossing brooks and dipping away from sight only to appear again in triumph five hundred yards later, shaking the valley off its back. Gently monstrous; roaring in the glory of spring or summer. This is how I think of that landscape when I stop to remember – although I know, before you raise a sceptical brow, the over-optimism of memory.

My mother had told me to take money from the cloisonné box on the kitchen dresser for the train fare. I was twenty-four but I had almost nothing of my own. This is what happens when there are cloisonné boxes in the kitchen and folded leather wallets in the pocket of a father who so brims with a love he can't fathom that he must give and give in order not to suffocate with the excess – a daughter who isn't so much spoilt as made resourceless and who lives life in a state of constant guilty gratitude. Though happy all the same; I wouldn't want you to think otherwise.

It would take at least two days for my parents to get back from India; that was why I left Morda early, because it was me, and me alone, who would see my grandmother leave this world. That was the first time I ever did something for which somebody else could be truly grateful and is why I remember that walk along the lanes and the journey to London and the sweat on my grandmother's throat. I remember it because it was the first time I felt neither indebted nor childlike, as if the whole kindly legacy that was my parents had been removed from the equation and left me freshly sprung on the sofa in the heat of the evening and the presence of death – defiant of death, but somehow courting it too. Now and again my grandmother would wake up, look at me, smile vaguely, then sleep.

The Buddhist stories I was reading that night were about discipline and faith and letting go of the things that are liable to pass. There is the man who grieves so much for the son he thinks has died that he refuses to accept, years later, the man who returns and calls him Father. Do not cling so hard to your own version of the truth, says Buddha, else you will fail to see the real truth when it comes knocking. There is the story of teacups: the student asks the master why Japanese teacups are so delicate and easy to break. The master tells the student that it isn't that the teacups are too delicate, but that the person who drinks from them is too heavy-handed. It's not for teacups or grass or mountains to change, says Buddha. It is for us to adapt to what is. Do not clutch, do not judge, let pass. Everything is impermanence.

It wasn't at this point that I saw through your *gauze of life*, though; actually, far from it. In my grandmother's hot, silent room, nothing had ever seemed more permanent. When I was a child I had played on the floor of this room, shifting tiny figurines of soldiers, horses and goats around invisible territories. I was ringed by the chocolate-brown velvet sofas and biscuit-brown velvet chairs and the standing lamps and occasional tables and the smell of burnt honey that had knotted even into the carpet, the caramel carpet; this is how childhood comes to me, in terms of sweet food lavishly spread, uneaten, slowly going to waste.

Nothing had changed since those days except that everything had degraded and two decades of light had beaten the colours back a shade. But here, the little change only proved the lack of any dramatic one, and it was the same with the dog – the dog that had been here when I was a child was dead, but here was its offspring lying in its shadow by the rockers of the chair, just as always. Don't you think – don't your senses lead you to admit – that nothing has ever been less gauzelike than this great wall of reality we're faced with, day in and out?

In any case, at one point I got up and poured some iced water for my grandmother, and turned out all the lights in the room except for the lamp next to the rocking chair. The pool of sweat at the base of her throat had dried up and her skin had flattened a tone – and I mean it this way, like a piece of music gone off-key. Her eyes were open and she'd taken my hand. 'You'll grow into yourself,' she said, and it was the first sentence she had put together for hours. 'Grow into myself?' I replied. 'Yes – in spite of everything, we've always looked poor, our family, it's the big bones and height and these dirty tans we get, but your mother became quite beautiful in the end, and so will you.' 'Yes,' I said, though I wasn't sure I agreed, either about my mother or about myself. 'Have you fed the dog?' 'Yes, Nana, don't worry.' 'He gets manipulative if he's not fed.' 'Really, what does he do?' 'He plays mind games, he gets witty.' 'How so?'

She closed her eyes and shook her head faintly. 'Well, it's okay,' I said, 'I've fed him.' 'Where is he?' she asked. 'Down here by your feet.' 'He's alright?' 'He's out like a light.' 'He's *alight*?' 'No – he's asleep.' 'Asleep?' 'Yes, fast asleep.'

Then her brow crumpled and the feeling was that she'd lost her footing suddenly and tripped another yard down towards death. It is hard to explain these things now, they sound invented, yet this is exactly how it felt – the tripping downwards towards death. I got the book and read her a very short story called 'The Burden', and as I read I could see the scene the two of us made:

two women, one, I suppose, in the prime of life and one about to leave life altogether, their dark hair and louring (so Nicolas once said) features making them unmistakably related, one dressed in beige and the other hardly dressed at all; my grandmother was right, my mother's side of the family had always had a degenerate and hungry look. My father's genes were more refined, but recessive. I think by that age, twenty-four, I still hadn't stopped hoping to turn out like him.

You know it is said, and has been proven, that people are more likely to die when they are left alone, a fact I didn't know then but must have sensed in some way, because during my reading of 'The Burden', which was not more than a couple of paragraphs long, my grandmother closed her eyes again and prepared herself for what it was she now saw coming. I did wait; I waited by her feet for an hour and did nothing but hear her breaths and pre-empt the last one. Sometimes there was a gap of fifteen or twenty seconds after the exhale when I was so sure it was the end that I'd grip her hand tighter in farewell – and then a sudden gasp and the air would go back in again. Each time this happened I became more tense and almost irritated until it felt as though I were willing her to die faster. So eventually I kissed her forehead, put on a dress and took myself outside.

She lived by the river a way downstream from Woolwich Arsenal and upstream from the old firing range at Rainham Marshes. A pacifist sandwiched by war, she used to say. She had a grand, decrepit terraced house in one of the wharfs before they were demolished and turned into what they call luxury dwellings. When we were children she would climb down the bouldered flood wall with us and take us onto the beach, and we'd walk or run in swirls following the oil that had marbled the mud and sand – and we weren't to tell our parents, who had forbidden us to go anywhere near that quick and filthy shore.

Because the summer was hot and the river low I was able to walk right along the water's edge that night of my grandmother's death. If you want to guarantee staying alive, my grandmother used to insist, you must stay high on the foreshore so that you don't get sucked into the mud. I went a long way east towards the marshes, walking an imaginary plank in the dusk.

Across the river there was the open scrubland and what looked like a huge shadow cast by nothing – the Gallions Hotel, where, in times past, people would stay before getting on steamships to India, to China. Just here the Thames is half river, half sea. A thousand pale horses frothing at the bit. It is close to a mile wide, they say, and usually churning and milky, with a driving wind; they also say that there is a primordial forest under the water where it bends at Gallions Reach and that the current swells over rotted upturned roots.

But on this night it was differently milky, it was low and languid as if basking. Maybe this was when the gauze started to show itself and things began to lose their ordinariness, with the moon fattening in the night heat and everything quietly expanding. On its south bank there is a stretch, or at least there was then, where a patch of woods and thicket comes all the way down to the shore so that, with the warmth, the sand, the silver light and the curious stillness, you feel like you could be somewhere tropical. A shifting, a partial collapse; I don't know. I might have just as easily been with my parents in India, or they might have stepped out of the trees barefoot onto the beach, my mother with her tan and Amazonian height, my father quiet and rangy behind her.

Just after the trees the river kinks right and the beach is narrow or sometimes gone, and every time I had walked that far before I hadn't been able to get any further. You can climb up from there and then drop back down to the shoreline after the kink, where the beach is wide, maybe at its widest, which is what I'd always done. That night was the first time I'd walked right round the corner of the river, and it was there that I found – or anyhow found myself walking on – something that wasn't sand or stone, but bones.

When you trod on them they gave a civil clink like a knife tapping a fork or a porcelain cup shaking in a saucer. They were hip bones, femurs, shin bones, tiny pivoting joints, a ball without a socket and a socket without a ball, the smooth plates of kneecaps, long scooped jawbones that belonged to something probably bovine, or maybe equine. It wasn't a scattering, either, but a pile that had lodged itself in the moonlit sedge by the flood wall.

I put some of them out on the sand. They had a low, resigned calm. Nicolas has since wondered if they were from an old glue factory that had been upriver, on the Isle of Dogs, and had washed up at the kink where the current is forced to shift direction. Just a guess, though. Possibly they had sat on that shelf of the riverbed for years and had only been exposed by the low tide. Or maybe they hadn't been washed up but had been dumped there, though who would bother? And what for? One way or another they must have been in the Thames for a long time, given how smoothed off they were by water and how hollowed and porous, as much shell as bone.

They were greyish-white and washed clean. These most functional of things, but so abstract when you look at them out of context. They could be sculptures. So I mused for a while on how beautiful they were, with a kind of self-conscious appreciation that annoys me, because really I am only thinking of how sensitive I am to be able to see their beauty. I scooped them up into my dress. I was overcome by them. Everybody is aware that the Thames is a great swallower of bodies and much loved by the suicidal, and that corpses and parts of corpses do wash up on its shores – but this wasn't the case here. May it be known that when I took them I knew without doubt that they were not human, and that if they had been human my feeling wouldn't have been what it was.

I filled the sling made by the lap of my dress and walked home to my grandmother's like that, with my skirt gathered up in my fist. My grandmother was dead when I got back, as I knew she would be. I poured my hoard onto the bed in the spare room she always kept ready for family visits, and then I sat at her feet and put my head in her lap. My parents later railed at me for leaving her there in the rocking chair all night and said I should have reported her death straight away, but I saw no rush, I see none now, and I would not do it differently if I had the time again. Her death was so powerful and calm a presence in the room – the same calm I mentioned in relation to the bones on the shore – that it felt as though her life and all its interminable errands and demands and dramas had waited for this ecstatic moment of its own end, so that it could revel a little in that end, so that it could know that all of those seemingly interminable things did eventually terminate. And it could be comforted by that and rest in its own familiar space in the rocking chair by the lamp with its dog, for a while longer at least.

And so, this gauze. When you talked about it before, did you mean that sometimes, very occasionally, everything that had appeared very solid about the world loses substance? I mean, one is sitting there perhaps, on the bed on a hot night with crossed legs, and there is an inversion. One feels – or I should say, I feel – as if I could put my hand through the window glass or the wall as easily as through fog, and yet I can barely lift my arm and move it through air. This is because it seems that there is no point. I seem to be only air myself, and there is no point in shunting air through air. Nothing to achieve in that. Is this the kind of thing you mean?

For example, I look at the bones I collected in what might have been a dream – except it cannot have been a dream because the bones are there in front of me – and I do not recognise them as bones at all, but as arbitrary groupings of matter that have no past or future or meaning of any kind. My own bare knee fits this category too, and I stare for half an hour at the orange street light that glows off the curve of the kneecap.

I feel no grief at the death of my grandmother because life as I'd always known it shows itself now as only the negative space made by a much vaster reality. When I think of my grandmother in the room directly below, fundamental and as still as a root, she is perfect in my mind's eye and the more my mind looks, the more she too becomes a grouping of matter, unassigned and timeless. To say she is dead is senseless, just as senseless as it is to say I myself am alive.

If this could be one example of seeing through the gauze of life, then the answer to your question is resoundingly yes, I have seen through it. I think I sat in a trancelike state for hours that night and it was only when the sun came up that I moved. Then I flannelled my grandmother's face with cold water gently, as if not to wake her, and called the hospital. It was about six-thirty or seven in the morning that she was finally taken to the mortuary.

As for 'The Burden', the story that became the last spoken words my grandmother heard, even now it springs so energetically to mind, and it goes as so: Two monks are walking down from the foothills of the Himalayas to the nearest village. When they reach the village it is raining and by the time they head back up towards the foothills with their bag of walnuts, rice, dhedo, vegetables, spices and the like, the streets are flooding and turning to mud. A beautiful woman is standing on the other side of the road trying to cross. The older monk passes his bag of shopping to the other, takes off his shoes and walks straight through the puddles to the woman, then he lifts her and carries her across. Later that evening after prayer the young monk seems worried and almost shifty and he keeps looking at his companion as if there is something he needs to say. Finally the older monk asks what troubles him and he responds, 'We aren't supposed to touch the opposite sex and yet earlier today you carried that woman right across the road.' The older monk thinks about this for a moment and it looks like he might have no way of defending himself. But then he glances over each shoulder, opens his arms to show how empty they are and he replies, 'Brother, I left her at the roadside where I put her down – it's you who is still carrying her.'

On the whole I do not think of you any more. So it was strange when you came into my mind like that, standing over my bed with your spine stacked tall like a wonder of the world and with the thighs of someone who hasn't eaten for a year, hovering as if you wanted something.

Thanks to this I am at my escritoire at just gone four in the morning with my hand welded to a pen with a split nib, suddenly curious about you after years of an incuriosity you might call callous. It's been a mild and dreary Christmas but now, on Boxing Day night, it has started snowing, and I've had to go and find a blanket from the airing cupboard. As soon as the first flake of snow fell I thought of you, as it landed on the pane in that ludicrous wet collapse that removes all the mystery. I tried to put you from my mind but you wouldn't go, so I got up. That was at about midnight, when the music from the jazz club a few doors down was coming to an end, and it was almost as if the first flake fell on the last note.

I sat on the edge of the bed trying to breathe in squares, the way a yogi or swami will tell you – breathe in for five seconds, hold for five seconds, out for five, hold for five, in for five. It made me thirsty. Does she think it was worth it? I wondered. This is what came to me when I pictured you there. Not: Is she happy, is she free, is she alive? – no. Does she think it was worth it? I would look to your face for an answer, if only I could see, in reality, in the flesh, that face. I got up for water, then for tea, then I sat in the armchair by the window and watched the snow. It has settled so thickly. Have you ever noticed the absolute chaos and panic of snow if you look up and watch it explode out of the sky? And yet it lands with order and without a hush, and sudden wellbeing is bestowed. How so? You can see people's happiness condensing in billows of laughter; the few people who've walked along the street in the last hour from the bars along Goodge Street have all been laughing.

What I mean to say is: I haven't resorted lightly to writing to you. It's just that you appeared so expectantly at my bed earlier that I wondered if what you wanted was an answer to something, and the only vaguely urgent question I could think of you asking in all our long years of knowing each other was about the gauze of life. My hand has cramped in the process of giving it, and I think it is an uncertain start, an overly cautious and laughably sincere start, everything considered. And now actually I realise that far from wanting an answer, you have probably forgotten you ever even asked. It was seventeen years ago, eighteen even; hard enough to remember what happened two thoughts ago, let alone back in a life since lost.

But despite having been up most of the night I'm not tired at all and an energy is coming from somewhere behind me that might be the snow, falling without pattern. I wonder now why I didn't just answer the question when you first asked it. I don't understand myself, or for that matter the passing of time. Seventeen years! Can you credit this? No, nor can I. It's late; I'll make one more tea and go to bed.

I didn't go back to bed. I went out in the snow because it won't stay fresh for long in London. I went along to see Yannis, a Cretan who runs the Greek store on Hunter Street and opens up every day at five a.m. to make his own pitta bread and custard pastries, and we took coffee out onto the road and spelled out SWELTERING in the snow with our tracks – or, I should say, swelt ERING because I did my half upper case, Yannis saved energy by doing his lower, and our halves didn't quite meet. Yannis loves the snow, I remember this from last year. He relishes its crunch, like biting into an apple, he says. He tells me that Crete is never purified by snow and so it grows ever hotter and more corrupt; I say that the snow does not purify but temporarily shrouds, and ends up becoming dirt if it covers dirt – but Yannis is not ready to hear this and tells me I am like his wife, unromantic; like all modern women, passionate as a pot plant.

Before you say it, I know. I swore I would never live in London, but that was because of the Cold War. Nobody would take the time to wipe Morda off the map, and if you are raising a child it is of genuine concern that the place they live is not suddenly wiped off the map. Times are different now that we are not waiting for the Russians to extinguish us, even you have to admit it – and people are different too. I think our hearts do have a chance to warm up a little when not so full of fear, and ever since moving here I have found London to have a kind of sincerity, safety and solidness, like a stout old uncle, like Yannis almost.

There is also of course the jazz club, Jimmie Noone's (Jimmie's, as most people call it, and which I can never help reading, with a certain sadness, as 'Jimmie No one's'), which goes on until one or two in the morning on a Friday and Saturday night. In the summer the saxophone wafts in through the open window, and below that the clarinet, and below that the river of piano. I drop to sleep with birds singing in my throat. There seems to be no specialism; one night it is swing, the next avant-garde, or big band, bebop, ragtime, or Charlie Parker, Nina Simone and Thelonious Monk tribute evenings, 'Ruby, My Dear' played with the tenor saxophone alongside the piano, which makes it far more beautiful to my ears. Countless nights I have gone about life, cooking or reading to the sound of this jazz, and occasionally there will be a singer whose voice will make me stop and listen, or stop and sing, or stand with hands on hips racking my brains for the name of the tune, or look out of the window as if I might be able to see the sound. Sometimes people passing by will dance together in the street, tipping from foot to foot if swing, or swirling limbs if Latin, something like 'Blue Bossa'. As I can confirm from my living-room vigils, people often stop to dance to 'Blue Bossa'. I can imagine you doing just the same. And at those times, amongst others, I will think to myself: London, God bless you! For the summers that are warmer and stickier than in the countryside, and for all this free music. And being here then will seem like a homecoming.

You will know the escritoire I sit at to write this – the one that used to be in the hallway in my parents' house, with its tambour top that no longer rolls smoothly, and the six miniature drawers full of pointless things my father found and could never bear to part with. I inherited the desk from him, and I have not got rid of those things. I am sorry to tell you that my parents both died by the mid-nineties, my father first, then my mother three years later. Really, they were better than me in so many ways – richer, happier, more travelled, more generous and loving, more panoramic of mind. Since being in my hands the escritoire is a mess. Of course, it was never a mess in their hands, except inside the drawers where it couldn't offend the eye. So I have invented a foolish little measure for keeping some order, to do right by my father all these years beyond the grave (in the way we do keep trying, all our lives, to do right by our parents, whether we know it or not): there is a piece of Roman jet, a conch and the oval of amber you gave me that sits on the beech like a spoonful of honey; these three are always on the desk somewhere, gauging the mess as groynes gauge the height of the tide, and if I can see them I know – with a sense of daughterly relief – that the mess is not winning.

I've lived in this flat for two years, which is not long in terms of belonging to a place but long enough to be exempt from the charge of passing through. This might account for the look that I know is often on my face, that I catch sometimes in the mirror, a look of wary attachment, suspicious belonging. But then maybe the look is not that at all but just the general cross-purpose muddle of the ageing face in which all kinds of incompatible things have collided. Surprise, torment, pleasure, peace, disillusionment. All of these separately and at once. And on the subject of surprises – and I would like you to contain your mirth and judgement if you can – I have taken full-time work in a care home; maybe this explains the wary look, suspicious of death perhaps, or what awful ambush waits for our bodies around the corner.

You are opening your mouth to object about this care-home

job (like some born-again Christian foisting your light upon the world, you will say), but what of it, my friend? For once you have no right or means to reply, and so I continue. Until I moved here I was living in my parents' old house, which I inherited from them with the escritoire and everything else. So large and alive with their successes and love – but you know the house was too big for one person, too big for two people even, and when Teddy and I were there we thought we could hear it expanding around us. When Teddy left home for university four years ago I stayed on for a couple of years until it became unbearable; then I sold it and came to this flat.

Even before Teddy left we had resorted to living mostly in the kitchen. The red room had fallen out of use since a family of starlings got bold and moved into the chimney stack, and in hindsight I think that was the beginning of their dominion. Those rare occasions when we did use the room the starlings' occupancy meant we couldn't light the fire, and so the room was for summer days only, doors open wide to the moths, dust, flies, mice and spiders; Teddy set up his tripod and photographed the room's gradual surrender to nature, a process that completed itself beautifully during the second winter of the starlings' stay, when the birds came down through the open damper and got into the house. He caught shots of them in flight above the dresser, in front of the television, in front of the mirror above the fireplace, and it was that one, that single fortunate shot of a starling and its reflection in flight in an Art Deco mirror, that got him his place on a photography course at university and prompted me – now that my only child had, as they say, flown the nest and I was alone – to leave the village.

I bought this place without looking any further: not so far from Russell Square, much beyond what I could afford, but I had looked on the outskirts and it seemed to me that it wouldn't do; so I had to use some of the nest egg I'd set aside for Teddy from the sale of my parents' house in Morda, and even then I couldn't say that what I bought is anything more than basic. It is one of those many London Regency buildings that lost its decency a good hundred and fifty years ago and was carved into flats, mine having two small bedrooms, a windowless kitchen, a big, light living room, but then this, this magnificent thing – a stained-glass window at the back, in the bathroom, with the image of a hummingbird braking hard at a fuchsia, all electric blues, greens and reds, an uplifting sight when the evening sun comes through and one that makes me think always of Teddy's photograph.

Playing cards, hand after hand. Bending willow, shaking boughs for apples, reading erotic scenes from our parents' novels. Drawing one another's faces. Drawing on one another's backs. Knees up in winter by the fire, looking at your father's sketches of plants and your mother's photographs of you as a baby clenching your fists. Bolting down the lanes at Morda, hollering, Come on then! It was all about your need to throw yourself at every corner in defiance of what was around it, and so we bolted and ran, and even when we walked it was fast, and even when we sat slouched over a task you were leaning into it, showing your back to whatever doubt said that you were not capable.

You were going to walk east to west across America, from Rhode Island to a place called Eureka in a straight line. One day you would lay out a map of North America and say, Done that. I would crop my hair like a field of winter wheat, and you were going to rewrite the Talmud in rhyming couplets or otherwise in limericks and publish it as a new religion. We would pave one of Morda's fields with slabs of granite inscribed over and over with our names. I was going to marry below me and live on love. You would not shave, or wear dresses. You were going to accept death long before you died. I was going to sing: Mozart, Handel,

Fauré, Joan Baez, Edith Piaf. I was going to sing and sing, and you were going to compose your new religion and not brush your hair or be precious about your body, which was given you as a strange gift that had come without a label and for whom you had nobody to thank.

Bolting down the lanes late for school, bolting down those same lanes year upon year late or drunk on your parents' firewater, which we stole and replaced with lightly brewed tea, knowing it might be years before they noticed. Breaking out like horses and shouting *Starka!* after the name on the bottle because we liked the way it sundered the Shropshire calm. You brushed off male interest whenever it came, scarce though young men were in our village of farmers and ex-miners. You looked at men sidelong and would respond to their interest by saying placidly, 'Thank you, no' and lighting a cigarette.

Your brother would hand over 50mg of phenylpropanolamine, or 40mg of amphetamine, and he would tell us with a liquid tongue that your father's assiduous cataloguing of English flora was a final treachery. He had stolen – confiscated – your father's handmade collections. I remember him (the dull clang as he sat on the piano keyboard, and the back of his shorn head in the mirror behind him, which didn't seem to belong to the same person as the face, which was wide and kind and always appeared to know something we didn't – this is how I always think of him, in two mismatched halves) – I remember him leafing through the pad of faint sketches of dandelions, campion, honeysuckle, aquilegia, love-in-a-mist, flicking the pages with the back of his hand as he talked about his friends in Lithuania who were staying to fight for the cause. Because it was one thing to escape communism as your parents had done, but another to deny where you had come from, to start drawing dandelions neatly labelled in the bottom left *Taraxacum officinale*. It was true, I suppose, that when he showed us the botanical catalogues your father had made of Lithuania's native hepatica, meadow rue, yarrow, gladioli, the drawings were more eager, the ink more mutinously pressed into the page; because they were not limp inventories like the English catalogues, but urgently amassed proof of what the Soviets were about to wipe out. To which you, who had left Lithuania as a baby and had never known the place, said uncertainly, 'And yet, who cares?'

Sitting in what would soon become the red room with the fire lit and our 40 or 50 or sometimes 60mg, while my parents were away for their long stints in India escaping the winter. We played hand after hand of Poker, 21, Gin Rummy, All Fives. These were not games but little parlays with fate; I remember the feeling that each card turned was a renewal of luck, that I could continually play myself out of dead-ends and misfortune, like flinging open a series of gates until one led to the great reward, the ultimate boon. We were surrounded, in the red room, by a sense of divine bounty, something mighty to aim at; so it was with this room. An intoxicating place. It was lined with shelves of religious texts – Christian, Jewish, Roman Catholic, Islamic, Buddhist, Hindu: my mother and father could not limit themselves to a single doctrine, they saw the mysticism of faith divide and emblazon itself like a firework, from the books of the Apocrypha to the Hindu moksha, in one explosive rejoicing. And you, marooned in the wet Welsh Borders, rising from our card games erratic and euphoric and irrepressible, plucked books from the shelves, sifted through creeds and, like some creature trying to shake itself dry of the swamp, settled on the Upanishads.

Brava! These raw songs of Hindu philosophy suddenly in your hands. Sitting once more, as we had as children, on the floor by the fire with your elbows on your raised knees, your top half slung forward, crescent-backed in the pose your mother always said would cripple you. Reading: *If everything is in man's body, every being, every desire, what remains when old age comes, when decay begins, when the body falls?* You would turn the two hooped earrings through your left ear in a full rotation as you read, until the lobes flushed crimson.

Cooking haphazard creations; you liked meat. We once tried to kill a rabbit in the garden but we couldn't catch it, and when one of your stones did find its target the poor creature turned a gaze on us that dissolved our appetites – such offended surprise, as if it had expected more of us, and then a moment of cold scrutiny that appraised our souls, and then terror and flight. Let us never do that again, I said, and expected you to dismiss me as sentimental. But you nodded, a certain softness and ruth settling in your pout, and tossed your remaining stones into the hedge.

Cooking pieces of mutton and steak that we found in my mother's freezer, a deep chest of frozen flesh; you would fry the meat and splash fat against the wall while scowling, as if a cold wind were at your face, and then serve it up on plates with nothing but a spoonful of mustard or Crosse & Blackwell pickle or home-made damson chutney. During those winters we ate pounds of fruit that we'd stored from the autumn, from days of footing up ladders in my parents' garden and shaking boughs and shielding our heads against the apple and plum rain.

Evenings spent during the winter that crossed over from 1971–2, painting the large room red on a whim. We painted it in one night with an energy that felt inspired, or at least that was how we pitched it to my parents when they returned home from India a week or two later. 'We felt inspired,' you said. 'Please forgive us, didn't we do a good job?' My mother stood there blooming an Indian health, a slim, calm, tanned radiance of incense and hard-won spirituality, then inspected the edges around the skirting boards and door frames and found in them something that satisfied her sense of perfection. You had finished them with a two-millimetre watercolour brush and had taken swabs of turpentine to every blemished inch of skirting board. My father just regarded me and said, 'You've grown tall, my love.' He looked like a man who'd found a prize, then found it again, again, and whose happiness at life was such that the colour of a wall was of the same benign lack of importance as the birth or death of a star elsewhere in the cosmos.

Then one night the following winter, when they were away again, you took the Safavid vase from the mantelpiece, laid it sideways on its great copper belly on the table and began arranging fruit in the enormity of its mouth. This task took you two hours. First a watermelon, a polished planet filling the opening, and in front of it plums, an apple, a quince, some damsons, some redcurrants that spilt out onto the table. You left it there for two weeks until the melon had collapsed inwards and sent a river of juice over the vase rim, and in this swam the flaccid damsons and the remains of the redcurrants. The apple and quince were withered and furrowed as anxious old brows. The plums were a low mossy outcrop. You pointed at the new darkness behind it all, the darkness that was the inside of the vase and which had been revealed by decay, and when you pointed at it, it was true that it emanated with a kind of force, a ravenousness.

The photograph you took of it was bawdy and bold. You called it *Still Life with Irascible Hole*, after Roger Fenton's infamous *Still Life with Ivory Tankard and Fruit*. Vanitas, you explained, was the art of symbolic still life to represent the passing of transitory things and the emptiness they leave. In Fenton's photograph the fruit was rude with ripeness and the dark opening of the tankard relatively small, like a carp's mouth agape. In yours, the dark opening of the Safavid vase was more a beast mid-roar. In his, the emptiness threatened in the way a beautiful red dawn threatens the day, but in yours the threat was fulfilled and the day was done. His was subtle, but halfway measures have never been for you. It was a photograph that threw death at your face. But all the same it was lovely to look at in all its sepia richness, the glowing of the copper, the glossy juices and shining, sagging pulp that were full of your fearfulness. 'It's yours,' you said. 'For you, my dearest friend, to remind us that our days on Earth are numbered, and the numbers are not that big.' You winked, you flashed a smile. 'Thank you, Nina,' I said.

Us in the tunnel, up the tree, by the fire, in the lane, on the sofa, at the stove, behind the camera, on film, the various nouns and prepositions of our lives over several years. You appearing one day in a cream crochet shawl that your parents had bought you for your twenty-first birthday and which seemed at once to confirm and reinvent you. You sauntered in tall and vulnerable and with an air of magnificent poverty about you, tossed your hair, flung the shawl like a matador his cape, and grinned.

You on the floor by the fire, roasting yourself until the silver cobra that wound up your right forearm began to burn your skin, which prompted you to turn and roast the other side. Your camera by your feet, your dark hair to your waist, your earlobes flushed and your back bent forward. Those strong, rough-skinned hands holding the Upanishads: *What remains when old age comes, when decay begins, when the body falls?*

B ut you looked so old and sad when we saw you last. I am plagued by this – by your crochet shawl, in particular, once creamy as a new lamb; when you came back for the last time it was filthy and torn, but torn in just one place, and this single tear – with the white of your shoulder coming through like some fallen rampart – betrayed a loss of dignity far greater than if you had stood naked in public. You were hunched, and there was something cruel about your face, though, when I think about it now, it might have been a cruelty reflected onto it from the world, and not one coming from within. But then what is the difference, when all's said and done? A face is cruel or it isn't, it lets itself become that way or it doesn't.

Are you better? I am not naive; it seems clear to me that there is something very wrong in a language that uses the same word to mean 'improved' and 'cured'. By better I mean only improved. You telephoned us from the station and I went to collect you. You were standing at the end of the platform with your head down and your weight off one foot, in the way I've seen wounded wolves stand in films like *Once Upon a Time in the West* – not that I have seen this film, but this is how I imagine it to be. It had been almost two years since we had seen you before that. When I got you home and we asked where you had been, you said, 'I've been in an elevator, going up and down.' So we sat you out in the garden at the mossy table and gave you tea, and asked you again. 'I've been in an elevator, looking for love.'

'For two years?' we asked.

'Love is hard to find.'

The garden was blowing with leaves and Nicolas put his elbows on the table with an attempt at anchorage and a seriousness that was almost morbid. He said, 'So did you find it?'

'I didn't find the *one*. But I found a lot of people I wasn't looking for, and I made do.' He asked, 'Who were you looking for?' and you told him, 'Laurence Olivier.'

He stood sharply and walked indoors. Your moods were the stuff of legend, and that day your mood could only be described as dangerous – languorous, facetious, self-absorbed; you were amused by yourself and this was the worst of all possible states, because it was the kind of amusement I imagine Caiaphas felt when he made a deal with the Devil. The amusement is a mask for the wretchedness we feel for striking up an unhappy alliance – in your case this alliance was with yourself, whom you had long thought badly of and were always escaping. But on that day it was as though you had recognised that you owned only yourself, were shipwrecked with yourself, and your mood reflected your disgust at this most desperate, careless misfortune.

Later that evening you went on the train to London and Nicolas went with you. 'I'm getting out' was the last thing you said to me when the two of you left for the station. He came back alone two days later, and that was that where the three of us were concerned.

Get out of what? This mess, this life? I have always wondered – and I will only ask you once – did you manage it, did you get out?

Teddy was here yesterday; his arrival made me put down my pen for the first time in days. He came to visit for the night on his way to see friends for New Year's Eve, but he brought no bags as such, just an extraordinary array of energy drinks and some crash weight-gain powder that he had as pudding with a glass of wine, as part of a prolonged attempt at gaining breadth. He has grown up willowy like my father, without Nicolas' sturdiness – but this strikes me as strange when I write it, because Nicolas was a slender man when younger and hardly (what would you say?) *burly* himself. It's just that, at twenty-two, Teddy is taller than Nicolas ever was and doesn't have that thickset neck and jaw, and the prominent Adam's apple, the sheer masculinity, and it bothers him. Wrongly, but all the same.

The thing is that I see very little of Teddy lately, and when he visited this time it was to tell me that I will see even less of him still. In four days, January 3rd, he is taking his camera and travelling around eastern Europe for a few months to photograph the forests, to travel to Lithuania in particular. Perhaps to find a wife, he said. English women stifle him. We were out on a night walk by the river at the time; the skies were clear after days of snowy cloud, and he wanted to show me the arrangement of Jupiter and

Venus on a rare cross-path, one above the other in the western sky, rather like lights on some stupendous radio tower.

We saw the planets sure enough. I thought they looked rather alien-invasion and wondered why I hadn't noticed them before. 'Things are rarely seen without being looked for,' Teddy said with that palladian, harmlessly arch tone that sounded strange coming from somebody whose nappies I had once changed. Yet I respect him and he shows himself routinely worthy of it in the things he knows or thinks or feels, for example when he insisted that we try to see the planets, and the sky in general, in reflection in the water, because a sky without a reflection is just the sky in profile. I discovered on that walk that my son loves reflections, he loves and requires symmetry. But though we stood at several points along the bank in the grainy mulch of mud and thawing snow, and though the city found some crude reflection, the river was too wide, full and flowing with meltwater to reflect any of the subtleties of the sky. We stood pointlessly in the way people do when they have come to see something and end up seeing nothing.

'But Lithuania,' I said to him. 'It's too far away.' He took my hand hesitantly. 'In the scheme of things, it's just around the corner,' he replied, and I could only say, 'Not in my scheme of things.' 'Well, I'll send you photographs, one a week.' But I knew that, even with the best will in the world, he would not, so I suggested, 'Send me one – just one – make it a good one.'

Five years after you finally disappeared I found a postcard from you in Teddy's bedroom. It was 1991, so he must have been eleven at the time. It bore a picture of a chihuahua on the front wearing a Tommy Cooper hat, and on the back a Lithuanian stamp. I haven't seen the postcard itself for years, but I do still remember the picture on the stamp, which was a castle, and I remember this because Teddy was very much into castles and fortresses at that time and had drawn a tiny knight in its turret and another on a horse approaching at speed from the far left, above the words *Dear Teddy*.

In the card's short message you claimed to be living in the desert, and it bothered him immensely that you had not said which desert; he had looked at his atlas to see if there were deserts in Lithuania and found there were none to speak of. When I asked him about the postcard, this was his only concern, that he might discover which desert you meant. He thought perhaps you were referring to the dunes along the spit, down to Nida – could people live in dunes? He had a look of respect and despair when he asked that, which implied that of all the women he knew, past, present and future, you were the one who could most plausibly live alone in sand dunes.

I did not have the heart to tell him that as likely as not there was no desert and that he had been flung a metaphor. It reminded me that, for all that you love to call a spade a spade, the spade is always a symbol for something else. You try to dig with it and it bends in half. This is not the kind of woman you can expect to get something straight from, I wanted to tell him. It made me feel defensive of him, because he was a child and still in the habit of taking you at face value, of worrying about and trusting you.

I am sure that his trip to Lithuania is a delayed response to the call of that postcard, but I decided not to bring it up. I have always wanted him to live life fully and not to be afraid, and not to put barriers in his way – above all else, not to be the barrier itself. Instead, as we left the river and walked up through the streets, I decided to change topic by asking him what was wrong with English girls.

'They don't know anything about the world,' he said. So I asked, 'And other girls do?' He ruffled his hair with his fingertips as Nicolas has always done. 'I don't know yet.' I suggested that maybe it is because we live on an island, and islanders are always more closed off from the world, and he turned to me with his grey eyes narrowed and said, 'Mind you, I do have a thing for Jean Shrimpton.'

I laughed. 'Jean Shrimpton! She's older than me now.' 'What, did she used to be younger than you?' he asked. He made a square with the thumb and forefinger of both hands. 'You know the picture I love best? The one of her with the white scarf around her head.' He loosed his hands upwards in adulation. 'Ah, she looks so perfect in that one.' I said, 'Where she looks like a young girl, you mean?' 'Yes,' he replied. 'Vulnerable, unblemished—' 'Underage.' 'Exactly.'

Then he gave that smile of disruptive mischief that I've known him to have since he was weeks old, and he stopped in the middle of the pavement, suddenly serious, and looked directly up at the clear sky.

'You know when I see stars I always think about . . .' He left a pause, so I invaded it. 'When you see stars you should think about stars, Teddy.' I said it with frustration, admonishment, though I had meant to be more delicate than that. And I regretted saying it, because he looked at the ground without reply and appeared to shrink into the old shape of himself as a child.

He was going to say, in case you missed the nuance, that stars make him think about the holes of light that beamed through your shawl the day you arrived at our back door. He has made the observation more than once before. It is funny how deeply affected we can be by the smallest things that happen in childhood – I have no doubt he still sees you exactly as he did that day, raising your arms against the spring glare and growing wings. His vocabulary was limited more or less to nouns in animal picture books then, and I will always remember his glee at having a word for what he saw: *butterfly!* This great, dark-winged vision leaking light as if bullet-holed. Two decades later he still packs the truth of you into this vision etched on his one-year-old retina and thinks of you as eternally magical and light-shot, so that even the stars are first and foremost reminders of you.

Should I, his mother, disabuse him of this view? Should I say to him, Teddy, Butterfly is not quite the creature the name implies. Or should I let him see the good in you and have him run with this glorious vision he has: you with your head thrown back in laughter, you with a copy of the Upanishads quoting *May we never hate one another* while your eye gleams wickedly, you wrapped in the shawl and stoking the fire in the woods as the sun comes up, you in the dunes, negotiating and renegotiating your terms with every shifting grain of sand so that they allow you to make permanent home amongst them.

Am I being unfair? Perhaps you are a tender creature after all and perhaps Teddy's notion is the truest. There are butterflies that survive winters. To be resilient is not always to be hard. If your nickname were purely ironic it would never have survived so long, surely, and you would have shrugged it off as you shrugged off everything that no longer suited you. I cannot say for sure that Teddy is wrong in his assessment, this is the thing, and so I let yet another subject go.

My own father once said that your children are beautiful to you in a way that nothing else is; as a girl I remember him telling me about my beauty as if he were outlining a profound fact, or setting out a singular truth. It was not a description, because that would suggest it was from his point of view; no, it was an *explanation* of my very particular beauty as known by him, the world expert on his subject. He knew something about me that I would never be able to know myself; he knew it because he was my parent and preceded me, and could see into all the voids from which I'd sprung. And as soon as I became a parent I could acquire that piercing vision and could know and see the same as my father had known and seen. It is such a steady love you feel for your child – bottomless and generous – and all afternoon I have missed Teddy, and every time he goes I miss him, as if each time he falls once and for all from the face of the Earth.

S omehow I feel fraudulent to have written most of the last few pages in January, after Teddy left the country, and to have made it sound like I was still referring to 'yesterday'. In fact I went back to work on New Year's Eve and haven't had time for this letter since.

More than this, I am aware that I haven't been completely truthful and I wonder why. How can it be that we can begin something wholeheartedly and slip, so quickly, into guarded omissions and liberties with the truth? Under the circumstances the goodness of human nature is very quick to buckle, don't you think? But then, of course you agree, and you hardly need me to point it out.

So a dilemma arises: let's say you lie in a letter, or maybe not even lie as such but just write something that is not completely honest, or omit something that might have been important to add. Do you edit that letter with an infill of truth so that the reader never knew there was a lie, which might mean removing or rewriting a page or two, or even starting again with a new, robustly direct approach? Or do you admit the lie, as I have done, and remove nothing, and be transparent for good or bad? And isn't the admittance of a lie more honest, anyway, than a truth arrived at through editing?

I have wondered about this kind of thing for the last hour, sitting here turning the piece of Roman jet in my hand and trying distractedly to think of ways of describing it. This is what writing does to you, it seems, it turns objects that used to be just things in your life into things that must be described, and at the same time makes them feel increasingly indescribable. This Roman jet, for example, which is a thimble-sized amulet bust of a man with angled cheekbones and gaze of steel, who might be an athlete according to Nicolas, and who might also be made of carbonised wood and not jet at all. I treasure him, but the longer I look at him the less able I am to say anything that would make anybody else feel the same, or even anything that justifies why I feel that way myself.

Yet this instinct, Butterfly, that I should simply record things for good or bad, as I said. I suppose I have gradually come to believe that what's written cannot simply be amended to suit some later preference and so I have decided this is the way I will go on, writing without amendments, transparently, yes, *see-through-ably*, as though any of what I wrote mattered in the slightest. All you can do is trust me, even though I might be writing one thing and thinking another. While I write my spare hand might be doing anything, for all you know; it might be driving a pin into your voodoo stomach. But of course it isn't, dear Butterfly! All I mean is: aren't written words strange in this way, so inscrutable, all hurrying together on the paper to cover up reality like a curtain drawn across a stage.

C ome on then, I hear you say. What was this frightful lie?

As I told you, it is not really a lie so much as an omission, and the omission is Nicolas. I went to great lengths to describe to you what happened on the night of my grandmother's death, including the bones, the falling away of the gauze, the pedantic detail of orange street light on my kneecap, the two monks and their groceries, and so on, and it feels now that all of this might have been just deflection, as if describing effects without mentioning a cause, and I don't know why I would have done this.

You see, as well as finding a pile of animal bones on the Thames shore that night, I also found Nicolas; he was crouching on the shale, by the water, and he seemed to be scrutinising something there. Of course, I didn't know he was Nicolas then, he was just a stranger without detail – a drunk, I thought, an eccentric, homeless possibly. He was there when I made my way back to my grandmother's house with the bones wrapped up in my dress, but we didn't speak. You do not want to come across a man when you are alone there at night. Probably I should not have been on my own there at all. But when I got back to my grandmother's door I realised I had dropped one of the bones, and I noticed because it had been one of the more unusual. A cow shin, I've since assumed, and the longest and finest of the heap I had picked up. It had been washed down so much by the river currents that it was perfect, without any torque, almost like a purpose-made musical bone or a razor clam – at least that is how I remember it. I tipped the other bones onto the doorstep and, without going indoors, I went back to the river.

He was still there when I got back, but this time he was sitting on the slope of the flood barrier with his legs outstretched and ankles crossed, gazing out – and he turned around. I saw him do that and I thought he was about to speak, then he turned back to the river. Not the murdering type, I told myself. Too healthy in the face: large jaw, dimpled chin, plump lips, dark eyes; not killing anyone, too kind. Young, handsome, proud-looking; he had looked at me uncertainly as if worried that he was worrying me, and that was when he turned away. I wish men would not do this. But it didn't matter anyway, because I suddenly had no fear of him. Somewhere between his intention to speak and his decision not to, I realised my grandmother had died it was as if my certainty grew out of his lack of it and, because of this exchange between us, I felt completely unafraid. I picked my way down the slope, just a few feet from him, and started scouring the beach. It was only after I had been looking for the bone for a minute or two that he called to me.

'What did you lose?' And so I said, without thinking, 'My grandmother' and I lifted my chin defiantly and took him in for the first time.

He had the hair of a king; I could imagine women running wax through it. Thick, curly and dark, and dark serious brows. 'Careless,' he said.

Then he stood and made his way down the slope in two sideways strides. He took something out of his pocket, took a torch from the other pocket and shone the light onto his opened palm. 'The tail of a peacock,' he said. I glanced it over and he explained, 'A broken half of a figurine from Victorian times, or maybe before. I found it a few weeks ago on the shore near Blackfriars Bridge.' So I said, partly because I was annoyed with his flippancy about my grandmother, and partly because I had no idea what else to say, 'I don't know what to say.'

He lifted one of those heavy brows and turned the peacock in his palm a couple of times before putting it back in his pocket. 'Do you mean your grandmother has died?'

When I nodded he showed an expression that surprised me – sorrow; no, not sorrow. I don't know how to explain it, except that you will know it anyway, that expression he has always had in which his whole life turns up for a moment in his eyes. He might be thinking anything, though in fact there probably is no thought he could single out. The most ineffable of looks – I put that down to the moonlight at the time, though I realise now of course it is nothing to do with the light. It is a look that fuses poles. It could be fear, then and again it could just as easily be peace; I always think, when I see it, of the way very hot water can feel cold for a moment – there is some point of intensity where one thing can be experienced as its opposite, and that is the intensity I am talking about in his expression.

'You know,' he said, 'if you lose something on this shore and you keep looking for it, one day it'll turn up. It's widely believed that the river reunites all things.'

I wasn't sure if this fatalism was supposed to be his attempt at solace, as if death unites all things, as if one day I would find my grandmother again; anyway, I was not consoled. I was needled. His openness wrong-footed me, his candid, unproblematic face, which I knew (consciously, even at the time) I would fall for because it was not like mine, and which made me bad-tempered because it had taken away my power to decide what I wanted and didn't.

'I suppose you think it'll offer up the other half of your figurine?' I asked finally, when I realised he had said all he was going to say on the subject of my grandmother. And he replied instantly, 'I do.' 'So will you be coming to look for it for the rest of your life?' Again, instantly he said, 'Surely that depends on how soon I find it.'

We crouched at the bottom of the slope, in the marsh grasses. 'I've come back to find one of the bones I dropped,' I said, and before I could go on he intervened with, 'I guessed.' 'A long one,' I said, 'I thought it was worth the return trip. Maybe I dropped it when I climbed up here.'

He said I didn't seem to have; I had to agree. I looked at him in profile, at the proud curve of his nose, at his lips that rose permanently at the corner in a smile, at his overall slapdash elegance as he sank deep and loose into that crouch. And me deep and loose in mine too, because I am a natural croucher, but not elegant, more functional, as if I have been designed to hinge at extreme angles for a purpose still, at the age of fifty-two, not discovered.

'The Thames is full of loot,' he said. 'Maces, axes, swords, half peacock figurines, coins, Roman shoes, pipes, pots, cannonballs, cufflinks. Bones, of course – as you know. Animal and human – some of them might have been Neolithic ritual offerings.' 'Do you think mine are Neolithic ritual offerings?' I asked, and he looked east along the river. 'Very much doubt it.' 'But you haven't even seen them.' Then, I remember, he reeled in his gaze rapidly until it was fixed on my mouth. 'So why did you ask me?'

He watched me at an angle as if taking in something extremely curious, and then we got back to our feet; my blood had rushed and I'd felt for a moment that the moon was hurtling. 'I'm sorry about your grandmother,' he said, and took my hand to help me up the slope.

'Please don't be, she was happy. She always fed her dogs fresh mince and red-wine gravy, and put two eggcups of brandy in their water to give them good dreams – her heart was good and big. Heaven will find room for her, please don't be sorry.'

'I meant I was sorry for you.'

I told him he mustn't be.

'When did she die?'

'When you first looked at me from over there.'

He opened and closed his mouth without managing to produce a word, and when he saw I was smiling he did so too. Mine was a smile dredged up from somewhere thick with the overpowering smell of incense. My mother had always burnt eucalyptus, holy basil, cardamom, ginger grass, lemon grass, palmarosa, brought back from her trips to Kerala, and that was the smell of home. Now it smoked up heavily in my nostrils as if I were catching my own scent.

When I told him I had to go back, he said, 'Come on then.'

If it struck me as strange that he was coming with me, that I didn't refuse, that he'd known about the bones despite never having looked up the first time I went past, that he'd assumed my grandmother's death without the slightest doubt, or even that I had assumed that death without doubt, well then this strangeness was nothing to be marvelled at. We were not living in normal times just for the moment. We walked.

We stopped when we had reached the pile of bones on the doorstep. When I bent to them my head filled with tears as if I were a bucket being emptied, and I sobbed, because I had no idea how I would move her or what to do with a dead person.

'Wait until the morning,' he said, and ran a thumb under my eye to staunch the tears. I blinked and the tears ran horizontally along his thumb and down into the well between knuckles, into the small hammock of webbed skin.

'I don't think you have a hope in hell of finding your figurine,' I said, and he thanked me, and said he appreciated the encouragement.

In my mind I have always since conflated his smile as he said that and walked away with the smile on my grandmother's face when I found her dead, both expressions of infinite contentment. In the morning, after I had called for an ambulance and my grandmother had been taken away, I was left sitting in her rocking chair, tearless and calm after that peculiar epiphanal night of seeing through the *gauze*, my foot stroking her dog's back. I hadn't wanted to go in the ambulance and I had agreed that I would walk to the hospital straight away to see to the papers. It was then that Nicolas came back; it couldn't have been much after seven a.m. but the sun was long up and when I heard the knock on the door I had no doubt it was him. I was still wearing my dress from the night before, which was streaked with the bones' dirt and the to-and-fro across the flood wall, and which in any case he took off – may I say it? tore off – once the door was closed.

I refuse to feel awkward telling you this.

Shortly after we met I gave him one of my grandmother's rosaries, which was made of beads of ox-blood red. He gave me a conch that looked like a harp. He had found it on that same bit of river beach a few years before, in the marsh grass. How did a bright queen conch from the tropics arrive downstream of Woolwich? It struck me, these strange relocations the things on our planet go through; but of course, Nicolas says, the Earth is a closed system, where else can things go? We live on a sphere with a roof and a floor. Things simply move from here to there either underground or across the ground or through the air, disappearing, emerging, decomposing, re-forming, transforming. All this, yes, but never ceasing, because ceasing to exist is not an option on offer to the things on this planet.

Beggar's spoils, you called all the useless things he collected. Broken relics of man's washed-up endeavours on the shores of the Thames, and the flint, coral and graptolite he dug up in the woods upriver from Morda. Nicolas' sorry old beggar's spoils, you said, which was frankly uncharitable. You told me, in his presence, never to trust a man who forages in the substrate. He answered only that I should never trust a woman who tells another woman what she should never trust in a man. It was not his way to rise to your or anyone's bait, and I respected this about him. He knew he had some lonely and pedantic habits that hardly needed a psychologist's eye to be seen for what they were – digging in the soil, scratching at limestone for fossils, mudlarking on the shores of the Thames for washed-up trinkets. Each boy needs his father; those who have lost hope of ever having one never stop looking for something else instead.

But even in full awareness of how open he was to mockery, from you especially, he was not ashamed of what he did. No, he only talked more about its subtleties, which felt to me curiously brave. He called these surfacings of fossils and flint *unmanned miracles*. He said that nature was pushing its bounty up through the soil, silt and mud and that people like him who collected it were less archaeologists and more flower-pickers. Sooner or later each thing under the ground would bloom above it, and whoever had his fingers ready to pluck would be the one rewarded. And he felt that if he waited long enough each treasure would have its season and what was missing would surface, including therefore the other half of his figurine; he didn't ever seem to doubt its appearance, or worry that his fingers would not be the ones hovering when it did.

'Flower-pickers!' you would tease. 'Our own little florist of the river shore.' With this reproach you would tussle his hair or press your thumb along his eyebrow as though neatening a child. To which he would respond without words, more with an amused smile – the sexily boyish, playful smile that you and I once agreed was his trademark. You will remember that once he went upstairs, brought down his box of beggar's spoils and laid them on the kitchen table in front of you. Flint, coral, porcelain, coloured glass, metal deer brooch, dagger, trilobite, gemstone, dog tag, watch battery, leather sandal, plastic button, gun, pin, bone. And he asked you to take your pick. Of course you picked the gun, a

Mauser C-96, a German piece from the First World War that he had found on the north bank of the Thames. You thought it was wonderful. You lifted it to your head with a rueful grin and pretended to shoot yourself.

This was something I loved about Nicolas, that he would not be bullied, that he made the bully rueful, but never took pleasure in doing it. He was – is – a sincere man at heart. That is the thing.

Yannis sells the best fried squid, marinated anchovies, salted sardines and unleavened bread in the whole of London – he says the whole of England. He also says this isn't saying much. He has a griddle in the tiny kitchen area behind the counter, where he fries the squid to order and sells it in a greaseproof paper bag. Occasionally I go to his shop in the evening when he is about to close and buy a bag at a discount, and eat it on the way home. Yesterday evening he asked me to stay for a few minutes because he had something he wanted to discuss, so we sat at one of the two high, round tables in the window, with a glass of beer each and a plate of bread and anchovies, and he asked me what a man had to do to get his wife back.

'I think begging is the only way,' I said, but he had tried that. He came to England four years ago because his wife had got a job as an oncologist in a hospital here, but now she was the one who couldn't settle and wanted to go home, while he had built a business from scratch and wanted to stay. She says it is his fault they can't go back to Crete, his stubbornness. He says she is unreasonable to drag him all the way here only to drag him back. He has been working through a stack of English modernist novels in a bid to anglicise himself – he has laboured through page after bewildering page and learnt phrases like 'a pint of porter' and 'the industrial epoch'; words like 'brat' and 'rascal' and 'ghastly' and 'nothingness'. She cannot tell him this effort has been for nothing?

After months of arguing to what has become a script, she has gone. Except not to Crete, but to her sister's friend's house in Muswell Hill. 'Muswell Hill!' he said to me. 'This is *bloody ghastly*.' Unknowingly he pressed his thumb into an anchovy's face as he said that, because he was gripping the rim of his plate. So I removed the thumb and squeezed his hand. 'It is not the anchovy's fault,' I told him, and he looked at his plate, at the wretched flattened fish, and muttered a string of apologies.

The upshot is that he asked me to write to his wife and point out his virtues. Like a letter of recommendation. I told him I could not; it wouldn't work. Let's put aside the fact that she is his wife, and if she hasn't seen his virtues yet she may never do so. The finer point is that women are loath to accept the recommendations of other women. He seemed intrigued to be told something about what women do and don't do, and looked at me brightly, like a dog that has seen its lead. But the truth is I have no other insights to share with him, and I told him that – not only can I shed no light on womankind, but I also know nothing about relationships except for some faint grasp of the multiple ways they can go wrong.

'But people like you,' he said, 'who have been married and divorced, you know things the rest of us don't.' I suggested that a special knowledge of failure is not such a valuable thing, and besides, I was never actually divorced, only separated. After a moment of surprise he seemed genuinely disappointed. 'You mean you're still technically married? After ten years of being apart?' 'Actually it's fifteen years,' I said, and I tried to explain that while it only requires a single yes to get married, to get divorced you have to say no so many times in so many different ways, and so expensively, that it does not always seem worth the trouble. Marriage is a construct easily put together, and painstakingly dismantled. The law makes it this way. To prise it apart, legally speaking, you have to take to it with a sledgehammer as if it were your worst enemy you were obliterating, and not the remains of your tenderest dreams. Not the little patch of fertile ground your only child sprang from. Nicolas and I could never bring ourselves to do that, that's all. Is it so strange?

You will see my cunning here, as if my agenda is to relate to you in passing a conversation I had with Yannis, when really of course I am using it as an opportunity to tell you something. I just thought you might be wondering what had happened between Nicolas and me after you left. Sometimes I wonder if you assume we carried on as if nothing had happened, and there is a part of me that likes you to think that, and a part of you – a caring part of you – that probably likes to think that too. And it is true that I do still see him from time to time now that we both live in London. Anyway, I suspect I overstated the point when I said what I did about tender dreams, because Yannis poured the last of his beer into my glass with great, warm compassion – and I suppose I should mention that for him to appear compassionate is a triumph of character over looks, because he is in fact made like a warlord, with a long straight nose that is almost vertical and a forehead that slopes back alarmingly – and said that he thought it must be chilly, to be in a marriage that is over but not ended. Because the other has left, he ventured. They have left, but not shut the door. It must be like living in a room with a draught always coming in. His big, savage, Cretan face winced at the thought.

They know me here; an hour or two after closing time Yannis drags the two tables together and a few of them congregate. Sometimes, once a month or so, me amongst them. When they sit together it is like the edges of the city have been drawn in, those with gold teeth and polished teeth and false teeth and missing teeth, those chased to England by Idi Amin, those who are the children of the *Windrush*, those who own a piece of the Berlin Wall. They come in comfortable shapeless hand-knits or beautiful suits from charity shops, except the one Nigerian who comes in beautiful suits from House of Fraser. There are always spirits and often coffee and sometimes bread. Each has fingers quick with cards; the usual is five-card-draw Poker played with a royal deck. Coppers and silvers and nothing above a pound, before midnight anyway, because no one has money to waste. It is just company and cigarettes and spirits and laughter, and an exaggerated communal love of the Queen – Poker is a royal game and she is their patron, Britannia, the matriarch it is better to love than be scorned by, the aggressor in a pair of brogues; they make affectionate attempts at mimicking her voice, which sends the ash from the tips of their cigarettes flying in gusts of laughter.

After midnight the real money comes out, small but serious sums, and then I lose interest; I still abide by the friendly pact you and I made, to play only for honour and never for money. So I sit aside with pen and paper, here by the glass display of the counter, leaning on Yannis' copy of *The Rainbow* that has a receipt as a bookmark, which is still towards the beginning of chapter one.

Yannis believes my Poker skills are better than they are, perhaps because he is not used to women being able to play cards at all; I have told him about the games you and I played and explained to him that it was never in the name of skill or even fun – no, only ever in the name of jeopardy, throwing ourselves at chance and seeing who was luckier, and who the universe favoured first. Our little deals with God, I told Yannis, and he said, God does not play cards (which may or may not have been a pun, with Yannis it is hard to tell). In any case, under this misapprehension that I have any talent for the game he always positions himself with his back to me when I sit out and go to the counter, so I can see his cards and stop him if he is about to do a catastrophic thing, but I never stop him. Lately, like now, I just sit here at the counter and write to you.

Do you remember that morning when you were sitting on the windowsill at the far end of the living room, going through some old letters and photographs of your ancestors? Leaning against the wall. I think it was winter. I don't know why but I often think of this when here with Yannis and the others. You found out that your great-grandparents had been part of a large influx of Lithuanians to Coatbridge in Scotland, at the turn of the century, all poor as birds and shipped in to work in the coalmines. Unlike the peasants who went to the New World in search of milk and honey, the letters and photographs of your ancestors did not give the impression that these Lithuanians expected anything beyond a reprieve from starvation; maybe not even that. There was only one picture of your great-grandmother, and I remember it well – do you? She is standing in a long, heavy coat in a grey street with a collection of saucepans hanging by string over one shoulder, a bundle of clothes or food in the crook of that arm, and in the other arm a baby – your grandmother – swaddled grimly. It appeared cold, she appeared cheated, but not surprised.

You looked at that photograph for a long time over a cigarette; you drank in the smoke slowly and steeply while you stared at this woman who was not really anyone. Her hard face and her scowl. The child in her arms would go on to marry one of the fortunate Lithuanians who thrived in Scotland, a Jewish man who became a doctor, so she is the one everybody starts with when they trace the family's history, being, as she is, the good news. But my interest was in the poor broken human being who gave birth to and held her, the one who didn't prevail, who nobody ever talked about and who probably died young in Coatbridge with bad lungs and no notion of any life that would ever yield anything but hardship and grind. You looked at the picture with a kind of fascinated contempt. You pitched your ragged beauty on our windowsill like a makeshift tent; really you never did look like somebody who was going to be there long, and I remember thinking that as I came into the room and saw you in silhouette, with your unbrushed hair tucked behind your ears. (Maybe this is the link, the thing that makes me think of you when I'm here, because Yannis and the others have this temporary look too, like they are staying and not living, even if they stay for the rest of their lives.) Behind you in the garden Nicolas and Teddy were running about in some weak Morda sun.

Your grandmother – to return to a happier theme – met your grandfather on a train to Glasgow; she going on a frugal shopping errand, he going to his last year of medical school, both immigrants, but he without any of the expectations of defeat that came with that title. They saw one another and fell in love with themselves, seeing in the other the heroic survivor they each thought they were. (Am I right in what I remember? I go over these facts sometimes in case they tell me something new about you, in the way people like to find out new things about the dead. But this memory of you on the windowsill is twenty years old and decidedly worn down.) Five, six, seven years later – your grandfather by now a specialist in lung diseases – they moved to escape the Scottish cold and ended up in the small mining community in Shropshire that is Morda, where he ran his own practice; your father was born, became interested in botany and, after the Second World War, in his early twenties, became the first in his immigrant family to go back to Lithuania, to fight for its independence from the Soviets.

This is what you told me – and that in going back he came to be involved with the Lithuanian Academy of Sciences, where he joined a project to archive seeds of indigenous plant species that were fast disappearing under Russian industrialisation. This is how he found himself face-to face with the intimidating beauty that was your mother, who was working as a typist at the Academy. Your brother was born soon and out of wedlock, but it was another seven years before you arrived, into a now coherent and happy family in a respectable area of Vilnius; born and then, before you could know it, left as the communist grip was tightening on people like your father, and came back to Morda.

I think of the day you showed me the things of your ancestors and in that memory you are the lazy little Jewess slung in the warmth of the window, the only one of your family for generations who has had nothing material to overcome and no danger to face. You don't even have a working religion, the Jewess is just a title that gives you licence to flirt inconsequentially with other faiths in the way a married woman can flirt inconsequentially with other men. Atrocity is going on over there, where your people are from. You just draw on your cigarette without appetite, toss the photograph onto the table and rest your head back against the wall. So I take the cigarette from your hand and sit at the opposite end of the sill, and think how strange it is, the random loins we spring from, the beauty that unfolds even from a sullen shuffling woman with clanking pans. That she left her country in 1901 and eighty-two years later it is still not free – yet that you are free, and I am free. We are free and here on the windowsill. You put your bare foot on top of mine; there are times when the very presence of another person can be a miracle. Your foot is warm, which is surprising. I suddenly remember this as I write.

A nd you would ask Nicolas and me, 'Where did you two meet?'

'On a filthy Thames beach,' we would say.

And then a few days later, or a few weeks later, 'Where did you two meet, anyway?'

'On a filthy Thames beach.'

You would sigh, 'Ah yes.' Which made me think that either you forgot the answer time and again because it wasn't romantic enough, or that you asked repeatedly because the answer was so romantic you wanted to hear it again. As children are prone to doing with stories they like.

I used to think your longing for other people's romantic anecdotes was just one of your many ironic gestures, or a strange nervous tic you hadn't been able to shake off from girlhood – but maybe it was actually one of your more conventional traits. We take all sorts of gleeful interest in things we would never have or do in our own lives, why else would my Wednesday afternoons be spent hauling in a pile of execrable crime novels from the mobile library to feed the appetites of those mild old ladies who read them in a little scented plume of rosehip and lilac? They lap up the stabbings, the disappearances, the trail of blood on the passenger seat. Their lumpy knuckles cannot put the books down; their faces become gentle and settled while they read about gore, as if they are back in their days of breastfeeding. Never so merciful or so reposed, and I can feel a moment of such warmth, such love towards them like that.

And so with you in your own way, if you heard that someone was in love, or had done something sweet. You were absolutely sincere, almost adulatory at the notion of one person loving and finding shelter in the life of another. You would declare, 'How beautiful' and then tilt your head off to one side in calculation of exactly how beautiful, and you might not move, and if you were in the middle of doing something like tearing a piece of bread from the loaf, you might stop with the bread poised halfway to your mouth. That same hand, so given to batting away any faint hint of romance for yourself, would float in quivering appreciation of somebody else's.

'And then what?' you once said. 'After you and Nicolas met. Your first date.'

I told you we went to the Serpentine, to see an exhibition; perhaps that was when he gave me the conch, though I really couldn't say. It was about a week after my grandmother's death and the day after her funeral. Perhaps you don't remember this conversation, but I firmly do. We were sitting at the kitchen table in the cottage in Morda one night drinking Polish vodka, while Nicolas was away for work and Teddy in bed – I'd drunk four or five shots while you'd barely touched your first. I told you about how I stayed the night in my grandmother's house with my parents after the funeral, and the next morning, while they were going through some of her things and deciding what to do with it all, Nicolas and I went to the Serpentine. We didn't touch one another, we only toiled chastely around the rooms, hands in pockets, and were polite, and feigned expertise.

You reared up, do you remember? You raged! An exhibition, my friend? My dear friend, who never much liked art or galleries or places that had to be crept around, who took some peculiar Platonic offence at the idea of a painting of a tree, when you could just go and see a tree. A first date at the Serpentine! This insincere use of art for courting couples who'd rather be fucking is a waste of everybody's time. You said, An obscene *squanderment*, and you said it standing with your arm flung theatrically. Men and women are born to share their bodies in a way that aeroplanes are made to fly; they should do it shamelessly, routinely. They may do it liberally if they wish, and in different configurations. Men can do it to other men, women to other women. Wives to other women's husbands, husbands to other men's wives. Let's not be prudish. But they should not do it while pretending to do something else. An aeroplane is never coy about flying. Imagine it! Down with the coquettish aeroplane! Somebody put a great deal of work into that exhibition, and all you could think about was your loins. You should have booked an hour in a cheap hotel and been done with it.

Your anger was very unreasonable, Butterfly. You were such a tyrant; just because my romance failed to come up to scratch, you felt your world had been betrayed. This is the problem with people who live vicariously, they ask a lot of their friends. In the face of your outbursts I would always clam up and make a decision to withhold things from you as a punishment for your unreasonableness; maybe you noticed, although, then again, maybe not.

But now I imagine you on your own in this so-called desert, trying to build a life out of little, and it hardly seems to me that it can hurt to step forward again into our conversation, even if so many years later, and end this petty punishment. It never made me feel good anyway. You once intimated that if only I had spoken up more for my relationship with Nicolas you might have behaved differently, and at the time that idea made me sullen with injustice. But maybe there was some truth to it; I have often had to consider that since.

Later on in that conversation with Yannis the other day, after I had refused to write to his wife, we got talking about our marriages. We talked about their early days and the romance. I suppose this is what prompted me to write what I just wrote – which incidentally, on a reread, I think is true in gist, but the outburst about coquettish aeroplanes might be a bit improvised and slightly unfair on you. However, there is the self-made law of honesty to abide by, so it must stay.

Yannis and his wife had their first and last real date at the age of seventeen at Lake Kournas in Crete. They skirted past acres of ocean in a beeline for one clear disc of lake, the only one on the whole island – all that land, and they headed for one tiny hole in it. This is what it is to fall in love, he said, there is a world of firm ground but we go for the gap. We aim for vertigo. In that lake were the inverted White Mountains, whiter and cleaner in the water than they were out, as if the mountains themselves were a crude afterthought.

He and his wife dived in for the mountains, thinking they would find them together. Love makes you very optimistic, he said. An intense day of basking on volcanic rock and slipping into water as pedaloes wove by, a few hours spent burning up with love and enduring the downsides of heat, of midges swarming to one's warm parts, and by the next day she was pregnant. They married so quickly they never had time for another date, and then their son Akis was born. Akis, who sprung from that day like the infamous Lady of the Lake, who purged Kournas of its sins. Yannis is romantic, like you; when he says that love makes us optimistic, he says so as if we are right to be optimistic. In a way he reminds me of you, and I think you would like him.

This was his turn; when it came to mine I told him about the night Nicolas and I spent locked in the Royalty Theatre in the West End, a night that stands out, one I spent a lot of time thinking about yesterday after I wrote what I wrote. It was October I think, or November, 1976. Nicolas and I went to this theatre, where he was doing the lighting for their programme of perpetual failures. He worked there for nothing to get experience, which meant he stood on a platform show after show training a light on a cast of disconsolate actors who played to a near-empty auditorium. One night I met him there after a show and he brought me in to wait while he packed up. I went to his platform and he introduced me (as if to friends) to the new electric spot-lights and tried to explain to me about lumens and foot-candles, gobos, the projection of a crescent moon onto the black backdrop of the stage. And while we were there the theatre was locked. The caretaker came in and turned off the main auditorium lights, and we saw him from our perch and said nothing.

Nicolas switched on a spotlight. There was just one column of white light spiralling diagonally through darkness to the left-hand side of the stage, which seemed a number of miles away. The Royalty was a big thousand-seater theatre, and the darkness took away its walls and made it a ten-thousand-seater, fifty-thousand. With torches we climbed down into the auditorium and Nicolas sat at the back of the stalls. He said, 'Go to the stage and stand in the spotlight.' I picked my path there slowly. I put my feet in the centre of the circle of light and laid the torch down. I asked what I should say. 'Tell me about the men you've known,' he replied.

There had been some men in passing, I told him, though I couldn't see him in the glare. Some men – or, rather, many men. There wasn't much else to do out on the Welsh Borders. You finish your A levels, you are so busy discovering yourself that you forget to go to college or get a vocation, you start working in a pub and, when your best and only friend leaves town, you become a loner and invest yourself in things that rely little on the company of others, like pleaching willow and learning how to slum it comfortably under the stars, and singing. You start singing in the pub on the evenings you're not working and people come to see you because you have a good voice and an unintentionally provocative appearance – it isn't your clothes that provoke but what is underneath them, despite your efforts to cover it. The singing is short-lived, you realise you love the company of others, but only when they are indifferent to you. You like trees and fungus and the challenge of making water boil in a tin pot, and rinsing the coffee cup in the river – rain even better – so that you can pour wine into it and sleep deeply and wake up thirsty and starving.

None of the men had been of much note, I told him, and to my surprise he found this sad. It was the only time he interrupted my speech, and his voice came from the dark and was thin with distance. 'Many men and none of note? Do you not think maybe you chose the wrong men?' But the thing is of course that choice had little to do with it. Shropshire is not London. Not that you take whatever you can get, just that you have to take some of what you can get, and what you could get then was severely restricted. Anyway, the need for meaningful solitude is sometimes best met by being in meaningless company, wasn't that the paradox? He probably baulked at the word meaningless, maybe because he imagined the possibility of himself being just such a man who delivered nothing to a woman. But they were not nothing, I tried to explain, they were just something without meaning and without note. All sorts of perfectly good things fall into this category.

When it came to his turn, and we swapped places so that I was near-invisible in the stalls and he was the one in the spotlight, he explained that he, himself, had been more reserved and thoughtful. He had been in love, but not often, and not the love his mother had told him to hold out for, but still, nothing meaningless. Well, almost nothing. Maybe one or two. His girlfriends tended to be small and slender with one particular part of their bodies of which they were mortally ashamed, though this had never been the eyes, which in four of six cases had been brown, bright and lovely.

They tended to have fringes, he said, and birthmarks. Fringes were like well-kept gardens and denoted a homely girl with an open, tidy face. You see, you are brought up in the Kent marshes, just you and your mother in a wooden house whose land has no boundaries, you just guess at where the garden might end and where the acres of treasure-studded flatness begin. It is just a changeable guess. Then a miracle: when you are fourteen you move with your mother's new husband – who has emitted from nowhere and married her so fast even you missed the wedding – to a wholesome suburb of New Hampshire where the sun is very often out and the large gardens demarcated and where the seasons arrive with clear intention in discreet unmistakable blocks. Glorious times of having and giving. Pumpkins as big as a full moon.

America! Where you find a home for your enormous smile,

where the gap between your two front teeth is no longer a defect but an open door through which girls hurl themselves, where the dimple in your large chin turns you from an awkward kid into an all-American youth, easy and jokey, where you learn that expression of almost permanent sardonic amusement, and take to wearing aftershave and growing stubble and holding your head proud, where people call you *dashing*; you take to amateur dramatics and discover that you have the kind of face that can do anything. It can suit a baseball player or an intellectual, depending on how much stubble and whether a T-shirt or a linen shirt, and whether the prescription glasses – once the bane of your life – are on or off. If off, and if bouncing a ball from knee to knee, you are the high-school heart-throb. And if on, suddenly you can be a New York Jew, clever and sharp and easy, playing life and winning; playing life and always winning.

Three years on, when the marriage collapses, you and your mother move to Deptford and live in a house next to a piece of derelict and apocalyptic ground bafflingly named Twinkle Park, and you seek girls with fringes to allay your homesickness. How do you really feel about fringes? How do you really feel about the scraps of New England accent that still hang around your speech when you are losing confidence and feel threatened? If America is what protects you, and if America is thousands of miles away in a life you barely even had, what protects you?

So now you are thinking about your future and your career, about lights, how to get a paid job doing lighting for stage or screen, and though you are twenty-five you haven't slept with anyone, fringe or no, for eighteen months – or hadn't, that is, until a month before and what could now be called the Night of the Bones, though you are not sure about the momentousness of this title. The affair might come to nothing and then it will be lumbered with a label that portends something big. Better just to say, since that night on the filthy Thames beach. Or more rightly, since the morning after that night on the filthy Thames beach.

Later on Nicolas turned off the spotlight and we found our way backstage with torches. In the wings we made a nest of blankets and drapes that we found in the dressing rooms, and an *Oh! Calcutta!* banner, which we used as a sheet. We stripped off without any mention of each other's spotlit sexual summaries, because he knew enough of my bored promiscuity to be determined to make it a thing of the past, and I knew enough of his outgrown fetish for the neat and the safe to be determined to make him kiss my fringeless forehead and wish himself well clear of his boyhood and his New England pumpkins. 'I will marry you if you like,' Nicolas said – 'but I have no money.' I asked him what it cost to get married but he had no idea. I said, 'I could sell some things, I have a bracelet, a bike I've never ridden, I have a piano.'

'*Oh! Calcutta!*' he grinned, and eased himself on top of me. We lay still. He asked me which particular part of my body I was ashamed of and I told him the part between the crown of my head and the soles of my feet. Maybe because he felt I meant it, he seemed pleased. Whole-body shame is part of a bleak and complex way of being that has nothing to do with gardens laid neatly to lawn. 'You're a baroque,' he said, 'an irregular pearl, one that isn't spherical or symmetrical.' 'The cheapest, then,' I answered. 'Unique, though, and beautiful.' I sighed: 'How embarrassing – in this torchlight you've mistaken me for somebody else. In the morning light you'll look at me and quickly dress and scurry away.'

'Like all women,' he said, 'you refuse to accept a compliment – why can't you?' 'Why can't I? – because at school they called me a giraffe.' He laughed. 'It must be those two horny growths on your forehead.' And then he asked, in a voice close to sleep, if I would go pearl-fishing with him one day.

History, of course, knows the answer to this question, it knows the long night-drives up to Scotland and poses the question in hindsight: how many holidays is a woman supposed to endure camping by the Oykel river in a freezing Scottish springtime while her husband looks for pearls? For that matter, how many trips to antique shops hunting out rubies or San Carlos peridot or Baltic amber, combing for jet, bartering at mineral fairs? Will there be a reward for this in the afterlife or has it all been in the name of selflessness? And yet at the time of course the answer rushed to my lips without pause.

He turned our torches out and told me to listen. Could I hear that high-pitched sound, that wailing? I answered no, too deafened by the darkness. It was the thickest, dustiest, most crowded darkness I have ever known. He told me that a year or two before there had been a show, the *Royalty Follies*, that used dolphins, and the dolphins had lived in a tank in the theatre for weeks. And now they haunted the theatre and could be heard. We lay in calico, velvet and dust, awake and asleep all night, but I didn't once hear them. I only heard the braking and whistling of underground trains until they stopped for the night and when they started in the morning, and had an awareness of a beautiful intention I now had for my life, the intention to be happy. 'There!' Nicolas would whisper once in a while, perhaps into my neck or into my mouth. 'A dolphin, did you hear it?' But I never did hear it. I just kept thinking, maybe saying, with a kind of anxious joy: 'I have a piano, a Bechstein I got for my eighteenth birthday, we could sell that.'

When morning came we had no notion of it. I held the torch up while Nicolas looked in his pockets for a watch. I stared upwards into that band of torchlight and saw dust caught and falling, in exactly the way meteors fall. Each particle of dust left a tail, and seemed to appear from nowhere as a burst of light and then dissolve. I don't know why it should be that such small things can sometimes take up so much of our attention and imagination, but this dust is one of the sharpest memories I have so far in my life.

I suppose the world is constantly producing things of wonderment, every moment, at every scale, and one time in every million or so our minds will be such that we will be open to seeing it. To see the silver effervescing of that dust was as beautiful a sight as any mountain or waterfall; but then, when I saw it, I was in love and as happy as a human being can be. Of course this helped. The world is heavily changed by the way we perceive it; in all my reticence and doubt, this is one thing even I haven't been able to dispute.

February 2002

A

nd you? Content?

No; somewhat less than content. If I think about this desert of yours I see trees rather than sand, but it is a sparse scattering of trees, which are very upright, pines or birches, and in the middle a house, or more likely a hut. In this hut a table with a single chair and a bed, in fact the charpoy my parents brought back from India for you, but the base has holes in it where the ropes have come unknotted. Here you lie at your maximum discomfort without a mattress and with your legs falling off the end; charpoys were not made for your eastern-European stock – nevertheless you do have a pile of blankets, not particularly soft, but thick and heavy enough to keep you warm. Under the charpoy on the floor are your clothes, a pair of shoes and a pair of boots. In this spare and functional scene your womanliness lives in one single object – the fine, soft shawl over the back of the chair, ingrained with years of perfume and pulled shapeless where you have worked your fingers through the crochet.

There are also a small number of books and a solid-fuel stove and, let me see, a sandwich toaster. My imagination grants you electricity. If you are to have electricity then there is also an overhead bulb and a pump to supply water from the spring and

– no, the luxury must stop there. On the whole you have a towering nonchalance about food and also the suspicion you reserve for everything that tells you you need it; but even so it is amazing what you've been able to make in that sandwich toaster. Toasted honey sandwiches are the supper staple and you also find that sliced apple and honey works, as does pear, and if those fruits, then why not vegetables – you boil them first on top of the stove and there it is: toasted carrot-and-swede sandwiches, or beetroot-and-cabbage, and potato dumplings; you've toasted a piece of gammon, smoked sausage, eel, and sometimes you've dispensed with the bread and clinched a filleted perch or herring between the ridged grills and eaten it off the hotplate. Who needs an oven? you mutter with a cigarette between your lips.

What is around you? Nothing. I see no neighbours or even a lake that would give the wilderness meaning, I just see these scattered trees for an indefinite distance. Early in the morning you come out of your hut and stretch. You collect pine needles from the ground to make a mulch for growing vegetables on the nine-feet-square plot you've dug over behind the hut, where you have some potatoes, carrots, mint, beans and peas, that sort of thing. Beetroot that keeps going into October, swedes into January. You grow them without gusto and with the almost reproachful lack of fuss that makes everything and everyone want to do its best for you, to be the one thing to hook your attention.

I suspect you walk for some part of the day out in the maze of trees and drop cigarette butts to guide your way back. By and large, though, you sit at the table and study the Upanishads. You appraise every word of them, each abstruse, unwavering and rousing word. Book II of the *Taittiriya* Upanishad, the book of Joy: Man's elemental Self comes from food: this his head; this his right arm; this his left arm; this his heart; these legs his foundation. You get up and pace. Food gives rise to the Self?

Food gives rise to the *Self?* The Self – Atman – is in food, and rises from food to vegetation to earth to water to air to Spirit to Brahman. Atman and Brahman are in the eel pressed indecorously between two pieces of stale bread! In the lowest things the glow of universal Spirit – but wait, the elemental Self, the living Self, the thinking Self. Legs are the elemental Self, but is the head, the brain, the mind? Is the mind elemental or living or thinking? They who think of food as Spirit shall never lack. Shall never lack! Brahman in the eel, the smeared pork grease, the beetroot!

Often, these little revelations. They give you a radiant smile. You proceed at one page a day, if lucky, and when you have finished the ten books you start again, Book I, The Lord: This is perfect. This is perfect. Perfect comes from perfect. At one time you'll close your eyes, sit back and hook your hands over the ridges of your hips in pure pleasure at those opening words; at another time you'll flatten your hand across the page in undiluted fury. What is perfect? Nothing is perfect! This is pompous. This is pompous. Pompous comes from pompous. Maybe you'll throw the whole volume on the fire like you do the other books you hate, except its lies would probably put the fire out.

Later you will deride yourself for your lack of cultivation after all this time and for the way you live like an animal, or less than an animal, because at least animals mate and stay busy. You – you are just killing time on Earth before you can be allowed to die. On the loneliest or most self-denying of days you will try to affirm yourself again by writing a postcard to the one person on Earth you find simple enough to love. Dear Teddy, I'm well and still living in the desert, you'll say.

Your last choice of postcard was exemplary, the chihuahua in the Tommy Cooper hat, and it warms me because I know why you chose it from whatever display carousel in whatever town you happened to be in. We watched Tommy Cooper die onstage in front of an audience who laughed because they thought it was part of the act, and though you never said it in so many words, I know you've felt this could be an analogy for your life. You were dying onstage in full view of everyone. This was the first thing I thought when I found your postcard to Teddy: she's making a point, and the point is that she's dying in such a way that everybody thinks she's deep in the act of living. She is dying. She wants me to know, yet she doesn't want me to take it seriously, at least no more seriously than you could take a chihuahua. No sooner does she make the cry for help than she lets loose the wry smile.

I see you pushing the half-written postcard to the side of the table and cooking up the mushrooms you foraged without the slightest idea of edibility. You pull the chair close to the table and take up your knife and fork with a serene hum. You eat with your back straight and your hair combed, in case it turns out to be your last supper.

As for me, most days I make an effort to do good. I flannel down withering bodies in baths and give insulin injections into bellies. I am asking a woman how it was to grow up during the war and, before she knows it, the needle has been in and come out again. Their poor bodies are pricked like dough with all the drugs in and the blood out. I help them get to their rooms to find a thing it turns out they never owned and which they wanted for a purpose they can't remember, so we go slowly back to the chair from whence we came and say nothing of it. I spend much of the day taking people to the toilet, pulling down their underwear and waiting for the movement that was so urgent a minute before but which doesn't come.

It'll come when it's ready, I say, which means nothing more or less than that. It isn't to say it'll come when we're ready. Maybe we'll have returned again to the chair and there won't be time to get back to the toilet. What does it matter? We speak of dignity, but dignity is nothing more than being accepted. I feed them, I clear the food from their laps, I dab the spilt tea off their collars, I help them on with their nightclothes and out with their teeth, I snap the lids off their vials, I see past their rages, and furthermore they let me. The pay is abysmal and it isn't true that job satisfaction, as such, makes up for it. It isn't like a hospice that aids people as restfully as possible towards death, but more like an alpine crevasse in which people hang as desperately as possible onto life, and increasingly one they don't even want. There isn't any satisfaction in supporting the insupportable. For me, the satisfaction comes from somewhere else. One day I lifted the loose flesh of an old woman's breast so I could wash underneath and I passed no judgement. I used to think: Why does it come to this? Why do we suffer? Why can't you piss now that we're here in the place people piss, rather than piss over there? If you pissed in the right place there'd be no pads, no rubber sheets. Why must our breasts collapse? Why must our teeth come loose?

I lifted that flaccid breast and all I thought was: Oh well, breast gone to the dogs. When I looked up at the woman's face I saw a person who had borne the brunt of a joke, and without thinking I squeezed her hand and laughed. She looked down at her chest and began to laugh too, and as I carried on washing her neck, shoulders and arms the laughter died down into smiles that were so full of the shared joke that each time we caught one another's eye we started up again.

What is it to be acceptable? Isn't it just for somebody to accept us? The thought comes: Why can't you feed yourself? Why does it come to this? Then the better thought comes: I accept you. But acceptance takes so much effort; am I really equal to the task? If I am asked to do overtime at work I refuse, because too long there makes you brutal. Sometimes I can feel it myself when I start seeing the place as an opportunity to scrape together a little more money and then realise in bitterness that the exhausting toil of it isn't worth the money scraped. I take it out on the bodies that generate the never-ending toil by being a little less gentle, a little less patient, a little more coercive, and then I hate them for being so easily coerced.

I always wanted a gentle nature. I was over forty by the time I realised I was not going to develop one. My father had one, my mother too underneath the effusive spirit, which meant that it was in my genes and that there would be an onset at some point in life – a sudden, incurable onset of gentleness. The day it struck me that this wasn't going to be the case was the day I saw Teddy being the diplomat, just like my father. I'd gone to pick him up after a night at the cinema and when I pulled up he was walking over to a group of men fighting. I watched him, a sixteen-year-old, extend his arms between the two factions and part them like curtains, without force or threat. Nobody would touch Teddy, he was dovelike; my father would have done just the same in that situation with the same effect, not only calming violence but converting violence into calm.

I know now that the gentle gene skipped a generation. It had come to Teddy by adolescence and most likely long before that. I heard you say, 'If a thing you want isn't coming by nature, then you must make it come by design; if you can't design it either, spoof it.' With this in mind I applied for the job at a care home just off the Finchley Road, up near Swiss Cottage – The Willows it's called, and I do not (am I too serious?) join the others in calling it The Wallows. At work I do gentle things and through them I feel more like my father and Teddy. In feeling more like them I act more like them, and then feel more like them; the circle is virtuous as far as it goes. I hear stories that repeat on ten-minute loops, I pluck the hairs from a woman's chin, I put dressings on a man's bedsores, I hold the hand of a ninety-year-old screaming at her bowl of stewed rhubarb and look patiently into the back of her mouth at the vibrating uvula. I shrug as I remove the bowl. 'I don't like rhubarb much, either,'

I say. I put a steady hand against her cheek, against all their cheeks. It's alright, I tell them. I don't mean it is going to be alright, I mean it is now, already, so long as it can be accepted.

Happiness doesn't come in the way I expected; not a massing of good things over time, but a succession of small, strange and unowned moments – the sun makes a hot oblong on the bedroom floor and I stand in it with my eyes closed. The coriander germinates in the window box and up comes the seedling. The bled radiators stop knocking at night. Just after the first bar of Coltrane's 'Naima' I'm reminded of 'Ruby, My Dear' and at the end of 'Ruby, My Dear' I'm reminded suddenly of Nina Simone's 'Sinnerman'. New connections! As if the world's hands are joined. I spent over half my life waiting for the accumulation of happiness and then I realised that it doesn't accumulate at all, it just occurs here and there, like snow that falls and never settles. Not the drifts that you and I imagined we would plough ourselves into, but instead gently, opportunistically, holding one's tongue out to catch the flakes.

Anyway, this morning when I caught my reflection getting out of bed, I was young; it must have been something to do with the movement, the transition that made me look it. I got dressed without looking again. Late morning I went out to meet Ruth, whom I know you'll remember because she delighted you; a paediatrician, you'd said with a nod when I told you. 'Oh, to be a sick child and be in Ruth's hands,' you said. 'Doesn't she make you feel comforted somehow, as if humankind is working? As if all the old loose ends are now accounted for?'

I saw her, and she gave me a ticket to a matinee that afternoon of a Pinter play that she couldn't go to because she had been called into work; she was supposed to be going with her daughter and she insisted that I went so that her daughter wouldn't be on her own. The play was *Monologue*, one man speaking for half an hour to the empty chair next to him where he imagined his friend of old to be. Ruth's daughter was rapturous about it afterwards, about the subtext and everything that wasn't said. For myself, for half of the play I'd fought the urge to go and sit in the empty chair. For the other half I'd fought the urge to leave and find an address to send this letter to. No good writing to Butterfly if Butterfly can never read what's written, no good. Not a form of expression at all, but a form of silencing. No good this man talking to a chair, better that he talked to his own navel than to a seat without a sitter.

I went to the map shop on Long Acre and bought a map of Lithuania, which I took home and studied. How else am I to start finding you? If I went to the Lithuanian Embassy and asked to see a phone book I know you wouldn't be in it. If I asked the handful of people I know who knew you, they'll have less idea about you than I have. It feels like a form of code-breaking to squint at this map and try to fathom you from the printed pixels, to try to deduce your whereabouts from things you said, did, bought, thought, things you hoped for, things you hated. There are areas I know you won't be, the towns and cities. I think you must be in the forest. Probably because of what you wrote on Teddy's postcard about living in the desert I'm drawn towards Nida and the west, though I know there are far too many tourists for you to be near the dunes themselves. The north-western forests maybe, close to the Latvian border where nobody will think to look for you.

By the time Nicolas came round in the evening I was cooking; I smiled when I saw it was him at the door. I had been singing to the music coming in through the window. I had drunk a little. We ate a split portion of pasta and mussels and played a hand of Whist. But as we were lying in bed about to sleep I thought of the map I'd folded and put on the bookshelf, and then of the lost cow shin somewhere in the Thames or on the shore, and of the lock of black hair in a box between two sheets of newspaper. Every gentle notion I'd trained myself to have deserted me for no reason, as if I were two people in one form. I do good, I sponge down aching backs, I inject insulin painlessly, I massage knotted feet. Most things have become alright by me, most arrangements, I don't distinguish between the conventional and unconventional or the good and bad, and I don't have any interest in judging. But sometimes still, even on a day that's going well, this lack of tolerance, what Nicolas this evening called the dirty fire: you burn and leave soot, he said when I asked him suddenly to go home.

But it was his fault, I told him. He came round on a whim, he ate half my dinner, I was still hungry as a matter of fact, I had nine mussels. Nine! I was starving. He had his elbow on my hair while we made love and because he was so deeply absorbed in his own pleasure I couldn't attract his attention to tell him it was pulling. My scalp was sore, in case he was interested, and I was tired of winning at Whist and didn't understand why he couldn't make an effort. Just a small effort to win! Would it hurt?

So he got out of bed and plucked his clothes off the floor. 'You burn and leave soot,' he said on his way out. 'My mother warned me about you, she warned me about beautiful women, their aftermath.'

'Your mother was a despot,' I replied, and I shoved the door closed behind him with my foot and sat down to write this, and have been writing it since with the map spread on the floor. Now that dawn is coming the feeling of intolerance has gone completely, and all I have, looking at the map, is a recollection of you talking about the disappearance of your country's forests, hacked down by the Russians and replaced with chemical plants and fertiliser works. Whatever upset me before now seems to have transferred onto these lost ash and oak groves and become more a sense of regret. Nicolas' mother was not a despot, she was soft-shouldered and charitable. When there are so many true things that can be said in life, I don't know why I say the things that aren't.

D oes this come hard to you, when I say Nicolas was here? Or does it make you laugh?

There is a particular thing he used to always do with me; I don't know if he ever did it with you. He would be bouncing a football from one knee to the other, or hurling a tennis ball at the back wall of the house and catching it on the rebound, or cooking, or reading *Private Eye*, and as I passed him he would tease, 'It doesn't matter how much you know, you will never know what I'm thinking now.' It pleased him, he would stop what he was doing – put one hand on my stomach, one on my lower back, and kiss my neck in delight at this philosophical ace he found in his hand; ah yes, we are each of us fortified palaces! There is a room at the centre that nobody will ever reach. It made the corner of his mouth twitch. 'Unless I tell you what I'm thinking, you can never know it. Even if you know everything else in the world,' he would say.

When I think of him being here, or wait for him to arrive, I think of him as if he will still be like this – with his boylike smile and his curved brow and his pleasure at this little game that was almost sexual, that said I could never drill down deeply enough to know what he was really made of, but which invited me to try. But it is nothing like this any more, as I have perhaps said. There is no longer this simultaneous invitation and denial; instead he comes round and we talk about Teddy and he sits on the sofa with his hands clasped and smiles as if all I see is all I get. At night, he used to wake me up to tell me something of no consequence – sometimes a joke, sometimes an anecdote, bubbles that rose to the surface of his mind when it was dark and quiet; now he sleeps as if he is catching up with all those accumulated years of wakeful moments, sleeping off the jokes, the little tales, while I get stuck in bad dreams.

(I say bad dreams, and I mean it literally, as in a bad book or a bad film – dreams that show no imagination whatsoever. I am about to sit an exam without having revised, I have to catch a flight and I am walking with my suitcase along an empty road, in search of the airport. I wake up and remember the dreams with grubby embarrassment; they call up a flash of otherwise defunct religious shame. I see the Lord shift and roll his eyes. Why, when he has given his people brains of extraordinary power and infinite creativity, must they keep dreaming about exams and being late for flights? And I see him finally forsake me, not because I have wronged him but because I have bored him.)

But you know, it is strange, since beginning this letter on Boxing Day I have started having dreams on your behalf, or at least I don't know if they are my dreams or yours – I dream them, but I am never in them. You're in them, and everything is felt through you. Like this one with the rat, which I've had the last three times Nicolas has stayed. It is a dream with certain small variations, but each is essentially the same. You are in a room with a rat, which is running towards you. A boisterous dog appears and it picks the rat up in its mouth and brings it to the single bed where you sit pressed against the wall, pleading with the dog to go away, which of course it doesn't. When it jumps on you, and lays the rat on your chest, you wake up.

Variations: a friend or parent is in the room and has let the rat loose on purpose to frighten you. Or you take the bedside table and smash the last ounce of oxygen out of the rat's lungs until its flesh is pressed between the floorboards and its blood is all over the walls. Liquid always seems to increase when spilt; it didn't seem like much blood when inside the rat, but now it looks enough to have come out of a goat.

I wake up when I have these dreams and usually get up, and Nicolas' rosary clinks against the metal bedstead where he hangs it. I associate this sound with him being in my house. This is when I want to write to you most, after the rat dreams, and I often do. Much of this letter has been written in those odd hours of the night, where the darkness is thick and airless and like soil.

So what is this rat? Why, in my dreams, are you always cowering from it? See how many pages it has taken me to tell you that Nicolas comes over from time to time, and has been doing so for the last year, on and off – this is because I feel ashamed to say it. I think you will mock our cowardice at breaking away but not breaking away. Or you will think we are feeding on your scraps. You who perpetually gamble everything on a whim, just to be free. You who hear the bear in the woods and open your door to let it in. You who can so little stand the scenery staying the same that you have to run through it. To keep running. But Yannis said something the other day, when I asked him about his wife – he said it is the cowards who keep running, and I wonder if he is right. The bravest people are those who are not afraid of things staying the same.

You didn't analyse personalities in the way I am analysing yours. Your strategy was to go to war with people first and ask questions later.

You sit at our table in the cottage in Morda, by the back window, dealing out cards for Solitaire. You take up position here for the best part of a year or two with your Go-Cat playing cards, which you picked up at a church sale in the village. Green-backed with a sinister picture of a tabby. *A Square Meal for Bored Cats.* You never meant to stay so long, certainly you never meant to live with us, but time bleeds. There is nowhere else you have to be, it is good for me to have an adult presence in the house when Nicolas is away, Teddy loves you for reasons nobody can quite identify, and anyway, time bleeds. You arrive, and before you know it six months have passed and then six more, and your money comes in useful and the back window would be empty without your silhouette.

Some days you are as plain and pale as the northerly light coming through the window behind and we leave you alone in the veil of smoke that makes you look like a sullen bride, bored at her own wedding table. Other days, like this particular and arbitrary day, your eyelids will be painted in heavy purples or oranges right up to the brow and sweeping wide towards your temples, lashes almost unliftably black and heavy. This particular and arbitrary day it is orange and Teddy touches the paint with his finger to see if it is hot. When you raise your eyes from the cards there appears to be an effort; already wide-spaced, these eyes look like they are trying to take off from your face like a weighty bird that needs something to launch itself from but is finally graceful in flight, an albatross, something that means to travel far.

Only your eyes are made-up, in contrast your face is naked and your lips as pale, plump and bare as a bottom, as breasts; I imagine this is what Nicolas is thinking when he says you are disconcerting to look at, like somebody undressed from the waist down. Some days you will be done up like this, some days not. For a time, when you are going most frequently back and forth to London, it is more often than not. You are too much for Morda, but then you always were. You hardly ever go out and when you do I am sure people comment between themselves on sighting you in a lane, as if you were exotica escaped from the zoo.

Instead you play our old table like a veteran croupier, sweeping up the Solitaire hand when I come along and transforming it in seconds into a Poker hand; you just want somebody to do light battle with. The combat zone, we call the table, and a ring forms in the oak grain where your ashtray sits, next to your right hand. You push half the matchsticks you have towards the centre to stay in the game, nails tapping while you wait for me to have a go, head resting languid in a cupped hand. Head surely heavy with the weight of your eyes. 'Your hair is alive,' you tell Nicolas when he sits with Teddy in his arms. The crown of his head touches the ceiling, which is lower in the alcove by the window, and his hair rises and waves with static like some plant on the riverbed. 'You could sell that electricity back to the grid,' I say. 'We will be rich at last.'

I push my last few matchsticks in and you murmur, with a smile, Hallelujah! and astonish Nicolas by folding; you had nothing in your hand. I knew you had nothing, you knew I knew, I knew you knew I knew. It is like this with us, no explaining it. Just that games are more interesting between us when we pretend not to know what the other is up to. Teddy stands on Nicolas' lap and pushes the static out of his hair, cackling with mirth. 'There go our riches,' you say, and gather the cards up as swift as a thief.

About four months ago, back in October or early November, Ruth mentioned that there was a shortage of life models at the drawing school she goes to, and two weeks later I found myself lying, as if shot, on crusted mustard velvet on an improvised bed in an old chapel with fan heaters turned on me, slightly aggressively I thought, like muskets. I didn't think long about this decision and I can't even say it really was a decision so much as a thing I found myself doing, and then doing again. The first time I went to meet the tutor for an interview her eyes lit up. Five foot ten of barely contained dilapidation! An elegance so surface that a pencil nib will scratch it away in no time and find the disaster beneath. This is all art wants, to scratch at the surface and find disaster beneath. You will be a perfect model, she said, and there was no interview, and now I am their emergency on-call nude body who has no regular class but goes when they need me and when work allows. After every class she says, 'You were so perfect' (like a bombed temple, she means), and gives me £20, which ought to be £21 for my three-hour sacrifice, but she never has the extra pound in change.

Is this one last act of vanity, I wonder? Yes, I'm sure. Vanity, and also its unlikely partner, surrender. It makes me feel like a piece of fruit in your photograph. I lie or sit (always on this mustard velvet drape that I think used to be a curtain back in its day and now has almost no velvet qualities at all, is more like the grit of a newly fired brick) and I can feel time acting on me, and I have the odd sensation that they can see me ageing as they draw. In some ways this is a tragic feeling, and in some ways wonderful. It's too late, I think. The days of being desired and being burdened by desire and competing for it, these days are over and now I am what's left. I give myself over as a sorry offering, I put the twenty-pound note in my pocket at the end and go and buy a book and some cigarettes and some ink, and feel cheap and free and taken from in some small way that I can't afford. Give what you can't afford, you used to say; give more than you have. Live in divine debt, it's the only way to get any return from life. I think in many ways you were right about this. I ache all over and I have shown my bare, pale groin to strangers, and that £20 is the sorriest amount of money I ever make. And it is wonderful really, to be so open at last about this rigged deal we make with life. It is wonderful in its own way.

'It's sordid,' Nicolas said when I asked him what he thought of your *Still Life with Irascible Hole*. He laughed at the title and said, with exaggerated purr, 'irr-ascible'. And with exaggerated pout, 'hole'. His mouth surrounded the word and closed it down. He is a man who has always leant a little towards darkness, and for him to call it sordid was no criticism. For him, back then at least, the world was too light, yet also never light enough. Even in the most literal of ways he craved darkness just so that he might shine light into it, and then resented the light for banishing the dark; but we are all paradoxical, aren't we? We all give ourselves over to these internal battles that we'll never resolve.

At dinner that evening with my parents I brought up the photograph again. I'm speaking here about events that happened almost a quarter of a century ago, so forgive some laxness with the detail – I remember so well the purr and the pout, and they seem to eclipse my memory around the point I'm trying to make. Because I am trying to make a point. I'm trying to tell you that Nicolas found your photograph sordid and that over the years this appraisal has changed, which I think symbolises something, the meaning of which might be too painful to face. It began when

I said over dinner, 'Nicolas finds the photograph sordid, do you think he's right?' When my father asked Nicolas in what way, he answered, 'Well, it's all juices and holes, is it trying to be funny?' 'Perhaps so,' my father said, 'perhaps it is trying to be funny in its own inadvertent way, but that would be its secondary function.' My mother said that more than sordid or funny, it was a waste of fruit, to which Nicolas laughed guiltily in a way people do when caught between the sacred and profane.

I stayed out of this conversation, having provoked it. My father was right, if the photograph was funny at all it was only by default. You rarely made any attempt at humour, more at depreciation, which meant stripping away the borrowed value of something until it was left with whatever was its own. If that deflowering made it funny, then so it was. I saw Nicolas looking at it several times over the course of that weekend, which was his second visit to Morda, with morbid fascination as if something in him were being pulled into the hole at its centre.

I don't recall him saying anything more about it for the next six years, even as it hung in the hallway of our home in London, and after that the living room of our miners' cottage near Morda. He only made a comment again after he had met you for the first time, and then he said that as a work of art he suddenly found it quite trite, quite obvious. He meant by that something grave – that any benefit of the doubt he had given it before was annulled by meeting you, in whose context the photograph was now made clear. He no longer called it *sordid*. Sordid meant that it and its creator might stir him in some way, obvious meant that neither it nor its creator had any such power to stir one way or another.

Do you understand me when I say it is possible to see a change in another person that they do not yet see in themselves? My grandmother said that insight of this kind was the Lord working through one's eyes, just as he may work through ears, hands and the senses in general, without limit and whenever so called upon. Lord or not, when Nicolas proclaimed your still life obvious I saw him, without knowing it himself, put up his first defence against his love for you. Two decades later and still it goes on. Recently, in a discussion of the photograph with Ruth and another of her friends from the hospital, he dismissed their praise of it and called it quaint. 'The light's good,' he said. 'But it's not radical or troubling or even meaningful; if it's anything, it's just quaint.'

With this final denouncement of course he turns to you the hard side of his heart, but in the fumbled manoeuvre we see it – the soft part, the part that is still in such need of his protection.

I have been thinking increasingly about your sudden reappearance. Today I was shovelling snow from the front door and I looked up from the ground with a notion that you were there. It was just somebody passing on the street, though I note with interest that this someone was a tall person, far taller than you, and a man at that, which suggests that my memory of you has become overly monumental these long years.

We've had a winter of fluctuations, first mild and dreary, and then there was a fortnight of light snow after Christmas and into the new year, followed by a thaw that seemed to swill water around the whole city and flush out its spirit. I've never known the streets to be as quiet as they were at the beginning of this month. Now, at the end of February, we have a foot of snow in the parks and some verve has returned, perhaps an exasperated energy from all those who thought spring was coming.

At work we've lost three residents over the winter. I don't know what curious biological programming makes a human who never steps outside more likely to die when the outside is cold. We're such simple life-forms, Butterfly, when it comes down to it. We see the days grow short and the branches bare and our enthusiasm for our own lives fades a little. Frances, under whose breast I found no judgement, is only just now recovering from five weeks of pleurisy and looked for a brief time as though she might make the sad tally four, which would be more losses than we've had during the last eighteen months put together. I was surprised by how much the thought of her death affected me. But slowly she's improving. While Bing Crosby and Frankie Laine drone in the background we're all given to turning our heads towards the big picture window that looks out over the garden and the summer house and waiting expectantly for a sighting of spring.

As you'll remember, then, you arrived at our back door quite literally out of the blue. A lucid, blue evening in April when the light is so glassy that it is almost a thing in itself, a surface, onto which you seemed to condense. Such was your reappearance: a manifestation. You knocked on the open door and I came into the kitchen with Teddy on my hip to see who was there. You raised your arms outwards in apparent joy at seeing us. The sun, which was low behind you and bursting from cloud, spun through the wings of your crochet shawl, and Teddy jabbed his forefinger into the space between us and you and called – almost sang – your new name in an eruption of happy recognition as if he'd known you for years. 'Butterfly!' he said, and for a moment I think you hesitated on the doorstep quite humbled, or otherwise cautioned, at having been so instantly assigned a label in this way.

You stooped under the low door and filled the kitchen with a perfume that was more tree than flower.

'Teddy, Nicolas, meet Butterfly,' I joked. In truth I imagined you would hate the name, but it was strange how it so instantly became you. You had always been Nina, and suddenly you were something other, reinvented by the light as if it had dematerialised you and rebuilt you into a new existence. Nicolas had come into the room at some point in this and taken Teddy from me. You reached out your right arm to its full extent and I was surprised, almost perplexed, to see that you still wore the silver cobra. You shook their hands, Nicolas' with a firm, haughty clasp that made something in his expression stand back as if challenged, and Teddy's with lightness. His one-year-old hand had never known such formality.

Once you had kissed my cheeks and hugged me, you leant back against the kitchen table and folded your arms.

'You're still wearing blue,' you said. 'You always wore blue.'

I did often wear blue, dark blue, which you once said made me look like an impending storm, like the rainclouds that come in before the monsoon.

'And you look like a tree that's gone green for spring.'

You were wearing a peculiar long green tunic, which you had tied around the waist with a piece of twine, and your hair was unkempt but lustrous even so. Once it would have been long enough to become caught under the twine, but now it was slightly shorter, and thicker, and though you were never the kind of woman one could call *ripe*, there was something in your thinness that passed for slender, something that, in another less self-denying person, might have been described as energetic or radiant.

'I can't believe I'm seeing you.'

'Nor I you.'

'After all these years.'

It had been nine years in fact since you had left Morda; you left in '73 when your parents moved to America, where your father had got a job as a botanist, or botany researcher – I never did quite know what it was he did – at the Smithsonian Institution. Off you went with them to Washington, but when I telephoned you a month later your mother said you had disliked Washington and had left to travel around America; one of your many typically abrupt departures. I can only think they were in temporary accommodation at that time, because by the next time I telephoned, a few months later, their number no longer worked. And neither did you call or write, but then, as we know, that wasn't exactly your way.

We had been twenty-one the last time we saw one another. And in my mind this was just after you gave me the photograph, although perhaps I have collapsed time a little to fit my memories – but it must have been something like this. You came forward from the table with a bright smile and held your hands out in front of Nicolas. 'May I?'

He gave Teddy to you. You held him as though you were weighing him for lovability, to see if there really was something in this fleshy little form that could sustain one's adoration for a lifetime. Teddy was afraid of you. He didn't often come across strangers. But you were never a person who asked for concessions and you tucked him on your hip in such a way that suggested you were providing a seat that he was very free to leave. He began to play with the great length of hair that fell over your chest and his expression changed from fear to resolve: after all, I will stay here. I will stay right here.

What a thing is this dispassion of yours, Butterfly, that causes everybody to make the same decision?

That evening we sat down for dinner. It was you, Nicolas and I.

You looked out of place in the cottage, which I thought was just the awkwardness of the situation. But actually, when I think of it now, you looked out of place almost anywhere substantial. You pulled out a chair and perched on it in a way that seemed to say you weren't really for chairs, for old oak tables and ranges. I don't mean to say you were contemptuous or ungrateful, you were just in transit. You looked trapped and as though you wished you could feel differently. Across the table you looked at me as if I were at once beloved and unknown.

'Is the food okay?' I asked.

You shook your hair, gestured abundance with your arms, and said to nobody in particular, 'You were always going to be the most able cook. The most splendid wife and mother.'

I admit to being almost embarrassed as we looked at one another along the table, with a shoulder of beef between us, and Nicolas quietly eating.

'As for you, Butterfly?' Nicolas asked, because Butterfly had become, in the space of an evening, what you were called. 'Do you have a husband or family?'

'I don't.'

'You were never interested in men,' I said.

'Is that what you thought?'

'You always ignored them.'

'I'm waiting, that's all.'

'You might wait for ever,' Nicolas said.

You put your fork down. 'Do you mind?' You pointed at a piece of beef on your plate. When I shook my head you picked up the meat and used your teeth, then licked your fingers. 'I'm sorry, I was born without manners.'

Your unused knife felt like a betrayal of sorts on my part; I'd forgotten that you ate only with a fork and that if food needed cutting you'd use your teeth. We have these canines for ripping, you used to argue. These are better by half than knives, which require two hands to operate. Man's overuse of tools is a mark of his stupidity, you'd said.

Nicolas had come to the end of his meal and brought out a pack of cigarettes that he laid on the table. Together we smoked, you whilst still eating. He leant back in his chair and put a hand in his pocket, or at least he probably did, since he always sat like that at the table after dinner, smoking, his face content in an interlude of quiet before he became restless. It seemed possible to me then that he did not see your tremendous beauty. At the most I thought he might see it in the abstract, but find it mistimed with his reality. It was an androgynous beauty of thick brows and strong nose and narrow hips, one that had lateral appeal, but which wasn't fond or nurturing in the way our lives had become since Teddy's birth. I'd had something of your androgyny too once, of course, and I'd had it still when Nicolas and I first met. But androgyny is a difficult thing to hold onto when a child has passed through your body, and not a desired thing, either. I worked on the premise – I'm sure very flawed – that people are wrong to believe that we desire what we cannot have. Instead we desire what we aren't, but can conceivably be. And neither Nicolas nor I could any longer conceivably be what you still were in your absolute lack of ties. If he saw your beauty at all, he saw it as a person sees something at the far side of a field, and then, after a moment of curiousness, carries on with his walk.

Nicolas went to bed soon after dinner; he said he would get up for Teddy in the night if he needed to. You opened a second bottle of wine and took it out into the cold garden, wrapped your shawl around you, thin as you were, and smoked and drank in the darkness. When I realised you weren't about to come back in I took a coat out and joined you. I spread the coat on the grass where you sat and gestured for you to move off the damp grass. We took half each.

'I like Nicolas.'

'He's tired today, quieter than normal.'

'You met him in Morda?'

'No, in London. We lived there for four years after we got married and while he trained. Then Teddy came and we moved back.'

'Trained for what?'

'He's a lighting man, for the stage. It means he goes off here and there to work on productions. Nothing major, we're always broke.'

'I thought you'd be in Borneo, Guatemala, America at least – not still here.'

'I don't even know where Guatemala is.'

'It doesn't matter, you get on a plane and the pilot finds the way.'

'Where have you been, *Butterfly?*'

You put your hand on my knee and squeezed, then let the hand drop back into your lap. I liked the irony of your new name, that of the most fragile and temporary of creatures, and I called you by it as a joke as if to suggest that we'd had no past together to speak of. Teddy had invented you hours before. Did you hate that? If you did you took it with a certain amount of goodwill and collusion, because you responded earnestly enough to the name. 'It doesn't matter where I've been,' you said. 'It doesn't matter at all.'

'In America?'

'No, no, not America, not there.' You exhaled headily. 'I was there for a few months but got swept out for working without a visa. They're very literal, you know, the Americans. Very pedantic.'

'But your parents are still there?'

You nodded, but had squinted off as if distracted, so I looked up, around us, at the night. 'It's beautiful here – better than Guatemala, wherever that is. I know the woods inch by inch, I know the shape of the river and how the sun moves, where the birds nest. We camp out a lot in the summer, even last year when Teddy was a baby. It's just us, me, Nicolas and Teddy, in the way it was just me and you. I wouldn't want you to pity my life.'

You tucked my hair behind my ear with resoluteness. 'Did I say I did?'

A new direction of thought seemed to strike you. 'My brother is trying to join the Lithuanian Academy of Sciences,' you said. 'Just like my father before him. Still trying to protect the place from the Soviets.' You gathered the surplus of your shawl and wrapped it around me. "This time it's a colossal nuclear-power station in the far east of the country, it'll have three reactors when it's finished. The Soviets have cut down all the trees; they're trying to turn Lithuania into a factory, according to Petras.'

'Has he gone back there to live, then?'

'Yes, for a time.'

'Is he safe?'

You shrugged. Because you had looked away and seemed suddenly restless with the subject, I took the tassels of the shawl in my hand.

'I remember this.'

You rubbed the wool between your fingers for a moment, then nodded. 'I haven't taken it off for nine years.'

'Nine hot years.'

'Nine difficult-to-play-tennis years.'

'It's clean, for something that's been worn ceaselessly for a decade.'

'I bathe in liquid wool wash.'

'Pass me a cigarette, *Butterfly*. Do you mind, if I call you that?'

You gave a generous shrug. 'Let's consider Nina dead.'

'Surely not dead.' I took the corner of the shawl idly between my own fingers. 'Just retreating from view.' And then dropped it. 'Are you going to stay for a while – a couple of weeks?'

'May I stay a longish while?'

'How long is longish?'

'A decade or two, I'm clean out of money.'

'I'd have to ask Nicolas. If I say two decades and he objects, perhaps we could haggle it down to one.'

'Well, a month or so would do. Put my case forward, would you? Tell him I can darn and iron and cook.'

'But you can't.'

'But tell him.'

You kissed me on the temple and gathered yourself up to standing like you had always done, a cross-legged handless transition that was the only vaguely athletic thing your drawn-out body ever did. You passed the cigarette from your lips to mine and said you were cold and were going to bed. I extinguished the cigarette and came too.

That night you shouted out from your sleep, as you did the next night, and the next. For three days you stalked about the tiny house in your tunic, talking about politics and death and the Four Conditions of the Self. Seriousness was your way, but I don't think it ever signalled unhappiness as such. Apart from the shouting out at night, my memory of you on that visit was one of a human being at ease with herself, languidly exuberant. It was true that the shawl didn't ever seem to leave your body, which gave you a curious swaddled, limbless look; only once did I see your arms, when they shot outwards to beckon Teddy to you and the shawl fell back. I saw in the crook of your arm some holes from needle use and some bruising, which I never asked you about. Teddy loved you. You crouched earnestly on the floor of the living room teaching him letters of the alphabet and names of animals with a focus and patience I had never had.

In the evenings you sat outside in the cold and it was me who sat with you, Nicolas only managed it for one evening. He was subdued by you, that was the truth. After you left I thought often of how you had arrived – there at the back of the house, knocking on the open door and raising your arms in unmistakable joy – though I wondered even then on whose behalf you were joyful: your own or ours. You had the grin of somebody who knows their arrival is in some way triumphant, a triumph of surprise, a momentous thing.

Increasingly I am aware of life as a kind of dream. I will be thinking or feeling something and the thing appears or happens, and it's as if the world, like my dreams, is a projection of my own mind. Today while walking I was thinking about what it will be like to be a grandmother, assuming Teddy goes on to have children. He is old enough; I could be a grandmother in a matter of months biologically speaking, and there I will be, not much over fifty, elevated into that final stage of being. As I was thinking it a toddler and her father walked past, and the child pointed at me and said, Nana. That's not Nana, the father said. Definitely not, I smiled. Afterwards I thought: Did this happen or did I imagine it? The truth is that it makes little difference either way to the experience itself.

That example makes it sound like I'm talking about coincidences, which wouldn't be true. Not coincidences but manifestations, ideas that resolve into form. I write down our old conversations, fanciful and ill-remembered though they are, as if to pretend that's exactly how they were, almost as a joke to myself, to take a sketchy memory and write it as if fact. But then, somehow, that sketchy memory takes form in the world. Not long after I wrote that last conversation I heard two men by the banks of the

Thames, peeling themselves out of wetsuits, discussing diving in Guatemala. One of them raved about diving down to the extinct crater of a supervolcano, the other said he didn't even know where Guatemala was. This is what I mean, you see, when I talk about the sense of the world projecting my mind.

And now this week a man called Gene has moved into The Willows, and I saw on his notes that he is Lithuanian, or of Lithuanian descent; so he appears, like the residue of a thought I'd had. Yesterday I saw what I thought was a piece of jewellery on the pavement and it was two green bugs back-to-back, beautiful beyond description, like a piece of gold-inlaid polished jadeite. There was no trenchant message here, only the sense that they had been set in my path as a reminder of the remarkable. The sense that I get, to put it another way, is that far from drifting through a world of arbitrary objects and happenings, I am tuning in through static to a collection of sensory things that have been put there to reveal my mind to me.

On the other hand perhaps it's the light. We're finally in spring and the light is as it was that April evening when you arrived at the back door. It's clean and sudden and at times it confuses me. Or confuse might be too strong a word – sometimes it distracts me, in the way the luminous words in a poem distract me from the poem's meaning. The ink on the last few pages of this letter is already fading from exposure to these unpredictable outbreaks of light. The first few pages are still unfaded, those from December. It gives the odd impression of the reverse passing of time.

Meanwhile, I keep looking but I do not get the impression you intend to be found. I have been tracing my eyes around the map of Lithuania, wondering where the bee-keeping farm might have been, where Petras was staying with friends. I am reduced to the wildest suppositions. What do I know about Petras,

Lithuania or bees? And yet, this is where my mind has decided you are and my mind is not a thing that is easily changed, as I have often lamented. You are not at the farm itself, bees would trouble you, as do all things in large numbers – no, you have found a spot half a kilometre behind the farm where the pine forest deepens and nobody goes.

There: you amble half desperate through the forest and you see it, a hut. Maybe there is a lake after all. For one short interlude the forest thins and gives way to a lake, but a lake that eases from the shore so gradually that you cannot tell where one ends and the other begins. You stay clear for fear of drowning. Inside the hut are his things, his shoes, his writings, his name doodled repeatedly down the margin, *Petras Petras Petras*, a childlike fascination with himself. You sit at the table and read his notes, but you can't read his notes. Too faded, simply illegible.

Then in my mind you come back to the Upanishads, which only serves to remind me of the poverty of my imagination. *The Self has four conditions*, you read, cupping the sides of your head with your hands. Always, just as this tentative, hypothesised you is about to break into action or do something instructive, she starts reading the Vedas, as if the whole of her life and future is snagged on their wisdom, as if she doesn't know how to operate any more in the world, how to have agency, how to live in time like the rest of us and suffer the consequences of her actions.

(Sometimes I imagine, out of sheer playfulness, that I am writing this as a kind of defence for having murdered and buried you under the patio. It turns out I am not at my desk in central London but in a cell awaiting trial without bail, because whoever bought the cottage in Morda decided to dig foundations for an extension to the kitchen, which was admittedly always too small, and the digger turned up bones and teeth and a silver cobra, which they believe would have been worn on a woman's upper arm, some small hooped earrings and some scraps of undecomposed leather and zip from a pair of winter boots.

People in the village mutter: How *could* she have done it? Which leads me to think: How *did* I do it? Suffocation is the kindest way, especially if you were in one of your stupors; strangulation unlikely since you would not have let me; knifing or bludgeoning impossible because you are, after all, a friend, one held dearly and much loved, and I am not a monster.

I will plead guilty to a crime of passion, something I have often imagined with fondness and craving, as though nothing could be more wonderful than such a crime. Some days I look around me at the hundreds of people all moving purposefully towards a blind fate, or not even at this, but at something more banal – the arch of the underground train tunnels, which are made with human hands and are as courageous as a swan's neck, or a swan's neck as breakable as a hazel twig, or the sheer, pointless, brilliant glare of sun on glass that makes you blink and long for something that vanishes before you know what it was – and it seems to me that this whole universe is a crime of passion. So reckless in its short-termism, wreaking such magnificent havoc on those who come to live in it, so unreasonable and grotesque and glorious and rampant and murderous, because nothing escapes it alive, yet nothing escapes it without having lived either, without having been zealously loved and brought to its knees – even if only once, for a moment – by it.

Oh, to have murdered you, Butterfly, with my heart on fire. And then to write out my defence just as the universe defends its crimes with a sunset. Happy days, happy, wild and playful thoughts. Meanwhile, both (probably) alive, I suppose we proceed meekly on.)

Yesterday evening after work Ruth's daughter was waiting for me. Or I should say I saw her outside in the driveway of the care home about half an hour before I was due to finish, so I went out to her, and she said she'd be happy to wait. She sat in the summer house until seven.

'You could have come indoors,' I said, when I was finished. 'The evenings are still so cold.'

'I prefer it outside.'

'Did you want to talk about something?' I asked, at the same time as she said, 'I'd like to talk about something.'

So I suggested that we walk towards the Tube, and go to a café there. By the time we got to the café it was closing, so we just walked up past the farmers' market at Swiss Cottage and made a loop behind Hampstead Theatre and back, and repeated it. She told me that she wanted to give up her religion, this was the gist of it. It had suddenly become very clear to her that she needed to leave it behind.

'Do you feel guilty for that?' I asked.

'Guilty? No, no.'

I was going to ask her in that case why she was telling me and not her parents, why she seemed to be coming to me for reassurance. But then I saw she hadn't come for reassurance, she had come to be heard as an adult. She must be twenty-one, a year younger than Teddy, but she has a plump dimple in the middle of her chin that makes her look perpetually childlike. All of Ruth's children have this, a look that is almost Amish – thick honey-coloured hair and smoke-grey eyes and fresh, gentle features. We hardly ever saw them when they were growing up, they were always at this group or that class, or staying with Ruth's mother in Suffolk. I can't even remember when you would have last seen Lara; it must have been when she was four or five, and I can't say she's changed much essentially since then. Goodly, we called Ruth's children; the *goodly brood*. All the same we – you too – were awestruck by their looks and kindness in our own way.

'It's since we saw the Pinter play,' she said. 'I watched that old man speaking to an empty chair and pouring a glass of wine for nobody, and it's exactly like speaking to God, and taking communion for God. Have a glass of wine, God. Here, let me drink it for you since *you* haven't shown up again.' She paused and looked at me.

'Is that how you see it, that God stands you up?'

There was a small sound that was almost laughter and she looked at me as if to say I didn't know the half of it. Then she asked, 'Did you think that man in the play seemed lonely?'

When I answered yes she said, 'Every Christian, Jew, Muslim is lonely. They speak to God, and God never speaks back.'

I had been moved, or maybe impressed, by her rapture at the Pinter play. It wasn't a child's rapture. Now I suppose I could see why, though I wasn't prepared for this kind of discussion or for how agitated she was. And I realised that she had chosen me to speak to about it, not arbitrarily or for lack of other opportunities, but very specifically, because she viewed me as the godless family friend who countered their piety with cynicism;

I wanted to say: But I am not godless! It's just that God has got tired of me. I could feel how much she wanted my cynicism now, and for that reason I couldn't give it – because I didn't want her to give up the cause so easily.

'My grandmother used to tell me that everybody *without* God is lonely,' I said.

'Well, that's what they say isn't it? That's the official thing, the—'

'Party line.'

'Yes.'

'But maybe the point is that we're lonely either way – sometimes anyway. Atheists and believers alike.'

'At least atheists aren't also stupid. I sit in church every week with my head all low like a bad dog, falling for the biggest joke that ever was.'

I couldn't help but smile. 'There's no shame in falling for a joke,' I said, and I might not have sounded sincere but I was, oh I was – because of course all life is a joke and falling for it is the best we can do. Better than refusing to laugh along, which I sometimes think is the route to madness.

I put my hand on Lara's shoulder as we walked, and I wondered at how much courage had gone into this conversation on her part, or how much going against the grain. If ever the phrase 'in the bosom of one's family' could be used without irony, it would be in relation to the belonging, wholesomeness and gentle piety of her family, its sheer warmth and durability. I remember Ruth once saying that she had created for her children a home that was failsafe; there were no needs, spiritual at least, that could not be met by the love they found there. And in light of that, Lara seemed to me, in the dusk, a fledgling that had crept out of the nest and up the branch an inch or two, and wanted to go neither back nor forward, nor up nor down.

'When I used to ask God to speak to me,' she said, 'I was always sure he did. I heard a man's voice, which actually is just my Uncle Billy's voice. Not God at all, just Uncle Billy, who Dad says is a gambler, a womaniser and a racist. And now when I ask there's nothing at all.'

I took my hand from her shoulder and put it in my pocket. 'Then withdraw your belief. If God exists he'll wait for you to come back, and if he doesn't you won't feel his loss.'

For a while she didn't answer, and when I looked at her she was staring straight ahead, and I thought she was irritated with me for being facile. Her cardigan was draped over her bag and the belt was dragging along the ground, so I picked it up and looped it around the bag strap. Then she said, 'I feel like I'm always carrying a sack of stones.' And she smiled, as though I had given her permission to put it down.

All the same I wanted to retract my comment, and I was sorry I had made it. I wasn't sure it was true at all that God would wait for her; he has always struck me as the life and soul, wanting to be where the action is. But she did look genuinely brighter and less racked, as Teddy once did when I lent him money he desperately needed.

'You won't tell my mum I've spoken to you, will you?' she said. I told her no, and I had the sense that we had just shared an entirely asymmetrical conversation in which one person idly muses while the other weighs up their life. All the same, I told her she could talk to me any time and I gave her my number.

It was only when she'd walked away and I was going down the escalator into the Underground that I wondered if there was a man involved in this religious crisis. I remember you saying that everything essentially is about men wanting women and women wanting men, that everything came down to this brute thing, no matter how heavenly it might have reckoned itself to start with. God himself is just the ultimate sexual fantasy, you said. The infinite, ultimate mover and maker and dominator. I thought of that as I rattled along in the Tube, which you also interpreted sexually. I thought of a church full of folk poised like naked bodies on beds waiting to be loved. A funny image, a sad one. A body wide open, and nobody entering.

*

What I mean (another day now, but I feel like I can't let this lie) is that Lara, who has never had much to do with me, has singled me out as an ally in her defection from God. Not just God, from religion. And as soon as I left her at the station I began to wonder why I felt uncomfortable in accepting that role. I don't know. Perhaps it is because I suspect that my reasons for being dismissive of religion are not very good ones.

Let me tell you something. In our house, growing up, God was a celebrity, and my parents threw lavish parties for him, which alarmed the church-going population. There was always red wine, whisky and ginger beer, smoked salmon and crackers, meringues, piles of fruit. I know you know this, but I write it to make a point you do not know. In our house, the question of religion was one of love and an open heart, regardless of denomination; everybody was welcome, whoever they were and whatever they believed. *The holy city of the heart.* The heart is where God, the infinite, takes his seat without jealousy, but with passion. All creatures can live there, all men, all their beliefs. All conflict is settled there. My mother's faith was firm, but she practised it with a pot-pourri of rituals. She burnt Indian oils in a little crucible under the rosary that hung from the wall light, and she wore attars of sandalwood and jasmine sambac, or majmua, meditative fragrances that kept the Lord near, she said. They gave the straight-faithed women of Morda dreadful headaches behind the eyes and in the temples – or so I overheard once in the post office. And so, in time, every member of the congregation fell out with my mother and father over their religious promiscuity and their lack of moderation, their winters in India and their drinking of whisky and ginger on the rocks, and their smattering of Sanskrit followed by quotes from the smokiest passages of the Song of Solomon, all of which made them seem vaguely lewd and aristocratic and incapable of an authentic feeling. The falling-out went only one way, though. My parents argued with nobody and continued to throw the parties, and people continued to come because they were fascinated despite themselves.

And so I lived with my open heart that had no religious preferences but was tilted towards God like the Earth is tilted towards the sun; just spinning harmlessly. I was wreathed in his spirituality, I never had to practise devotion because my life itself was the devotion. When I was born I was given to him, my mother said, like a drop of rain is given to the ocean. When did I lose my right to this faith? When did I question it? You imagine we question and lose it gradually, that it seeps away. But not so; I think I can name the moment, on a hilltop overlooking Bala Lake, with you, in the late summer of the year you arrived at our door.

(Ah, it would have to involve *me*, I hear you say. To which I reply, yes, it all involves you, of course. I see you put your elbows on the table and lean your chin on your fists, to fortify yourself against the coming slander.)

You had been in a buoyant mood all day, which was unnerving at the best of times, but alone with you in the Welsh hills on a fifteen-mile walk while you pranced in those terrible purple loons that you had salvaged from the rubbish after Nicolas threw them away, this was like being visited by a jester on Death

Row. By this point in life your ups never came without downs, nor did they often come naturally.

So you strode about in some suspect interval of high spirits, in Nicolas' trousers and Petras' cap, which you said you were not wearing, but storing on your head until he came back. By the time we got to the top of the hill, before our last climb down to the lake, we had been talking about war, which had somehow moved on to religion. It was a hot day and we had drunk all our water and the valleys were stale. I know that you were feeling helpless: Petras in Lithuania, and people he knew being sent off to some or other Russian labour camp for speaking against the state. You never did say where you had been in the years since I had last seen you (you were singularly, bloody-mindedly silent on this subject) but I know there had been one trip to Lithuania because the baggage label had been on your suitcase when I finally – perceiving you were not about to leave – put it in the loft.

But this would have been nothing more than a short, unwelcoming visit. We heard about these things back then, Westerners travelling behind the Iron Curtain, funnelled towards tourist hotels and eagerly encouraged to part with their strong Western currency, and then just as eagerly encouraged to go home. I doubt you ever saw your brother, or anyhow if you did then briefly, over a coffee or brandy in a hotel bar where he came to meet you. Any longer with him and you both would have been considered suspicious; any trips into the countryside to his farm would have had you questioned. I think those times in your so-called homeland, supposing they happened, only confirmed to you your lack of belonging. By anything but birth it was not your country. Britain was, this mannered land that was too small for you and which you were striding across in cap and bright flares.

As we got stickier and more tired you started, with an inversely proportionate enthusiasm, to talk about how little there was to be done about war; it was always and everywhere and man would never learn. I took issue with this, maybe because, in part, we could see from that point the abandoned Frongoch Camp, where German prisoners were kept in the First World War and then Irish dissidents after the Easter Rising. My father had taken me there when I was about ten, when it was redundant and ghostly, and it had left me with a feeling I am proud to own: that we are better now than we were. No longer do we accept war with our neighbours. A childish thought, but as I said, I am proud to own it, it is my one optimistic vehemence: our politics are more peaceful now, we are better than we were.

You dismissed the idea. Politics could never solve war because it created it; asking politics to be peaceful was like asking a gun to shoot droplets of sunlight. And man – man! Man was not better, he was what he was and always would be: frightened and selfish. We were toiling up the hill at the time, you ahead of me. I was surprised by how well Nicolas' trousers fit you, snug across the hips where they had been looser on him, and tight and long on the thighs before they flooded outwards. I am glad to have had no cause to think of them for years, but now that I do I see you striving up the hill and telling me about the Hindu trinity, Brahma, Vishnu, Shiva. Brahma the creator, Vishnu the preserver, Shiva the destroyer.

They were not idols, you said, they were not supposed to be worshipped as real. They were merely illustrations of ideas that could not be conceptualised otherwise, almost like dreams. I remember you saying this because the more time that grows between me and that conversation, the more I realise how true it is, that we are forced to invent form to understand the formless, time to understand the timeless. Religion has trinities, you said, because a triangle is the holiest and most elegant of things; with two lines you can only create two lines, but with three you can create a shape. This is why three is a transformative number. Brahma and Vishnu – creation and preservation – these are two lines. It is Shiva that transforms them into something new. And then, just as abruptly, you said, 'By the way I have a new lover.'

You knew I would be pleased. 'Who?' I asked, as we were reaching the summit. 'In London,' you said. 'Does he have a name?' 'Don't they all? One man is so very like another.' The summit had a view over the lake and a different, more hopeful kind of air that made us both turn our faces upwards. You sat at the base of a cairn. I remember this very well, the way you brushed your hair back behind your shoulders and looked down towards the lake and town. You said, 'Nicolas is coming to get us from Bala, yes?' and I nodded. 'Are you happy with him?' Again I nodded, or said yes, or of course, and you stared out with something that was almost a smile, and almost sad. 'You're lucky to have him, he's a good find.'

I watched you. In the four or five months you had been staying with us you had never spoken about him in that way before, in fact you barely referenced him at all. 'Two is not a holy number,' you said, and you leant across and put a rock on top of the cairn. 'Maybe that's why I get tired of relationships so quickly.'

'Come on. You're not tired of yours already?'

'Like I said, you're lucky.'

I became aware that the conversation had been sliding between subjects until I no longer knew what it was about. First politics, then the trinity, then your inadequate lover, then Nicolas; and when you talked about Nicolas a kind of repose took over you. I felt that you were moving in on me with your talk of Hinduism and perfect triangles, and this was when I began to feel threatened, not comforted, by religion. I watched you sit and I knew you were thinking of Nicolas. The breeze flapped the bottom of your loons. This was the early eighties, nobody wore such things any more. But you had joined me in the bathroom that morning and put them on uncertainly, asking for approval, as if they were a new fashion. You could be so naive and guileless, so out of step that, at those times anyway, I always wanted to give you the approval you asked for in the same way I would give it to Teddy when he showed me a drawing or an attempt at handwriting.

Very suddenly I felt outmanoeuvred, and I was. Wasn't I? You were going to work your way into my marriage and you were going to call its new three-way shape *holy*, and I, pinned like a snared bird to one corner of a triangle, would have to watch it happen. And it felt to me, if you will forgive the overblown metaphor, that in religion I'd had a magnificent wild cat, which I fed and watered and loved and to which I granted respect and freedom, in return for protection. And then, when I came under threat, when my house was besieged, it did not protect me but glanced back once, skulked away and gave itself to somebody else.

It astonished me that I saw your 'trinity' coming so clearly, yet didn't stop it, as if, in a way, I chose not to stop it. I said nothing about this to you at the time, though; as I remember, the two of us just looked down into the valley we had to reach, thinking of Nicolas making his way along its road. We walked down, didn't we, quietly, and I think I slept in the car on the way home while you and Nicolas played Twenty Questions. Or did I pretend to sleep? I honestly can't recall.

Here you are, miles from your hut. 'Get up! Stir Yourself!' the Upanishads have said. (Book I, *Katha* Upanishad, in which Death tries to evade difficult questions.) I imagine how it is – you read those words, '*Stir Yourself!*' When the book urges you along the hard path of wisdom, the *sharp edge of the razor*, you stand from your charpoy as if stung, throw on your shawl, leave the gloom of the hut and walk.

Let me see. I think there are the beginnings of a track you have worn through the forest, which snakes inefficiently between trees, twice the distance the crow flies. And amongst the spruce and ferns, suddenly a camellia. Its flowers are deep pink and the rain is drifting into them. You crouch and rub the sandy soil around its roots. You smell it, then sift it between your fingers. I know what you are thinking now; you are thinking of the time Petras told us about the genocide in the Polish forest of Bieszczady, not one act of genocide but several, in the hands of the Nazis, then the Ukrainians, then the Soviets. If you found sudden outbreaks of camellias or willowherb or rhododendron you would know that was a patch of soil made acid by fires where a family's home had been burnt down. There would have been residue of blood in the earth without doubt. At that time he would have been in his early twenties and we fourteen, fifteen at most, and we had been walking through the woods at Morda in a perfectly relaxed mood. He said these things and then commented brightly on the soft loam underfoot, or the crunch of the beech leaves.

You stand and look around you for more; the isolation of this one camellia makes it all the more fabulous in the otherwise bare forest, among bonelike trees. Why have you never noticed it before? Maybe it is Petras reborn, his soul transmigrated. Of course, this is not the kind of soul-cycle bullshit you believe in, and yet. The Upanishads say it, don't they? We hatch from the seed, we hatch from the seed, we hatch from the seed, until we no longer need to do it, and then we are finally free. Petras was, wasn't he, the kind of person who made the unlikely probable, the one who shone a rare light? Or was he? The problem is that you have glorified him as people do with the dead, which is something you observed in others even as a teenager reading the obituaries in the paper. 'All the people in the news today are liars, cowards and criminals,' you said. 'But all the people in the obituaries are loving, loyal and full of joy. It seems the wrong people die.'

Maybe Petras was not so much a gallant freedom fighter, but a dog blindly following a scent. There you go again – you are thinking about the walk in Morda, when he told us about Bieszczady; to think he had, for years, been writing dissident material about the Soviets uprooting local people, destroying the Lithuanian countryside just as they had done in Poland. Even you, who were not easily surprised, were surprised to see the book he pulled from his bag, full and battered by the onslaught of his private words. Then, a year or so after that, in 1972, he heard about the student who set himself on fire in Kaunas while proclaiming 'Freedom for Lithuania!', and he promptly added to a list of heroes that included Gandhi, William Wilberforce, Dos

Passos, Jesus and Elizabeth Fry the name of Romas Kalanta, a
student with long hair and a shabby jacket who, seen in some
ways, might have been the softest, gentlest visionary of them all.
He left to attend the funeral and, as we know, he never did return
for any length of time, as if he thought he had to take up a cause
Kalanta had left off.

You have never been able to stop imagining Petras out in an
ethereal woodland examining and cataloguing indigenous bark
samples, his pen his sword. It is only now that you have found
yourself in a woodland that replaces the likes of that one, following
your own blind scent, that you wonder if your brother and Kalanta
were really visionaries at all, or just young men who saw their
unhappiness and labelled it Russia. You have often considered
how useful it would be to have something to blame that is not
yourself, but you have not found a compelling victim. Am I right?
I see you looking at the camellia bush and biting your lip in
thought. You don't know how you feel about it, so you stand in
the light rain with your hands in your pockets. You are thinking
several things at once, as humans – to their detriment – can. I
cannot second-guess what they all are, but one of them is another
line from the *Kasha* Upanishad that you read just a few hours
before: *Do not run among things that die.*

First thing this morning when I was walking from the Tube to work I caught the smell of marzipan that comes off new gorse. It's early for gorse, but possible, so I looked around, even detoured up a side street to see if I could find what was giving that scent. There was no gorse and anyway I lost the smell, but when I got back to the original spot I could smell it again.

So, in my mid-morning break I went back to that same place, just to see if I could still smell it, and I couldn't, and I couldn't account for why I had even thought I might, or why I had bothered to try. But it was the most curious thing, because as I was about to walk back I saw my bracelet on a low wall at the end of somebody's front garden – the silver bracelet with the pearl inset. It must have somehow come undone when I was standing there earlier this morning, maybe when I turned my watch round to see if I had time to go and trace where the smell was coming from.

Again, that strange sense I described before, of tuning in through static. You see, the pearl in that bracelet is the one Nicolas found on our last pearl-fishing trip in Scotland, and I always associate this trip with the smell of gorse, because we went in late spring when the valley of the Oykel river was rife with it. We woke up in the morning and unzipped the tent to the smell of marzipan and heather, of water, sky, bracken.

I am writing this in Gene's room – the man who has recently moved into The Willows. It must be almost nine at night and he is sound asleep. He sleeps a lot, and badly, waking up anxious every hour or so, but we have discovered that if somebody sits by his bed while he goes off to sleep he will probably go for hours, maybe all night, before waking up again. I'm writing by the shaving light, and I have been sitting here quietly in the chair with my eyes closed, listening to his breath. This is what remains of a big, strong man after eight-and-a-half decades on the planet – such a small amount of time relatively speaking, eight and a half decades. Really nothing cosmologically, an eye blink, and yet it completely undoes a strong man.

There was an almighty storm on that last trip to Scotland. It has always felt to me that we ripped the pearl from its jaws, plunged our hands in and pulled it out a minute before the landscape collapsed. We arrived on the Friday night in good weather, pitched our tent by the river in the dark and got up just after sunrise. The sky was a pale, vast blue. Before bed, I had boiled water in the pot over the fire and filled up hot-water bottles, then dug the hot-water bottles into our bag of clothes so we could put them on warm and dry in the morning.

There was nobody and nothing in the valley, and every sound was of water, flowing through things, into things, around things and against things. Teddy probably ran the short distance down to the river beach where Nicolas stood and began shovelling the shingle into piles; he, like his father, loved to dig. I built a fire with the dry wood we had brought. Nicolas waded knee-deep into the river. To fish for river pearls you need shallow, fast-flowing water. You lower a glass-bottomed bucket into the river and scan the gravel bed, and if you find a mussel you use your hands or a cleft stick to pick it out, and you break it open. There will almost never be a pearl inside.

'There,' Nicolas said, and I too waded in and squinted onto the riverbed at the cluster of mussels. They were shallow enough to pluck from the gravel where they had been filtering the rushing water for food. In his palm I could see their exposed siphons, liplike and wide open, as if suffering an unbearable thirst.

We took them to Teddy who was standing at the river's edge ankle-deep, stuffing his small hands between rocks to feel for mussels there, and we helped him prise them apart. 'Look!' he said. He ran his finger around the inside of a shell, the thick and silky layer of nacre. I told him about the nacre and how the pearl is made. 'Isn't it beautiful?' I said. 'The purples and blues.' I held the dead mussels in my palm while Teddy squatted, nose wrinkled, and peered at them.

Before we discarded the shells I sat with him and counted their rings to see how old the creature was. 'Like trees,' I explained. 'The more rings, the older it is.' Some must have been sixty or seventy years old, a figure that astounded Teddy into one of his stern, focused silences in which he would stare blankly and meanwhile prod at something with his thumb – the ground, his thigh, in this case the hollow of the shell. He would prod almost painfully. Then reanimate and leave the thought behind, whatever it had been.

We fished from daybreak until mid-afternoon. Often in the Highlands the very early mornings are clear and blue and then become gradually duller as if, I always thought, our human presence clouded the landscape like breath clouds glass. So by mid-morning the clouds were grouping around the mountains. The duller light made the mussels more visible – the water's surface no longer glittered and reflected or threw down phantom shapes to the gravel bed. Nicolas handed them to me in fistfuls and I took them to Teddy on the shore where we sorted through them. Teddy would peer deep into the open shell. 'Nope,' he would say. And, 'Nope again', with a sceptical sigh that was adult and borrowed and, I knew with some embarrassment, was my own.

Nicolas could spend hours in the water without rest, and he did that day. Though he had always found pearls when he fished for them on his own, on our three or four pearl-fishing trips together we had never found one. It was a matter of pride to him to find one this time, and proof of purpose: I don't assume this, I know it. He tells me that it is common amongst boys who have grown up without a father, in an environment of mother and sister and mother's friends and sister's friends and conversations that considered in depth the precise nature of men's shortcomings, for the boy to be almost pathological about pleasing women, as though he might, and must, single-handedly right all male wrongs. In the cool, head-shaking statement, *Typical men*, which he heard so often after so many a story of maltreatment, selfishness and recklessness, the boy grew up wishing to be anything but a typical man. So he divests hours in the cold task of finding this proverbial needle in a haystack, turning himself inside out to find a pearl in this river for his wife.

You might not recognise this picture of a labouring, tireless man, because at home he was looser and lazier, whereas when he was pearl-fishing or mudlarking he interrogated the earth, he was almost merciless. There were no breaks in duty; I took tea out to him midstream and he drank it only because he had nowhere to put the mug down. For lunch he ate a bacon sandwich out of the same necessity. Otherwise he submerged his bucket into the monotone of his own reflection and waded slowly down-river and up. His shoulder bag would fill with mussels and every so often I'd go to him or he'd come to me to empty it, and we'd replace it with an empty bag.

One of the strongest memories I have of this day is of a moment that came just before we found the pearl. Teddy and I were breaking shells open on the shore. I looked up and for once Nicolas wasn't leaning into the river, but was standing upright in the water with one of his feet in the bucket to stop it being taken by the current, and he was staring at us. He has a tendency to make the softest and saddest of faces when thoughtful, which I have never been able to interpret. Maybe they are real moments of sadness but, if they are, they come from somewhere else, and not from the moment at hand. And sometimes I am inclined to think I misread the expression altogether and what seemed sad is just pensive, or not even that. Just the way the flesh falls. Do you know the face I mean? Did you ever have a way of interpreting it? That was the way he looked at us then.

A moment later there it was, in the heap of mussels I had just taken out of the bag, a pearl. I laid it on the flat of my hand and our fingertips rolled it around. Like most freshwater pearls it was a baroque – like I mentioned before, an irregularly shaped pearl that is slightly pitted. It was no bigger than a back tooth and had a faint lilac sheen, coloration from the peat, Nicolas said when I called him to the bank. A good lustre, he said. A good pearl.

What you will know about Nicolas is that he has a simple way of seeing. Anybody who has spent any time with him will know this; he sees in images that can be held up on cards, sometimes unobvious but visual and graspable. I used to tell him that he has a mind like Japanese food: simple, yet strange. A pearl appears inside a mussel and we pick it out, killing the mussel. Along the way we squander hundreds of creatures for the sake of this one pearl, and we pile their shells up on the shore without shame. And when I comment blithely on that waste he says that taking a pearl is only like taking a perfect photograph, you get through hundreds just for the sake of one.

Days were always short on those spring trips, but this day got hunted down mid-afternoon by a highway of violet cloud that had come charging over the mountains. As soon as we had found the pearl we looked up and seemed to notice the cloud for the first time. The tent was rippling in a wind we hadn't even been aware of. Nicolas put the pearl inside a matchbox, which he put in the pocket of his coat. As the rain started we went inside the tent and huddled together with the flysheet open so that we could see the storm. But when the wind began funnelling down the valley, blowing our stove and cups along the riverbank, lifting and shaking the tent, we made a run for it to the car, which was parked fifty yards up the track closer to the road. The rain came and pelted the insects and blossom off the windscreen, the thunder shook the old windows, the sky came down as low as the roof, a tree half a mile away across the river caught fire in a lightning strike. Nicolas rolled the car away from the apple blossom we had parked under, down the track towards the river.

It must have lasted the best part of an hour; the three of us clasped hands and laughed. Teddy cried as well as laughed, in little uncertain bursts. It was a kind of wonderment to watch the trees bend and the river turn mulberry and spin round the rocks. Our tent had collapsed but somehow stayed pegged, and we watched the rain hammer it to the ground. The rain itself was a wall shifting endlessly down the valley, and it was only apparent where the mountains were when the lightning earthed itself at their summits.

When the worst of the storm cleared, the rain continued and the thunder rumbled around quietly. We drifted off to sleep in the car, waiting for it to end so that we could go and assess the damage. I rested my head against the window, thinking, half awake and half asleep, of that small, dented pearl. Inside the pearl was whatever tiny thing got stuck in the mussel, the grit or dirt or parasite. Inside it was a fragment of the life of the river, the life of the river constituted by the salmon and trout, all the particles and the rocks that made the particles, the plants, the eroding mountains, the clouds, rain, sun, the cosmos stretching back through time. May we never, never stop wondering at this world we're given. An image keeps coming to mind: those iterated shapes, a pentagon within a pentagon within a pentagon, say, and this is the form my feelings take of that trip now. Us inside the tent, the tent inside the landscape, the landscape inside the pearl, the pearl inside the tent, the tent inside the landscape, repeating onwards, iterating and reiterating.

When we woke up I thought for a moment that the river was all around us and we were floating down it inside the tent. And it was only when a man's voice came from outside the car that I realised we were on dry ground and that he, the man, was impatient. Nicolas wound down the window.

It was illegal to fish for pearls, the man said. He was a salmon fisherman who had come down to the river after the storm and had seen the discarded mussels that the wind had scattered near our pitch. If we didn't want him to report us we should pack up and go home. Nicolas said he didn't know of that law, he hadn't been aware. It was a new law, the fisherman said, and not a day too soon in coming; people like us were destroying the livelihood of people like him, who depended on the salmon, which depended on the mussels. We packed up our soaked things. We swept the pile of mussels into a bag and put it in the car. When we drove off, with the matchbox in the glove compartment, I said that I felt like a smuggler. Perhaps more accurately, a victor. The storm had passed and something of that bright day had come back. It was as if a great door slid closed behind us on that most lovely of lands, but that we had come away with a piece of it, a pre-formed memory. And that then we could take that memory and see if we could go and find the life to which it belonged.

*

Meanwhile Gene is still sleeping and it has just started raining here, pouring in fact. I can hear an owl-call, that hollow flute of the male, and then the female's sharp reply, as if she is excited to see the rain drum the mice out of hiding; and Gene's breath changes every time she screeches, it gathers up at the top of his chest and he looks like a puppet whose strings have been pulled. Then he relaxes, his strings fall around him. I will stop this and turn off the light.

T oday at the life-class I accidentally said, out loud, 'See me as God sees me!'

Butterfly, what on earth was I thinking? It was just that the tutor kept asking the students to measure the distance between my neck and my navel or my ear and my muzzle (yes, she calls it a muzzle), until all I could see were twenty people squinting at me with their pencils outstretched. Can my existence really be sized up in this way? When Teddy was born, did I squint at him with a plumb line? In fact I widened my eyes and devoured him in one go! And as I stood there this afternoon with my weight on one leg and my right hand on my left shoulder, gazing at the foot of an easel, I could feel the blood push suddenly through my limbs where they had been half dead and cramping, and my life moving in me – the most curious sensation, when you stop for a moment and fully realise you are alive. That your heart is beating, I mean, and your gut is processing lunch, and you are producing heat.

In the drawings my grandmother did of me I could see I was alive. She could peer at me over her glasses, take up her charcoal and strip me bare of everything I pretended to be. You are not your ego, she would say. And then, tapping my earrings with her fingernail: You are not all this nonsense, you are God's handiwork. He made your flesh, your blood, your viscera and your soul. I see you as he sees you.

I have never seen anything like my grandmother's drawings of me. They make me look raw and perfect like the preserved bog people dug up from the peat. So much time dead had made them urgent again. I remember an archaeologist on the radio saying how eerie they were to touch, as if they would sit up and start speaking – so ancient that they were closer to the moment of creation, more surging with life than us. When I walked around the life-room at breaktime today I didn't see myself once. So when we were twenty minutes from the end and the tutor was telling them to finish off my hands and not to forget my hair, I only meant to say that this might be the time to try for my essence rather than my hair, to see me all at once. I had not meant to say what I said about God, and I sat for the rest of the twenty minutes seeing the distaste on their faces, and tried to suppress laughter.

On the way home from the class I called in to see Yannis and to get something quick for supper, and to my surprise Nicolas was there. He was just sitting at one of the tables with a coffee, waiting, he said, for me to come home. He and Yannis don't know one another, so I introduced them and Yannis came from behind his counter and clasped Nicolas' hand with both of his own. When he realised that it was me Nicolas had been waiting for, he gave me a curious look whose meaning I only discovered a few minutes later, when Nicolas and I left.

'I have something to tell you and something else to ask you,' Nicolas said when we were walking along the street to my building. 'I'm leaving tomorrow for New York for ten weeks and I wondered if you would consider marrying me again sometime after I get back. What is your friend called? Yannis. He suggested I should give you until then to answer.'

Yannis is gregarious and nosy; he will talk to anybody about anything. There he was, counselling a stranger in his shop on how to go about proposing to a woman, probably offering a little oval dish of calamari while his customer chewed over the options. No wonder he was surprised to find that I was the woman in question. Later, when Nicolas and I were eating Yannis' infamous salted sardines on toast, I told him that he had taken advice from a man whose marriage was itself in a state of crisis, and this seemed to please him, as if it made it all the more authentic. I also told him what I had blurted at the life-class and he sat back, with a piece of oily toast on his fork, staring at the table in thought for a moment. 'And how *does* God see you?' he asked finally. 'I don't know,' I replied, 'this is what I want them to show me.'

He smiled and touched my cheek briefly, and I know that this act of wry softness said: You mean, you want them to make you look noble. That touch of my cheek was supposed to convey, by way of comfort, that all hopes of nobility were past, and it didn't matter. Between us we have nothing splendid left, it is lost in all the cowardly little offerings we have made over the years. He looked somewhat triumphant in this loss of burden. I tell you, he chewed long and peacefully on that sardine as if hunger were no longer a reason for eating.

We spent most of the evening talking about New York, and the Brooklyn Academy of Music where he would be working on a touring production of Euripides' *Medea*. He laid out his metre-square map of New York City, Manhattan on one side and Brooklyn, Queens, the Bronx and Staten Island on the other. Turning it back and forth, he marked it up with points of interest in his guidebook. He wanted to go to Columbus Park to see elderly people playing Xiangqi, he has wanted to do that since he was a teenager and his erstwhile stepfather told him about it. Also the Public Library Reading Room, the Hunterfly Road

Houses in Weeksville, the Chelsea Hotel. All of these places had been put in his mind by his stepfather, whom I have never heard him speak about before in anything but passing. When it was late he folded the map one more time than it was supposed to be folded and said he would not contact me when he was away. He forced it into his back pocket and stood; one of his typically abrupt, proud conclusions to a vulnerable topic. Then he took himself to bed.

Once again it has come to the early hours of the morning and I must get to bed too. I seem to be sleeping so little at the moment and finding myself restless or hungry at strange times of the night, especially when Nicolas stays. Then the urge to come back to this letter is stronger, or at least makes more sense, although I can't explain how. As it is, he just came in from the next room, half asleep, to find out what I'm doing. I told him I was writing to you. He turned his back quickly. He sends his regards.

April 2002

March happened, I forgot to mention it. Forgive me.

*

But really, if honest, I could have seen Nicolas' offer coming. Something firm, almost intolerant, came over him when I asked about a month ago if he knew where you might be living. The question was more hypothetical than anything, I had no doubt that he wouldn't know. He was looking down at a newspaper or, no, dinner. I think we were eating at a cheap Italian place called Ciro's. He raised his eyes only and said, 'In the desert.' Then he went back to eating.

It was the first time he had acknowledged that he knew about the postcard from you to Teddy, a postcard that had dropped through my letterbox ten years before. He speared his food as if he had suddenly had enough of everything and wanted to draw a line once and for all. Enough suffering, enough separation, enough silence. Last week, when he asked me to marry him, he said, 'I want us to just get back on with our lives', which made me laugh before I had time to stop myself, because his tone implied that the fifteen-year break in our marriage had been just a bad fortnight that we should forget. And yet I agree, and I want to get on with life too. The question isn't about whether or not to get on, but what constitutes getting on.

It is curious for a person to think that for a long time they might not really have been living – curious, I mean, for them to not *know* if they have been living. When do all the activities of living add up to a life? I can tell that Nicolas thinks my flat is an admission of defeat, my job an evasion of responsibility – that I have given up on myself. My letter to you was probably the last straw; she is stuck in the past, he thinks, and not even a wholesome bit of the past. She cannot move on. The more I think about it, the more it feels that he wants to rescue me from my sad unreconciled state and make me add up to something.

At the same time he also seems to tread very carefully around my life as though he sees it as something self-contained and sustaining; he is wary of my independence. I know this because he comments on my hair being short, where short-haired women are for him slightly dangerous creatures who might not need much from a man. When I had my hair like this in the past he always said he preferred it longer, but when he comments now it is to say, with a hint of trepidation, that he thinks it suits me. There is something in this movement from him and what he likes or prefers, to me and what is good for me, that gives me the feeling that he views me now as something separate and worthy of his respect. He said we had each grown and become much more fully ourselves, that this is the basis for a strong marriage. And so I asked him, What will happen if we get together again? Do we remain fully ourselves and, if not, will it be grounds for divorce? He said I was trying as usual to solve the future before it had become a problem. But it seems to me, Butterfly, that men have never really heard of forethought.

One of the few clear things I know about Nicolas' life these last fifteen years is that he spent some of it in Japan living with a woman he met in the theatre. A year after he met her he moved to Kyoto to be with her, on a visa sponsored by her mother's theatre production company. And he told me that although he had only just now asked me to marry him, he'd made the decision a couple of weeks ago, while we were walking in the Isabella Plantation. He said the idea had come to him suddenly as more of a suggestion than a proposal, and one he hadn't planned on having. What I think is that his idea was prompted, consciously or not, by the row of azaleas and Japanese maples we were walking between at the time; he saw those early azalea petals and he thought of his lost romance, just as we are all reminded of romances and losses every day of our lives, and he sought instinctively to fight back against it with the offer of something new. What's more, I think he either recognised it then or has recognised it since, and he knew I knew he was doing it. He has always been that way, a man whose future is an impulsive reaction to or against a past he has just remembered and cannot accept, with the hope that comes in the absence, as I said, of any forethought whatsoever.

He has told me virtually nothing else about that relationship, though I know it lasted three years and that he spent a lot of time alone in her family's holiday home at Cape Ashizuri while she toured Japan with her productions. I have no concept of what Cape Ashizuri is like, though I gather he found it beautiful. To my mind Japan is made up of impossible intricacies and subtleties and isn't capable of any kind of epic cape, but I kept this facile observation to myself. He said that while living there he would come back to England once in a while to work on a show for a few weeks, or he might do the lighting for some of her productions, as was the plan, but his lack of good Japanese made the process too slow and confused, and he gradually stopped asking and being asked.

He said she became tired of being his translator. I get the impression that it was a relationship that promised a lot and offered a little, in the way exotic things do; I think he misses all that it never was, the possibilities. And I have tried so hard myself to live in a way that doesn't deal in possibilities so much as realities, but I understand how easy it is to come under the power of an obstinate dream, and in a funny way perhaps it is this that makes me want to say yes to his *suggestion*, not because I think I can fulfil any of his dreams but simply because of that flicker of empathy, which for a moment lays itself down like a bridge between us.

I do at least know that her name was Chihiro Mori, because it was written in the back of his passport as an emergency contact, and for whatever reason his passport had once been lying open at that page on his kitchen sideboard. He might have left it like that on purpose to save me asking the question. Such a peculiar relationship we have now, made up of things that aren't said and dodging anything that might come from the other's heart. We have been carrying on like this since Boxing Day, because that, of course (maybe you knew it from the beginning), is the real reason I started writing this then. He came round late on Christmas Day after Teddy had gone, to pay nothing but a friendly call with a bottle of brandy and some monkfish to cook, on the off-chance that we might escape the dry tasteless curse of turkey, and it was when he left on Boxing Day night that you appeared like that in my mind, so intrusively, perhaps jealously. Looking at the bed where some curious love of old had been invoked from nowhere, like spirits summoned by witch doctors. Looking at my face left irritated by his stubble, and the glasses of sparkling water by the bed, because as we know, where Nicolas goes, so goes sparkling water. Seeing, and shaking your head sadly, saying, My friend, do not – only the weak slip back.

It has been four months now of new quiet routines, trying out recipes on one another, making love with a certain defensive intensity, bickering where we used to argue, but bickering harmlessly, and remaining, both of us, completely unwilling to talk about the past. We simply deflect all matters of importance. Even when he asked me to marry him I just told him, with a small break in stride, that I didn't know what to say. He said I should not answer yet, even if I could. When he came back from America in mid June he would expect an answer, but before then he was actively uninterested.

When we were in the Isabella Plantation a fortnight ago I said something like, 'Look at this tupelo tree, we should come back in autumn when it's bright red.' And again, that mention of us being together in autumn might have been casual or weighted, even I don't know. It was simply evasive. Perhaps he has got tired of the evasion and decided it would be better if we just owned one another again, rather than dancing strangely in and out of one another's vision. I also believe, based on his muted response when he found me writing this letter, that he had known of its existence for a while.

I used to feel there was comfort in remaining Nicolas' wife even in our complete estrangement, and he must have felt the same about being my husband, because neither of us ever pursued a divorce. And the truth is that there is comfort in being somebody's anything, and in a person even saying that of you: my wife, my husband, that little word of possession.

But possession, Butterfly. A word that didn't impress you. Husband, wife, also words that failed to impress. You once threw a fork at Nicolas when he suggested that a husband owns his wife and a wife her husband. He ducked out of the way and then held your gaze as he laughed.

There is a sound I associate with the country rather than the city – the humming of electricity lines. In the city you can't isolate this sound from all the others, but in the country, where the wind throttles along the lines across open fields, you can hear and feel the vibrating song, and it seems to me that the grass in the fields stands on its tiptoes.

I have in mind this sound and an autumn dawn, which is when the hum is amplified by wet air and by billions of droplets of dew on blades of grass and spiderwebs and on the cables themselves. There is Teddy running ahead and Nicolas' strong back and the bits of leaves in his hair. This must have been the September or October of 1984, before the January you left, and we had all got up for a dawn walk. You were nocturnal by then, and night after night you upset the calm of the house with your silent restless skulking. The morning I am thinking of, Teddy woke up and there was no more sleep to be had for anyone, so we went out into some golden God-flung humming vibrating mist that had appeared as if to show humans they knew nothing about the Earth.

Along the lane you tried to part the mist with your hand. There was Teddy running ahead with Nicolas, bits of leaves in Nicolas' hair, though why I can't say. Had he lain down somewhere, had one of us stuck them there? Teddy perhaps, when piggybacking. You were talking about the deities of the morning, eulogising the breaking of the day; why did people get up after the day was already broken when they could stay up at night, watch the transformation of darkness into light rather than always light into darkness? There is Aušrine, Lithuanian goddess of the morning star. Aurora in Roman, the rosy Titaness Eos in Greek. In Vedic philosophy the goddess of the morning, Ushas, is a kind of portal for awakening, we pass through her into enlightenment. Why do people not want to be enlightened, why do they only want to be endarkened?

I remember this word in particular, and your sullen wild nerviness, which had an energy of its own; you clung to your cigarette like a climber to a rope, you kicked at a stone and let it roll into the verge. I remember the mist, the smoke and the steam from your breath all at once. I think this was when you took my arm, pressed the wet wool of your shawl against me and said, 'Have you ever seen through the gauze of this life?' Or no, perhaps I said something first about how early morning is thinner, less real, how I felt I could pass through the mist, steam and smoke, through the wet wool, into a reality beyond. Maybe it was me who started it, but in any case you asked, 'Have you ever seen through the gauze of this life?' And I said, 'Is there a gauze?' and you said with a small smile, 'You can't tell me this is the sum of it.'

Whatever I might have been about to answer, I didn't when I saw your face. I can hardly say what it was. Something in the very idea of dissolution seemed to calm you, in the same way you were calmed when you used to talk about your first memories – real or borrowed – of life in Lithuania, a life that was gauzy at best, shifting and lost. As if you found something of yourself in the loss of the world around you. You, you have wrestled with this religion and that, this love affair and that, from god to god and man to man, with prayers and needles, to try to see your way to something true;

139

you have been like a heron thrashing a fish against the riverbank
– you would say so yourself. But your face lit with the notion that
it might all be unreal and might not matter after all.

So I did not answer, though I could have. Instead I let you
speed up our pace to catch Nicolas and Teddy. As we climbed the
lane the mist was thinning and the sun spun through the trees in
spokes – wet, golden light, and while the hilltops were basking,
the mist was still thick down in the valley. Grey, bottomless trees
rose from it. Church spires floated in the distance.

'In Hindu mythology,' you said to none and all, 'the sun isn't
the mother of dawn, but the lover. He chases her across the sky
and the day starts with a burst of romance. The flowers bloom,
the lotus blossoms . . .'

'The wheat is lovestruck,' Nicolas said.

'The bees are drunk.'

'The streams are laughing.'

'The monks are hungry.'

'The clouds are giddy.'

'The temples are buckling.'

'The crickets are strutting.'

'Time is tripping.'

This was evidently a conversation the two of you had had before
in some form. You spoke like lovers; you had returning topics and
private games. As we walked further, off the lane and up through
the fields where the grass was pulled upwards by the vibrating hum
of electricity, the light made strange glowing arcs around us. As if it
were rucked by the vibration. I had never before and have never since
seen this effect of the light. If I looked at it, it seemed to disappear,
but if I looked at the ground or at Teddy or you or Nicolas, I could
see it, a hoop, glowing. I still have no idea what caused this, but in
my memory I see Nicolas a few steps ahead, ringed by this light. He
walked tall with the carelessness and ease of a younger man.

T oday at work Gene spoke for the first time about his Lithuanian roots, though it was me who brought it up. Such a private man, and yet not cold, not at all. He does a lovely thing when he is thinking of an answer to a question – he levitates his eighty-five-year-old hand upwards to demonstrate, I suppose, the rising of the thought from heart to head. Up it goes, shaky and slow. And when it has risen he speaks, but only then.

'The trees,' he said, when I asked him what he remembered about the country. 'The oak, hornbeam and what else? Lindens. Lindens.'

'Where were you from?'

'Ariogala.'

'Where is that?'

'Oh, central-ish. A small town central-ish, in the middle. But I haven't lived there since I was a very small child, you know, so don't trust what I tell you.'

I smiled; I was helping him on with his clothes at the time, pulling socks over his papery ankles. He has asked for a female assistant to do these things and we've no grounds to refuse; his notes from the hospital back up this request, which suggests to me male abuse or bullying of a kind as a child, maybe. In his torso, his chest, his arms, he is a big man and still quite powerful for his years, yet so small and crumpled in his underwear – he the child, I the adult. 'I trust what you tell me implicitly,' I said, but he wafted away my faith in him. There are times, I suppose, when your lack of authority in a situation is so complete that you must come to doubt your expertise in everything, even the whereabouts of the town you were born in.

'As fate would have it, I've been looking into Lithuania recently,' I told him. 'I'm trying to find out about an old friend.'

I expected him to be interested but he wasn't particularly. He just nodded.

'Have you heard of the Lithuanian Academy of Sciences?'

He shook his head.

'My friend's brother, Petras, had something to do with them, that's all.' One white leg into the trousers, the other leg, an awkward hoisting of them up around his waist while he leant on my shoulder. I added, 'He was investigating something specific, about the effect of radiation on algae in lakes that are used to cool nuclear-power plants. You were not allowed to openly investigate these things then, in case you discovered something the state didn't like. But I'm sorry, you'll know all this.'

Naively, I thought that Gene would respond somehow, or find in Petras' gallant fight a shared cause, but he just pulled himself up from leaning and buttoned his trousers. 'I wonder if it's still the way you remember it,' I said, with one last attempt at engaging him. 'The lindens and all.'

I have noticed how elderly people acquire an unpredictable, unreliable look, almost impish in some, as though they are slipping between gears. Gene looked at me in that giddy way and then he said, just as you did that day, 'The Soviets cut most of those down.' And he said it so readily that I wondered if this was the stock belief, the people's mantra, perhaps a way of summarising a set of complex losses. But nations can define themselves by their landscapes, this is certainly true; a tree can signify liberty, a tree felled by a foreign hand can crash to the ground as loudly as any army can invade. Sure enough, as he made his silent way into his shirt, he looked out of the window at the trees there as though they had just asked him a question.

'Gene isn't a Lithuanian name,' I said.

'Nobody could pronounce Juozas. My mother loved Gene Kelly, she thought I looked like Gene Kelly. Well, it was just her opinion. And later in life she started calling me Gene sometimes – perhaps she was confused or just joking with me. So when I came here and needed a name, that was the one I adopted.'

'When did you come to England?'

'When I was five-and-a-third.'

'To be precise.' I stood to get his wallet, which he always likes to have on him once dressed. 'But you remember home?'

'This is home.'

He was working his arms into a cardigan by this point. He asked suddenly, 'What's your friend's story?'

'Her story? You see, I think she isn't the kind of person to have a story, maybe that's her problem.'

'We were Hasidic Jews,' he said, as if on a separate plane of thought. 'Many Lithuanians were. Do you know what Hasidic means? It means *Loving kindness* – and that is what our religion is about. We told stories and sang and prayed. In Ariogala we had a place called the Valley of Songs because there were so many music festivals there; you see, Lithuania is a place of prayer, song, myth and folklore, and stories. Stories.'

'You remember all that from before you were five?'

'Of course not – not all our memories are things we remember.'

Again he smiled, or maybe he'd always been smiling, and I made some comment or another about this being true; I think how many memories I have borrowed from my parents, even from you, and built them up as if they were my own. I eased his foot into a dark-red shoe, his favourite pair, that he insists on wearing to the exclusion of all others. He looked down at me so sober and placid.

I asked him, 'So where would somebody *without* a story go in Lithuania?'

His kindness remained, but he watched me blankly.

'I'm looking for my friend.'

Still he watched me blankly. Was this to say, Your question is foolish. Or was it only that his thoughts were already elsewhere?

T hough unsentimental by nature, a memory comes to you. You are outside your hut when a breeze catches you and takes you back to a time when you were not much more than a baby, in the dunes at Nida with your mother, father and Petras. Petras is around eight or nine, a towering brother tall as the hills, fearfully loved. Your mother and father are burying him in the sand and it makes you screech with laughter. They laugh at you laughing; this is what Petras most often recounted about you when you were older – your baby laugh, which was a cackle of pure joy requiring a mouth open to its fullest and a complete suspension of breath. Even when he emulated it we laughed too, so infectious was it. You were game, as a child. Feral, Petras commented, and your parents countered, Delightful. The foulest temper and the sweetest, most coaxing love of life and adventure, and nothing in between except sleep, which was deep, determined and uninterruptible.

Petras is up to his jaw in sand, and the sand keeps falling away from his face because he is laughing at you laughing. Your parents scoop it back but it flows away. Then you feel a breeze – maybe it picks up, or maybe you've turned your head into it – and you become quiet at the feel of it over your skin. Grains of sand rush across the surface of the dunes like lunatics, like drunks. Of course you do not think of it in terms of drunks and lunatics at the time, but you think it as you remember. You close your eyes and open your mouth to feel the air touch places it can never usually reach, and the laughter around you stops. The air is on your gums and your handful of new, sore teeth and the insides of your cheek, filling up your mouth as if you have eaten one of those cottony clouds up there.

This breeze, which is warm and balmy, but edged with a northerliness that never allows you to forget where in the world you are, has returned fifty years later. It touches your right side as you bend over the vegetables in your plot behind the hut. Holidays, you think. Holidays! At Nida, in the long spit of dunes where the sand flows like water but is dry as bones. How can bones flow? How can water be dry? You stand up, flick your ash on the soil; good for the pea shoots, they like it. And so they ought; you've filtered smoke through your very own lungs to make that ash.

You have taken to watching a video of geese flying, and you go indoors, suddenly provoked by the memory, and switch the video on. You found the video player and the tiny, portable TV in a skip in the village, so you took them. Inside the video player was this short film of geese flying, just a film without commentary, and at first you had it in your mind that the film had no sound. You never checked to see if it was the sound on the TV that was defunct, because you would rather that the film were silent.

Except, after days of watching this film, you realised it wasn't silent at all, it was rich with the honking and squawking of the geese. You muttered incredulous profanities at yourself for this oversight – it is abysmal, wholly unnerving how deaf, blind, dumb, hubristic and arrogant you can be for assuming that a lack of human noise means no noise. You won't survive in this world with thinking like that, amazing really that you have survived this long. But I'm telling you, you should forgive yourself. Life is like this; the senses are instruments that go out of tune. You have been surrounded by non-human sound for so long in this forest of yours that only something different and out of the ordinary counts as sound now. The owl-call, the throaty crow, the snorting bison, these are no longer sounds in themselves, but part of the fabric of the air.

Anyway you watch these geese in formation. You have no idea why you find them so interesting but you could sit and peer into the screen all day if it weren't for the fact that, quite unconsciously, you chain-smoke while you do it. Even someone with only a very scant regard for her own life would baulk at the saucerful of dog-ends these sessions yield. Besides, not enough money to smoke this much. So you watch the geese for an hour or so at night, usually, to get you off to sleep.

On this occasion, though, the memory of yourself and your family in the sand dunes has taken over, and the V of geese sheeting across a chalky sky is not providing much distraction. Neither do the Upanishads have anything to say that can take you out of yourself, because the memory resists and pulls you back. The Upanishads say abstract things about time and about childhood, but what you feel is not abstract and the memory crashes through their verses as a ton weight through mist. So you turn the book aside.

It is peculiar to think of yourself as a child. As an adult you are a one-woman nation state. You do not consider yourself a person with a history and allegiances and moral frailties, but as a set of religious, political, social, physical principles, a stockpile of abstractions that have to be met periodically by base needs like food and sex, and here in the clash of the rarefied and the base you find yourself. It is a gritty little thing, this self, and not worthy of much, but it defends its borders all the same. You never expect perfectibility, you expect to be troubled because, after all, everything complex is troubled.

But as a child, with the breeze on your eyelids and the back of your tongue? Could this simple pound of happy flesh really be you, and is there any road you can take between this self and that and, if you could, what would it achieve?

Your thoughts turn away from yourself and towards those curious dunes, and to Petras. Ironic that he went on to dig himself into the Lithuanian landscape for the rest of his life, throwing his cause against the diggers and drillers and axes and chainsaws, dear old Petras, hero Petras, dear Petras, the drillers, the axes. Your thoughts run together anxiously when you think of him. Who would have thought a love of botany could set you against the state? You look out of your one rectangular window at the woods, what used to be oak and is now quick-growing spruce, larch and pine.

You remember all the battles he fought against the power station at Ignalina, against the deforestation of the countryside, against the obliteration of indigenous flowers, trees, birds, and finally against the oil-drilling at Nida. The Russians might try to stamp out our language, take over our schools and businesses, but – you hear him say, white-lipped – they are not going to ruin our dunes.

And they did not, you say to the geese on the wing. They did not! You pour out the last few drops of steeped nettle tea from the pot and slice a piece of cheese from the rocklike remains of a block. You sit back from your thoughts. Funny how that memory came on the breeze and, now the breeze has gone, how the memory is gone too. What was it about the way the loose sand was speeding across the surface of the dunes, around the legs of your parents and over the mound that was Petras' buried body? It made you calm and ecstatic; when you think of it now it fills you with electrical energy, and you wonder if your hair is standing on end.

T his is tantamount to assault, you are now saying. The cheese on my table is not rocklike; I do not even eat cheese. First the imagining of my life, what I eat, how I sleep and what I sleep on, and now of my memories themselves. The air around my baby teeth, this preposterous fantasy about geese! Do you not think that you and your *letter* have gone a step too far?

Sometimes when I look at the drawings at the end of the life-class I see that the bad ones are those in which a student has stopped looking and started making things up; in those drawings I acquire a rigorous little face that isn't mine and a pair of breasts that belong to somebody and anybody else, and there is a kind of cruelty in the pencil marks, a violence at the way I have been hijacked and misused.

I do not feel bad about inflicting this violence and cruelty on you. If you had not run away I would be able to see you, and would not have to make you up. When I think about it, there are so many sentences I could begin like that: If you had not run away, I would be able to . . .

*

It is true, you do not eat cheese. I forgot. You came downstairs one morning when you were living with us in Morda and said you had dreamt that a cow was standing before you. You had heard its bell clinking along the lane, then it drew up to the door like the milkman. *You shall not drink of me*, it said. Its breath crept warmly around its nostrils. So in the morning you made yourself the first of a thousand black teas and dry toast.

But you'll still eat of it? Nicolas said later, over roast beef. You took a piece of meat in your hand and shrugged: Unless I receive further instruction, yes.

W hen I look back on our years of friendship it seems to me that you are a person who, with fair consistency, has had more interest in others' happiness than your own, though you had volatile ways of showing it.

But what am I saying? Can I really mean this? Sometimes you peer at me through the dark as I write and the familiarity of your face forces my hand into words that are kinder than they are truthful. To rephrase: you did not go out of your way to make another person happy, but you did not go out of your way to make them unhappy, either. You never went out of your way. It isn't even that you are a selfish person – in fact isn't the opposite true, that you are fundamentally selfless? By which I mean somebody who lies low like a card in a pack, until the cards are dealt. Sometimes her appearance in the hand will be good news, sometimes bad, but she herself is neither. She is just offered up, and played or not.

I am thinking now of the time you were staying with us, two or three months after we got back from the pearl-fishing trip I told you about. Ruth came to visit for a day and night – to visit Nicolas, that is, because I hardly knew her then. She was one of his friends originally, from childhood, and I find it easy to forget this fact now that we have our own decades of friendship between us. You must have been staying with us for three weeks or more and in my memory these were happy times. It was a rogue, hot May day and we were all in the garden, sitting around the old wrought-iron table and chairs that we inherited in the move.

I am sure at first you didn't want to be there for Ruth's visit, but obeyed when we insisted you stay – and I mean obeyed, because you sat with all the subservience of a tethered dog. But I could see that you liked Ruth instantly, and I knew why. She is capable and one of life's doers – dark, large, deep-voiced, lovely; she is lovely still. She can wear big brash jewellery with finesse and she will never ask how you feel, or ask you to account for yourself. Not a human *being* but a human *doing*, Nicolas used to call her. In the weeks prior to that, since your arrival, you had deflected all my questions. Where have you been? What are your plans? Have you been happy? You had said only, 'None of it matters, all you need to do is tell me when you want me to leave.' (To which I replied, 'I never want you to leave.' I repeated it so many times, was so relieved to have your company in the loneliness of motherhood, that you did my bidding and stayed; have I only myself to blame?) But my point is that Ruth was exactly the kind of person who would remove any burden of explanation or justification and simply accept your existence in the garden as a fact amongst any number of other facts that were neither here nor there to her.

When you discovered that she could sing you came to life; there was no mistaking the moment you became interested in something – the image I have is of accelerated footage of a fern opening, where something inward becomes outward and unstooped and ready. I remember that she sang the Solemn Vespers so strikingly that the neighbour came to watch, and we were never to forget it because that neighbour, Christina, didn't again manage to have a conversation with us without mentioning it. Ruth's voice wasn't trained, but it was churchy, rich and capable of almost anything. Each time she got to the end of a song you would pick whatever flower or weed was growing in the bed next to you and toss it towards her with a 'Brava!', an 'Encore!' You went to her and put your fingertips on her throat to feel her vocal cords vibrate while she sang, and when she finished you did something that I imagine must have been extraordinary to her at the time, you kissed her on the lips. She mentioned it once recently and I pretended I couldn't remember the occasion at all.

I think we all went to the table then and poured drinks. Having witnessed that kiss, Nicolas sat back, impressed and threatened. There: that one-sided smile I liked so much, which was the containment of a pleasure that compressed not quite invisibly in his mid-chest, and rose far enough to twitch his Adam's apple as a horse-flank twitches under a fly. Meanwhile he leant back a touch more and linked his hands in his lap so that his masculinity could defend itself. He did this combination of half smile and retreat whenever he saw something in womankind he liked and couldn't control, and because he did it only with respect to women and nothing else it made me see in him, by turn, something I liked and could not control. He then said, more assertively than usual, 'You sing, Butterfly.'

'I can't sing, I'm flat as a pancake.'

'That can be remedied.'

'It can?'

'Of course.'

'People can be divided into two categories,' you said. 'Those who think everything is fixable and those who think everything is breakable. You are the former and I'm the latter.'

Nicolas smiled; I had the impression that he was satisfied

to have been noticed and judged by you, regardless of the judgement.

'Let's try,' he said.

'Try to fix me?'

'Come on,' he shrugged. 'It can't hurt.'

To my surprise you stood. 'Very well, I'm yours.'

The two of you had coexisted politely those previous weeks with little to say to one another, and with a paranoid awareness of the other's space. I do clearly remember that phase of courteous sidestepping because I remember being touched by it – how, with me, you were vivid and quick and caustic, and yet how with Nicolas you and he both became awkward. You in particular seemed to have all the confidence pulled from you: you bent your head more, which made you long-necked and grebelike and apparently meek; you were always glancing up from the floor. You were not coquettish, I wouldn't want to suggest that any of this was planned on your part. I think you were genuinely pinned by a social ineptness I've seen in you before, with the others at school, say. Yet you stood, and said – not just to Nicolas, but to Ruth – 'I'm yours' and you waited without mockery for them to make of you what you knew couldn't be made.

They straightened you. Ruth put her fingertips on your shoulders. 'Draw them back,' she said, and then, 'More.' She tucked her fingertips lightly under your chin and asked you to look to the horizon. She asked you to breathe with her. 'You can't sing well if you can't breathe well,' she told you.

'I can't sing well regardless,' you said, but you were not frustrated or impatient. Nicolas lifted your arms and let them drop, uncurled your fingers from their fists. He put one of the plucked flowers between your teeth, so you could not protest. I remember that Teddy found this funny and let out his thrilled cackle, and I see you standing there winking at him, thin and upright in the cut-off shorts we had made from my old jeans because the weather had turned hot. Long, pale legs patterned at the back with chair swirls, toes clutching at the grass. You had even forsaken your shawl and were wearing a long-sleeved cheesecloth shirt. Ruth sang a note and asked you to match it; yours was flat. At the next attempt it was a semi-tone higher, but still flat. There would be a return to breathing and a general re-elevating of your posture – chin up, shoulders back, chest open – as though this would rally the note from a higher place.

I knew, as did you, that it wouldn't. We had sung together enough in the past to know that the cause was hopeless, and hopeless because you didn't care to be in tune; just as you had said, you were not a person who believed things could or even should be fixed. They were as they were. But how could Nicolas or Ruth know this about you? To them, you were a painting that needed restoring, which implies that they thought you had come from a perfect state of harmony and could go back to it. Foolish assumption, this one we make about beauty, to assume that it must have come from perfection. Sometimes, to use your word, it's the result of pure randomised chancery, some happy irreversible spillage.

Between Nicolas and Ruth it was agreed that posture was your problem. Probably you would be a lovely singer if only you were not one of life's slouchers. I remember you looking at me with a collusive smile when they started straightening your back and asking you to envisage a plumb line through your core, and your vertebrae stacked like a ladder. You called: Do not let us grow crooked! You were then forced through some lessons in comportment, and you complied, walking up and down our long, narrow garden with an ashtray on your head whilst smoking. You would raise your arm and flick the ash around the vicinity of your crown. I don't put this compliance down to your good nature particularly because, though I think your nature is many things, it is not good. I know you will be the first to agree. I put it down to this neutrality I talked about before. People want things from you because you interest and confound them – so, unbothered by any sense of self-preservation, or any sense of self at all, you offer what you have without analysis, expectation or defence. You deal yourself up, they play you.

That said, I think you were amused by that afternoon. I have often admired how careless you are with yourself. You walked up and down the garden with an ashtray on your head, then an empty glass, then a full glass; you ended up with ash and gin in your hair, you let Teddy blow the ash out. When you sat you resumed your wiry slouch with your foot up on the table, your ochre-tipped fingers tapping your knee and your beauty unknown and uninteresting to you.

'You see, I'm not good at anything,' you said, more with victory than self-pity.

'Oh, come now,' Nicolas replied.

Ruth leant across and put her fingers on your throat, reciprocating what you had done to her earlier. 'You'd have a very good voice with training. But if you don't stop smoking, God knows what will happen to it.'

'Whatever it is,' you said, 'it won't be half as bad as what'll happen to my will to live if I do.'

Nicolas gestured in the direction of the house. 'Not true that you're good at nothing.' And then to Ruth, 'She takes good photographs, there's one in there, if you want to see it.'

How hypocritical we can be; he spared you his previously stated view on the subject, his view that your still life was sordid, and then trite and obvious. And you spared him your knowledge that he was sparing you. 'Oh, come now,' you said simply.

'I think you don't believe in yourself enough.'

'Oh, I believe in myself, I believe in almost nothing else, that's my problem.' And then, to Ruth, 'But you are good at things, I can tell. Let me see, you're a sculptor, or a lawyer.'

'A paediatrician.'

'Exactly,' you said, and a genuine pleasure lit your face before you became suddenly inward – not sullen, but removed. I knew you had disliked Nicolas' attempt at consolation and congratulation. You wanted to be obliterated, you wanted us to agree that you amounted to nothing, that you, your self, was eclipsed by your own fumbling, vulgar ineptitude. You would have been delighted to know that Nicolas had used the word sordid – you *are* delighted to know that, and as you read it off the page I bet a small thrill goes through you at this opportunity to take yourself and your sordidness out of the range of good people and cease to exist. And this is what I mean when I talk about your desire for others to be happy, just as you were glad to find that Ruth had a good voice and a vocation and was, as far as you had decided, happy. Ruth's self was big enough to make yours redundant.

Soon after that you went to your room and stayed there until the next day. What I am guessing you don't know is that later, when I went up to you, I found you lying on your bed still in the shorts and shirt, but with your shawl over your legs. Your left sleeve was rolled up above the elbow and that arm lay soft side up on the bed in surrender. I could see clearly the puncture from a needle. Your head was thrown back and your face unnervingly placid. At first I thought you were dead, but when I felt for a pulse it was firm and regular, if anything too insistent. There was no syringe, tourniquet or folded pocket of powder, but it would have been consistent with your sense of manners to put those back in the drawer or in your suitcase or under the bed, or wherever you kept them.

You were not asleep, but you had little idea of where you were. You knew somebody was in the room but I'm sure you didn't know who, or which room. 'Oh, to be a sick child and be in Ruth's hands,' you murmured with a smile. 'Doesn't she make you feel comforted somehow?'

'Sshhh,' I whispered deep into the well of your ear.

'Do you think the name Butterfly becomes me?' you asked from some blind depth. 'Do you find me especially *becoming*? No, you see, Teddy was mistaken. Me, I prefer Fly. Like John Clare in his poem to a butterfly. *To see thee, Fly, warm me once more to sing*. Ha! He takes her down a peg and owns her. *You, Fly*. Otherwise she'll get above herself and flitter off to another poem, I think you know what I mean. Please, if you will, call me Fly. It is better. My feet are dirty, my feet are covered in shit.'

I pressed my hand on your head. 'Sleep, Fly.'

Do you know, I always thought that perhaps Teddy wasn't so wrong when he named you Butterfly, but that was a vague thought that I had out of motherly generosity. And yet just now I realised (I have just been standing at the window, thinking about it) how mistaken Teddy *wasn't*, as if he saw something true that had always been there. That name actually was becoming, was un-ironic. Butterfly: settling on nothing, at the windowpane basking or trying to get out, batting at the light as if baffled by this lovely form that is (so it thinks) some fragile decoration of its ugliness. Do you know what I thought when you were lying there that evening? Instead of being angry that you had brought drugs into our house, I felt an unexpected sense of gratitude towards the needle that had given something back to you. Ah, I thought, so this is what is making you look so well! So bright-eyed and flushed with life. And I am certain you felt that exact gratitude when you guided the needle to the vein. For once you were not dealing yourself out, but were being dealt to. Nicolas said one time, when we were talking about your addiction, that you were a coward for escaping yourself, but I think that the opposite is at least worth arguing – that you were reclaiming yourself.

You looked so strong, well and calm, and I didn't want the drug to ease off and drop you back to a slouch. *Do not let us grow crooked*, say the Vedas. *We that kneel and pray again and again.* I moved the shawl to cover your shoulders. We are all looking for miracles and small mercies, I mean this. Who are we to decide on another's behalf what is miraculous, what is merciful?

That shawl of yours struck terror into the hearts of young men. You, aged twenty-one, would sit amongst the handful of young people from the village, around a limp fire in the woods or amidst a pile of beer bottles in a field or at the bottom of someone's garden, and you would hardly speak. Just smoke, and play along at cards if the rest of us played. At that time you were in a phase of wearing Petras' clothes, simply because, you said, you had grown into them and he had grown out of them. His brown and blue cords, his drainpipe jeans, his boots. You had not really grown into them, they were all too big for you. And always you wore your shawl, like a blanket laid neatly over an unmade bed. Through this complex crocheted honeycomb, this thick, soft network of deflection and obfuscation, sometimes, sometimes, sightings of your bare arms or inklings of female shape. But instantly lost again to the greater shapelessness that was your too-big shawl, this flocking of wool around your birchlike frame. As if, almost, you were giving shelter to the shawl and not the reverse.

You can tell I have thought about this – how you looked, how you were to those boys (although I couldn't even name any of them now; they don't warrant remembering). I have thought about it probably too much. The honeycomb, the flocking, et cetera. I have wrestled with ways of explaining you. They tried to draw you out, those boys, but you were undrawable. They thought that your thick cloak of hair was an encouraging, whole-some sign, as if it were flagging up welcoming semaphore. Yes, you were formidable and silent and strange, and yet your flushed skin – your soft hair – serene in the firelight – like warm wax – you were a Mary, a mother, no, a girl, a maiden, a kindly creature, a possibility. I know what they saw. I think of it like this: a herd of wild horses stampeding across a plain throws up a plume of dust, and through this plume the horses' ferocious and muscular beauty is gentle, almost romantic, the stuff of pleasing paintings in living rooms. You plumed like so; your beauty was so fierce it kicked up its own haze, something dulcet, like a myth. Those boys squinted at you with a giddy sort of look while they tried to work out how to approach you, and tried to balance risk against reward.

You accepted their cigarettes without thanks; you handed out your own without regret; you won or lost at cards with equal indif-ference. Gradually they became suspicious of you. I say gradually – it was a short time thinking about it, a summer and an autumn, and that was the end of our tentative spell as extroverts. It was '72, the year that Petras left home for Lithuania, which of course was the real, if unofficial, reason you wore his clothes – because you missed him; or, more rightly, appropriated him – because, seven years his junior, you had finally come of age by growing, almost, into his jeans, by becoming worthy of him, I suppose you could say. Not his equal, but at least worthy.

So the boys began to mock you; you were a dyke, a whore, you were filthy. Of course, we always insult what we do not understand, especially if it has rejected us. *When the moon sails out*, you quoted, from Lorca, and I misremember and misquote, *the waters spill over the earth and our hearts are little islands in the infinite.* Poetry was your only response to anything they did or said and you used it as wastefully as somebody emptying a cartridge into grey sky. The poems would leave local indents of silence, like hammer marks on metal. The others might laugh, they might miss a beat and then carry on talking as if you were not there, and you might carry on quoting poetry as if they were a paying audience, or otherwise, likewise, not there.

Then one evening in August or September, in the Morda woods, the matter of what was underneath your shawl was raised and became pressing. 'What do you think is under there?' you said with your own languid brand of scorn. You were kneeling by a crude small fire pit that had been dug earlier in the summer, to which we often returned, or anyway if you were not kneeling then – if you were sitting on the ground – you came to your knees fast when you felt the questions strengthen. They beset you with their curiosity. They asked and then demanded and then asked again, and all you said was, 'What do you think is under there?'

They jumped on you all at once – three or four of them – to wrest your shawl from you. It was not easy, you bent yourself double, your chest pinned to your knees. Finding no way in, they pulled back at your shoulders and tried to hoist your body up, but you had wrapped your arms under your legs and made yourself unopenable. They pulled your head back by your hair, and when they realised that they could get no further without real violence, the kind of violence that would be shameful towards a woman, they instead tried to tug the shawl upwards over your head – not straightforward, because the shawl too was pinned by your body, which had locked itself down.

I stood up, but as I came towards you to help, you turned your face to me and shook your head: left and then right, a short, firm no. I will always remember that. It was an affirmation of all that seemed to define our friendship – the way we asked each other to be left to our own fates; people intervene when they think the other person has no fate, or only a weak one that can be changed – just as those boys supposed with you. You have never purposefully interfered with my fate, nor I with yours. And I knew that by sitting back down as I did I was not neglecting you, but affirming your autonomy, your control, and that at some point in this battle for your shawl you would win; I wasn't sure what you would do to win, but I knew you would.

Such a strange sight to see them only half laughing as they tried to rid you of this thing they were so afraid of. Two of them were holding you down, one or two trying to pull it up over your head. Of course they would get it if they persisted long enough; you were outnumbered. But your soundless, motionless resistance appalled or disappointed them, I think, and there was a moment, just a moment, when they all seemed to pause, to step away and look at the back of the shawl pulled over your head and spread on the ground in front of you like a pool of spilt cream, and entertain the faintest thought that you were not worth it.

Another moment and they would either have torn it from you in aimless frustration or backed off, sat, drank, concluded: Stupid dyke. Either way, you would have lost. But just as that moment was approaching, you raised yourself up a fraction and straightened your arms in front of you as a child does when being undressed. You offered yourself. There was some laughter and hesitation; one of them stepped forward and rolled the shawl calmly off, then stood, unsure of what to do with it. You sat up and neatened your hair. You were wearing – and I remember it, partly, because it was mine – a white vest top with lace edging that could not have been more feminine or disarming to them, which followed closely the fragile cage of your ribs and the flatness of your stomach and, most crucially for them, I suppose, the great surprise, the ampleness of your breasts, plump and shapely against all the odds. You came to your feet, held out your hand and clicked your fingers for the shawl, which was given. The silver cobra coiled around your upper arm might as well have flicked its tongue at the giver; Petras' trousers hung at your waist with sudden elegance. *It is a beauteous evening*, you said, as you eased the shawl back into shape with light tugs here and there, and picked bits of leaf and twig from the wool. *It is a beauteous evening, calm and free; the holy time is quiet as a Nun, breathless with adoration.*

And you smiled at them, and they – what did they do? I don't know, I don't remember. Did they speak to you again, did they watch you walk off? Because you did walk off, into the woods away from home, declaiming Wordsworth; you must have been shouting by the time you had gone from view, because we could still hear you, you will be glad to learn. But they, what did they do? Who can guess. They slide into the shadows as men do when you have had your final say.

I skim back over the last few pages of this letter every so often
and I usually wish I could change what I wrote.

When I wrote, for example, about your indignation at my
so-called memory of you and your family in the dunes, and the
sand blowing across a buried Petras, I implied, I suppose, that I
had made the memory up. But something about that memory is
true, isn't it? I can definitely remember you telling me about this
once in the red room at Morda, or in the lanes at Morda, or on
the trunk of the fallen horse chestnut in the school fields, or in the
cottage at Morda, or in the garden, or in the car, or in London, or
in Spain. I'm sure you scuttled your fingers to imitate the bone-dry,
flowing sand, and you said, How can bones flow, how can water
be dry? And didn't you even put your head back and open your
mouth for a long minute while I sat or drove or cooked or tried,
with a cheap parasol, to win back a square foot of shade from the
Spanish sun?

You see, I over-emphasised there my forgery and invention, and
under-emphasised the very thing that drove me to write the
memory in the first place, which was a sense of sudden closeness
or complicity. The truth is that trying to get to the emotional
heart of things is so difficult, because emotions morph into one

another with such confusing subtlety that what was elation is now fear is now rejection is now rage is now wonder, all depending on the agenda we come at them with. So how can we get to the heart of them when the only heart they really have is our own? And this heart is supremely inconsistent and liable to irrational turns.

For example, the pearl-fishing trip in the Oykel valley. Sometimes the centre of this memory is the pearl itself, which represents happiness, a joint achievement, and a time in our lives when we were a family at one with itself. Sometimes the pearl slips to the background of this picture and what emerges as forefront is the moment I mentioned – not more than five seconds long – when I caught Nicolas staring at Teddy and me from the water. For a number of years this was all I could think of when I remembered that trip, because I couldn't decide why he was staring or what his expression meant. It was a look of love, I knew that, but was that pain behind it, or fear, or intense happiness, or . . . ?

I began to be troubled by a lack of facts, namely whether this trip happened before or after you first appeared at our door in Morda. I know the pearl-fishing trip was in the April of 1982, and I know you arrived that April, either soon before or soon after, but nothing I did to force chronology onto these events made any difference. I would go over the scene in my mind, but the problem is that the mind is a bad loser and can never accept it doesn't know best, so what it doesn't know it invents. Hence it invents, at one moment, the spectacle of our camping equipment spread over the grass in our garden to dry out before we put it away: therefore, you arrived after the trip happened. Yes, you were sitting, not on my coat as I'd previously mentioned, but on the edge of the groundsheet. You wrapped the guy-rope round and round your thumb as you spoke, and never once asked about our camping trip or where we had been.

At the next moment, it invents the opposite scenario. It does so as soon as I question the veracity of the last, because I'm certain the garden wasn't full of camping things, or at least if it was it means we had only just that day got back, since Nicolas was always prompt about packing away. So the mind rebounds. It says, Ah, no! We hadn't just got back after all – we were about to go. The tent was in a heap in Teddy's bedroom, where Nicolas had removed it from its bag to check it was all there. You were sitting on the floor in Teddy's room reading stories with him, wrapping the guy-rope around your thumb while the two of you mouthed sounds with lips pouted.

The chronology mattered so much, or so it felt then anyway, because the interpretation of Nicolas' expression that day as he waded in the river completely depended on it. Did he look at Teddy and me with such love because he had just, while fishing, had an image of you in his mind and was guilty and threatened by what he felt? Or was it because he hadn't yet met you and was still happy in his marriage, at an optimum point of devotion before it ebbed away?

And then sometimes this image too fades to the background and the storm is all I can think of. More recently this is how I tend to remember it, with less and less personal emotion and more as an abstract awe stirred by those incredible tantrums of nature. And now I think: Did I share too much with her? Am I cutting her too much slack? Am I making her think I care more than I do? Because, as I said, I think about the pearl-fishing trip now with detachment, little more, and somehow I wish that when I wrote about it I hadn't got so carried away with how it was, and had written more about how it is. Just a storm, is how it now is. I should have written a few rudimentary details about when and where, leaving out the digressions about Nicolas' upbringing and his expression and the salmon fisherman and the hot-water bottles; just the storm and a tree on fire, and our plastic cups tossed into the air, and an eagle plummeting sideways to snatch the bacon rind from the water as our plates reeled downstream. And three bleary little glad faces hardly noticeable behind glass and a veil of rain.

The longer I go without word from Teddy the more I imagine him with you in or around your hut, out taking photos of the trees or swimming in the static lake against the hum of a generator. You sit outside at a fold-up metal table that squeaks at the joints, on a day that is two degrees short of warm, and gaze into the light. This was how you were with him, benign but largely indifferent. Even when he was clanging a wooden toy against the fridge or screaming at a minuscule injustice, you never minded his presence. But you made no effort to engage in his world, either. I thought of it like the relationship between a human and a dog; human throw stick, dog chase stick, human shall never chase stick. Different types of beings equally united and divided by stick. Teddy appreciated your lack of likeness to him, and rarely missed a chance in the evening to curl himself against you in your armchair. You neither cuddled him nor shrank from him; maybe you would rest an arm across his shoulders.

So you are at the fold-up table, trying to build a Japanese torii out of snapped twigs, and are contemplating how vertical everything is – the trunks of the spruce, the secondary and tertiary branches that shoot straight up in search of light, the light itself falling like a plumb line in faint beams that make you look up for a UFO. Ah, how you would love an alien in this moment. The pitter-patter of intelligent life across the forest floor; you would sit your alien down and ask it to be honest about what it thought of Earth. Honestly (and here comes your frank, unsparing look) – do you think this Earth is wondrous or absurd? You contemplate briefly the possibility that it doesn't speak English or might be as dull-witted as a stone, but don't like to bother your fantasy with these trifles.

Over there Teddy stalks through the trees photographing lichen and leaf veins and insect dances. Or he threads through the water, always a good swimmer. The problem with Teddy is that he bears a false love, and his loyalty is misplaced. He loves you because he thinks you were exiled unjustly, and he prides himself on being the one member of our family who fights this injustice. Edward the fair, Edward the peaceful, watching over you with unquestioning belief in your goodness. He would strip the pines bare one by one if you asked him, just because you asked him.

Evening comes. There is incense and frying kippers and God beating about in the reddening sky. The sky looks sore. You are wondering why God must be so forceful with everything. You are wondering about Teddy too, how a four-year-old boy grew into this dark, intense man walking the forest with a camera and how from such chubbiness came high cheekbones, carved nose and sharp eyes. If only he would go away and care about some-thing else; it makes you feel guilty that he loves you still, and you hate to feel guilty, the most wasteful of emotions. His very presence is making you waste yourself. You take up a bit of tobacco from the table top and chew it – don't you – with your shoulder turned against him.

(B ut why do you write to her like this? Yannis says. He is taking me around Borough Market, his favourite place in London. A place of modern worship, lofty and vaulted, more populated on a Saturday morning than the church is on Sunday, its roof more light-letting than the great Gothic windows of Southwark Cathedral.

It's unhealthy, he says, that you should be writing to her like this, as if she were a *friend*.

I wonder if he remembers the comment he made a few weeks ago, about how I live in a draught? The other has left and – what was it he said? 'They have left, but not shut the door. It must be like living in a room with a draught always coming in.' This is how he put it, or how I said he put it. So when he takes a sample disc of cacciatore salami from the knife at the Italian delicatessen and asks me why I write to you like this, I say, Do you know, Yannis, that in life there are people who give shelter and people who take it; do you know that the people who take shelter come in from the cold and eat and drink from the cupboards of the people who give it, and sometimes they even make promises about staying and formulate in their minds a future in which they put their dreams to bed, their dreams of long, empty roads leading away from everything that ever tied them down? These people say, to themselves and sometimes aloud, I would like to give up my wandering, finally I would like to be one of the sheltered.

But one day the givers come down from a night of uneasy sleep and see that the door (which, come to think of it, had always been left ajar) is wide open, and the person who takes shelter is gone. Visible through the opening is a cloud that looks like a fast-dissolving highway. The days go on. The weeks go on and the months. Sometimes – this is more common than you might think – the ones who give shelter think about that highway themselves, this highway of freedom. But they have a temperate and cautious way of living, which means that no sooner do they visualise the highway than they see it dissolve. So they stay in the draught of a room whose door has been left open; they live in and endure the draught of somebody else's escape for freedom.

And then, Yannis, I say (as he handles appraisingly some miraculous edible rocks of cheese), you can see perhaps why one day one of them tries to close the door by proceeding as if the past made no impact and the old course of life can be resumed. And why the other one, entirely unconvinced that the past is really in the past, gets up, stands at the threshold of the door and looks for a shadow. A sound or something moving. And calls after the taker of shelter who has left their life so draughty and stripped; stands there calling out.

What? he says – you are calling for her to come back? No, I tell him, I don't want her to come back, I just can't be sure that something of her is not still there. So then I hope your letter is full of abusive swearing, he says; and when I tell him it is perfectly civilised he concludes sadly, Pot plants, you see. I told you. You modern women, pot plants.)

I suppose you might think that Yannis is not real. See how often he makes a convenient appearance when I have something I want to confide, something it would be awkward to say directly. What stops me having invented him for that purpose? How do you tell the difference between a person made of flesh and one made of words? I know this thought will have crossed your mind once, if not many times, because that is the way you think, by which I mean you think as if everything is a symbol for something else – like God being a sexual fantasy, or a triangle the symbol of creation. For you, nothing is what it actually is, even the desert you live in is an allegory, even the beetroot you eat is a transcendent notion; the more of it you take in, the thinner you get. No wonder you fell into this unlikely devotion to Hinduism and its purposefully symbolic gods, Brahma, Vishnu and Shiva – but I know I was talking about Yannis and I know I have started to go off-track.

Far from Yannis being made up, almost nothing in my life currently is more real than he is. And there are lots of conversations we have that are banal and trivial and signify nothing, which is why they don't make it onto the page – in fact Yannis is exactly one of those people who can gossip inanely all day about the racing odds, the unpunctuality of buses, the treachery of women, et cetera. Of course I wish his wife would come back to him, but I also wish it won't be for a long time, or I wish it would always happen tomorrow – you see, to be complicit with somebody is such a thing. He is the only person I have really talked to about you and he billows with opinions about it with typical Cretan hot-headedness, but when the conversation ends it ends, and he pours wine and makes some injurious remark about the government or the health-and-safety people who are always on his back, then asks me if I – if anyone – has actually read D. H. Lawrence. He has been trying with *The Rainbow* for over two months and his bookmark – not a receipt any more, but a KitKat wrapper – has found its way just past the middle.

'Could you give me an idea what it is fucking talking about?' he asks gently.

Is the flesh which was crucified become us poison to the crowds in the street, or is it as a strong gladness and hope to them, as the first flower blossoming out of the earth's humus?

He frowns accusingly at the page. 'Humus?' He swipes his finger into an imaginary dip and feeds it into his mouth. '*Humus?*' 'Yes,' I laugh, 'the first flower blossoming out of the thick wet chickpea-and-sesame soil.' He throws up his hands. 'Oh, I don't care, Lawrence was a lunatic,' he says, and he covers the book discreetly with a copy of the *Racing Post*.

*

I say this as if it's what he does in general, but it's what he did once, this week, when I told him about your job as a photographer of fake weddings. As an immigrant who has done everything he can to abide by the law and respect his host culture and learn his host language, he felt affronted by a livelihood predicated on dodging the law. By your little business that operated from a newspaper booth under the arches off Villiers Street in Embankment, by all the people living in squats and trying to get passports by whatever means. He believes these are the kind of people who give immigrants a bad name.

But I think if he could ever have seen the photographs you took he might have changed his mind, or opened it a little. Those photographs were not the stuff of hasty loveless services in registry offices. They looked pricey, an extravagance the bride's father had paid for to commemorate what would be a lasting union. No immigration officer could fail to see the sudden, bright and unlikely cross-border love that had sprung up between this louche, wiry Londoner and this lovely young woman from Port Elizabeth or the Karoo, with the luscious orange orchid bursting from her right temple.

Nobody was to know how the one-size-fits-all dress was gathered in at the back with bulldog clips, or that she had no shoes unless she provided them herself, or that the venue was the tiny back garden of a friend who had an arched iron love seat under a quince tree, and behind that a wall running with passion flower, and not much else besides. Out of frame was the washing line and a child's tricycle. In the frame, though, you made not just a wedding but a marriage; this was how I put it to Yannis, and it seems I stumbled on exactly the right phrase. Your lens married these people. The photographs were devotional and passionate, just like your *Still Life*, but also the opposite – because while the still life flaunted the gaping hole at the centre of things, your wedding photos disguised it, or even, I sometimes thought, dispelled it. I always imagined that some of those couples must have fallen genuinely in love when they saw how you had photographed them.

'Then I need a photograph like that of me and my wife,' Yannis said sadly. And then he added, with renewed objection, 'But still I think it isn't right.' When I suggested that it was different back in the eighties, he began on one of his righteous rants about deference to the law and level playing fields and the sanctity of marriage, all of which come from a place of goodness in his big, honest heart, but none of which I really listened to. I had started thinking about those times, because they coincided perfectly with the three years you lived with us in Morda. I thought about all the trips you took back and forth to London, the diary you used for bookkeeping, the way, for a year or so, this little business gave you purpose, friends of sorts, a notoriety – or so you once said – when you walked through Embankment Gardens.

Sometimes you took payment in kind: jewellery, clothes, shoes, drugs. You would come back to Morda with your hair pinned in place with a Mexican silver barrette, or in an elegant, outdated silk shift and trousers, or with a sachet of pinkish amphetamine that you would tap tentatively into a soda water after dinner with a kind of generous sense of experiment; you were just trying out a gift, after all. It would be ungrateful not to. I might find a bottle of Chanel No. 5 on my bed, or a book – yes, you passed on to Nicolas and me an unwanted illustrated book of South African diamond mines. You accepted the strangest forms of payment, if you don't mind me saying, and they became ever stranger as time wore on. The return leg of a two-way ticket to Johannesburg, should you ever want a holiday you couldn't come back from. Shoes that you would never wear, a handmade patchwork bedspread someone's grandmother had toiled over; and of course the little sachets, the pinkish yellowish greyish or bright white powders, the tiny pricey offerings of amphetamine or cocaine or heroin; they amassed over time and you hid them in a locked box at the back of your wardrobe so that Teddy could never find them.

This is what I was thinking when Yannis spoke – about your London life I never really saw, but which ate at you in mouthfuls. I saw you, in my mind as I was thinking, as a firework opening up and fading out. At first it was hair clips and dresses and stockings and clasps, so that you came home dazzling ironically, smiling, laughing, smearing orange grease on your eyelids. Nicolas hinted that he thought you had several men waiting for you there, several lovers, although he did not use that word. You handed over money each month for your keep. And then, over the three years, you would come back ever more jaded and falsely brisk, your wages seldom in the form of cash, more often in the form of folded sachets squirrelled away into the lockable box, your mood held up increasingly by a synthetic hum of restless energy that had a disappointing lifespan which, when it wore out, left you for days in your room.

Ah, but none of this is the heart of the matter, is it? Surely the heart of the matter is a guest-house in Earls Court where Nicolas stayed when he was working in London. The Ellis Guesthouse, run by Mrs Ellis, stand-in mother to Nicolas, poacher of perfect eggs, server of hot buttery toast (a toast-rack denier, a loose-tea evangelist), who judged not, who ran her house with discretion and honoured her guests with privacy and tried to pay attention to the small things – plenty of toilet roll in the bathroom, clean, sharp cutlery, extra blankets for winter.

All sorts of people went through Mrs Ellis' house and her door was always open, so long as you could pay the minimal prices. The regularly homeless, the recently divorced, the runaways, illegal immigrants, failing writers, out-of-work actors, those fresh from jail. Nicolas liked her liberalness and her quiet revolt. She would have been exactly the kind of person to turn a blind eye to the woman who sometimes went up to his room and left his pillows smelling of cypress and smoke, and exactly the kind of person to supply scissors when he asked, without a pause or a question, and to not comment the next morning when, alone at breakfast, he looked stricken, a lock of dark hair wrapped around his hand. That woman's dark hair, unmistakably; there it was, the same smell, piercing through swirls of warm milk and breakfast butteriness.

I almost asked Yannis, there and then, to come with me to Earls Court and see if the guest-house was still there. It was late, and the errand pointless, so I didn't ask after all. At home, after I'd left Yannis bemoaning the loss of morals, bemoaning you and Lawrence, slipping *The Rainbow* under the *Racing Post*, I did the things one does for bed – clothes off, teeth cleaned, face washed – and then I took that lock of hair out of the desk drawer, where it lives between newspaper in a shallow cardboard box that once housed a portable radio, and I placed it on the desk and stepped away from it. Years since I've looked at it. The fascination is still with the same particular thing – not the foot-and-a-half of hair itself, not the buffed-leather cavalry-boot black with its mahogany surprises, not the unkempt ends, not the cypress, the smoke, the coffee, the trapped life in the dead strands – but the top of the hair where the scissors made a clean swipe. A straight line, a decision; this is how I see it, a *decision*. Whose decision? Whose hands held the scissors and sliced that clinical line in the lamplight or dark? Yours or his?

May 2002

J ust this last week at work I was told a story that I'd like to recount for you. It was Gene who told me. The two of us sat outside in the wind and sun, and he told me that when he was in his early thirties he became involved with a married woman. He wasn't married himself. When he came home from war aged twenty-eight after three years' service he didn't feel he had enough humanity left to marry. Many felt that way, he said, even the ones who were married already. An affair seemed the most and best he could manage – this in a world in which casual relationships between men and women were not the norm, but also in a world in which war had forced years of celibacy on young men.

A year after the war he met a woman whom he called, mysteriously, M. I will always be left to wonder – Maria? Martha? Madeline? When he told me how he felt the first time he saw her, he started to embark on a theory of attraction. It is Plato's theory of the missing half – a famous story, but I will summarise it anyway. Once upon a time a single human being was both genders, with eight legs, eight arms, two heads, two sets of genitals, each human both male and female and also a third gender, androgynous, and each parented by the sun, the Earth and the combination of these, the moon. Fearing their power, Zeus cut them in half so that they became distinct, one man, one woman. The combination of both, the third gender, disappeared. He cut them – here Gene quotes Plato – *as you would cut hard-boiled eggs with hairs*. Ever since this separation, men and women have longed for one another, and the longing has been a desperate one for completion and for the healing of the wound of separation.

I think Gene referred to this theory because other more earthly explanations completely escaped him when he thought of his attraction to M. He ran out of words when he stopped referring to Plato and he just stared ahead for perhaps as long as a minute. When he started again it was to take up the facts: they met, they went out for dinner and a drink, they met again, they slept together, they slept together again. Though she was married she was childless; nevertheless, she said she couldn't, wouldn't and didn't want to leave her husband, and he told her he understood. He told himself it would have been disastrous if she had wanted to, since he had nothing left in him to give a woman except his lust, which, despite its tyrannising power, he would always try to be gentle enough in giving. You don't want to become one of those brutes, he said, and I nodded, though I can only imagine what brutality it was he had seen and was refusing.

She was a good woman, he said, and he seemed to want to bring this point to the fore. Good as in kind, gentle, compassionate, decent. When he told me this I think he was challenging me to disagree, but I nodded. I expect she was all of those things. And it went on for a few months, he said, seeing one another once in a while, and it seemed a convenient arrangement. For him it was something physical, and although their opportunities were scarce, even in the weeks of no or little contact it was enough that he still had in her a place for his desire to go, somewhere for the thoughts to land. For her it was the intake of fresh air in a life that had become otherwise still and – stale. Then he recanted: No, not stale, that's my word, M never used words like that. If she referred to her marriage at all it was briefly, with tenderness and without judgement. The only impression he ever got of that marriage was that it was still. Not stale, not bitter, not going to pieces, just not going at all.

But you fall in love, he said. This is the problem. That attraction – and again, when he tried to describe the attraction, it fell to his hands to do the talking; they came tensely towards one another as magnetically loaded things do, and he pulled them apart and they came together – that attraction doesn't come from nowhere and is not accidental. When you feel that the other person is your missing half, you will fall in love. And then . . .

He let his hands drop to his knees and he let his gaze drop to his hands. They were not charged any more, they were a pair of old man's hands, which were used, but not used up. The fact is that the affair went on for years, he said, and was full of love. It became, almost, a marriage in itself, one that rode out circumstance and evolved in massive, unnoticeable shifts, and passed with quietly celebrated anniversaries. Where it was most unlike a marriage was in its physicality, which never waned and which changed only in order to intensify. No doubt this was partly down to its ongoing novelty; they once went for over two years without sleeping together. M would enforce laws of celibacy on them once in a while in despair and guilt, and they would see one another every fortnight for a walk, for tea, as if friends. It was like trying to push the rain back up into the clouds. How could it ever do anything but fail? Their bodies were very insistent on one another, and it never waned, never. These were his exact words. Never waned, never. No amount of abstinence or self-control ever did anything but increase the insistence.

He asked me if it was normal to feel like you had died while making love. I told him I didn't know. He said: To feel like you had died and passed beyond your body into the mind of God. Then he retreated from this line of enquiry, as though speaking these clumsy words had got him only further from the phenomenon they described and which he was trying, somewhere in his old body, to hold onto.

As for M, there were any number of theories about her that might shed light on why she didn't leave her husband, and how somebody so otherwise loyal and fair had managed to construct a life of deceit. He had his theories, she had hers; they exchanged them. But people are not reducible to theories, isn't that true? This was more true for M than for any other human being he had met, M who was so curious and oblique and held together by her inconsistencies. M who was very witty and loved a joke, but whose face became almost laughably serious at the smallest thing. She told him once that she had always wanted to be one of those women who threw their heads back in laughter, but that she always forgot, and when something funny happened she instead wrinkled her nose and smiled soundlessly into her lap. It's very hard to escape who you are, he said, and in saying so he implied that M could not have done or been anything other than what she did and was, and, loving what she did and was, he could never have wanted her to try.

Yet when we slept together, he said, then she threw her head back, then she became fierce and free. Once again he approached the depths of this thought and retreated, and only said – by way of shorthand perhaps for this baffling carnal force that so evaded words – that he had never much wanted to be a father, but that he wanted to be the father of her children. Furthermore, that it made no sense for him not to be and for them to create nothing together. These were things he didn't tell her, or if he did he told her in diluted and un-urgent ways that were easily dismissed as abstract talk. Which they did, repeatedly, dismiss as abstract talk.

After six years the affair ended; why? Why then? No particular thing happened to force its end and neither did it peter out or drift away. It seemed that it simply buckled to inevitability. The love became too big, the time for it insufficient, and he believed that she felt the same. It sounded so perverse and pitiable a reason. If their love was so big, why didn't it forge for itself a relationship it deserved? Why didn't she leave? Why didn't he insist she leave? Why didn't he tell her husband? Why didn't he fall out of love with her for her cowardice? Again he looked at me as if he wanted me to judge them. When I didn't, he seemed galvanised. It just doesn't work like that, he said.

Gene is not a weak man. In his room he has a photograph of himself in his thirties or forties and he is strong and sturdy and his skin glows, and he has a smile that shows a mixture of childish pleasure and adult forbearance. In that mix I can see perfectly how he might be the kind of man to hunt treasure with unfading optimism, and at the same time to be able to keep his hands off that treasure with unfading patience. Both characteristics come from the same place, an absolute belief that, one day, the treasure would be his reward, at whatever cost to himself along the way. When he told me he slept with no other women during those six years, and that he waited for her without regret, and that in some way he went on to wait for her until the day she died, he told me as though simply to convey, without sorrow, that this was the structure his life took. He could more easily live with the knowledge that he never quite had her than he could have with the knowledge that he lost her through greed and snatching, which pushed her out of reach.

As it turned out, he did not ever marry. You don't, he said, it wouldn't ever feel right. I think I can understand what he means.

It is not that you can't settle for anything less, because you do, several times. I know he has a son because his notes from the hospital say the son had been to visit him there, though only once – and I suppose he must come from a later relationship. Yes, you do settle for less, it's just that the things you settle for never make sense. Somewhere deeply felt, you can never understand why you couldn't have that simple thing you wanted so much, and your whole life is pervaded by this incomprehension. You come to look like somebody who is blinking into bright light.

Butterfly, for the first time it occurred to me that you might have felt some of the things Gene felt, that the years you spent on the periphery of Nicolas' life might have been spent waiting for something that never happened. I have always been so convinced by the notion that in some way both Nicolas and I were victims of you that I have never stopped to consider the possibility that you might have been the victim. Suddenly I wonder if you loved him, and if you ever asked him to leave me, and whether, by the time he did, it was too late. Perhaps you wanted a child. I entertain this thought just for a moment; I try to squint the wrong way down the lens and see you small and consumed, a half person looking for her other half, and there, momentarily, you are. And I feel a compassion for you I cannot describe. And then you throw your head back in laughter in the way M never could and I think: No, this is not how it was. Gene's story is Gene's, not ours.

Yes, our story is quite different; our story is splattered with the blood of bulls. Gene's was the quiet emotional aftermath of war, ours *is* the war, the war itself, one soul grinding repeatedly against another.

You are exaggerating, you say. But I contend that no exaggeration is equal to the task of summing up the battle between us. We are in southern Spain, in Almería's Plaza de Toros, a Friday evening in July. We watch six bulls die; the rule is that if the bull shows special courage he might be saved and put out to stud, but this is rare and it does not happen for any of our bulls. Each of them is dragged out of the arena and the blood trail is covered with sand.

At the time I thought it was like watching an Argentine tango. You remember the videos my mother had of European dance-hall competitions when she was learning (briefly, before she bored of it) to tango; you remember, specifically, the reproachful magnetism between the two dancers as they flicked their heels up around one another's legs. I thought – though I need to make it clear I no longer see it this way – that the bull and matador were tentative like this; the matador flicks the cape, the bull advances, the matador toe-steps away, the bull quivers.

But then, who would not quiver? The picadors come out on horses that have their eyes covered and their ears stuffed. They gather in on the bull and lance its shoulders and neck, and that is when it becomes tentative, demure, as if wooed into an unplanned engagement. It lowers its head. In one of the fights the picador is too enthusiastic and lances it to its knees so that by the time the matador enters the ring it is barely able to stand, let alone fight. The crowd jeers and throws cushions; they wanted to see a fair contest. You waft your polka-dot fan restlessly around Teddy's sleeping head. But this is only one of the six fights, and in the others the bull is lanced into a kind of taut energy. The banderilleros run into the ring and towards the bull with their spikes. These sticks, like the feathered arrows in Teddy's archery set, festoon its shoulders. It looks like a morris dancer, Nicolas says, with his chin drawn back in concern.

By the time the matador enters with his cape and sword, the bull is already swaying sideways and forwards as if at sea, with punctured and twitching muscles – surprised, I think, and offended, but here is the thing – seeing itself for the first time in true relation to something else, no longer alone and dominant, but suddenly half of a two-way exchange. You can see this in the way it makes and keeps eye contact with the matador and maintains both closeness and space. They circle one another; the matador swishes his cape, the bull scrapes at the ground. The blood on its flank thickens in the heat, everybody is hot inside the bullring.

Maybe the bull has a moment of love then. You might laugh, but if all you ever do is live unthreatened in the bubble of your absolute autonomy, eating, shitting, inseminating, replicating yourself over and over, what can you really love? Now it has the man at eye level and it understands the invitation. The cape communicates between them, beckoning, repelling, this way, that way, charge, hold back. The band plays. We shouldn't think the bull is just meat thrown into a ring, it is an intelligence and it wants something it sees, it wants to be reckoned with. And the matador – we shouldn't be fooled by his gold silk, he is an animal and he wants to be reckoned with. You see that for a moment – only a moment – the bull recognises himself in the man, and the man in the bull.

Why can't this moment go on longer between them? As in the tango, which never resolves. When the bull finally realises that the man is cruel, there is no longer recognition. The bull is not cruel, why does the man have to be; why must it end like this? The matador draws his sword and pushes it down through the shoulders into the bull's heart, or lungs, or whatever meets the sword first. The bull's eyes become humid. In two fights the kill is clean, in the other four a second sword has to be used to cut through the spine. The result is the same: one way or another the bull staggers and drops like a rock into its short shadow, and is dragged away to music.

The heat is flattening and Teddy has slept through the whole thing, with his head on Nicolas' lap. Your thumbs twitch in rage but you have become otherwise still and quiet. Nicolas has been watching you out of the corner of his eye. I have been wondering why a sword had to be drawn; slaughter is so unintelligent, so colourless, it forces us to think the least interesting thoughts. It makes us think that the strong one wins and the weak one loses. It makes us think the winner does not limp.

Y ou look pleased with yourself. Have you been out
stealing hens?
You have that blush you get when winning at cards,
which in this case might be to do with remembering Spain; you
mentioned that holiday for a long time after – the villa we stayed
in with the big, cool, marble-floored living room and virtually
nothing in it, save for five cheap armchairs and a vast table that
converted into a platform for table tennis when the net was
clipped on.

You liked the villa, didn't you – the villa and its garden. Cool
and uneventful inside, hot and busy out, with its wild grasses
rubbing drily together and its geckos darting and cicadas creaking
in the juniper tree and its – as you put it – slatternly flowers.
You enjoyed our daily struggle of sun versus parasol as we tried
to construct movable shade on the beach. We made a circle of
shade and it became an ellipse and then a sliver. We made another
and another the entire day long and the sun hovered and swooped
in on each one. I think this thankless task appealed to you, probably even amused you – when Nicolas, Teddy and I went in the
sea, you stayed onshore to crawl about spearing the two parasols
into the sand, draping towels or T-shirts across the gap. Then

you would sit in the sun and let yourself burn. In the dried-up riverbeds of the Tabernas Desert you found a sprawling oleander and what you thought was an edible prickly pear, which you tried to pick, before our guide bent and stopped your hand. Squinting up at the gallows in the main street at Fort Bravo film studios, you held your blouse away from your body, red-faced, hair wet with sweat, and grinned at a crack of gunshot as though you were the happiest you had been.

Yes, I'd say Spain has flushed you. On the screen your geese are sheeting, gliding out of frame. Sliding, gliding, slipping through a narrow gap in existence towards freedom and something more real than all this table-hut-bed-forest-city-man-woman debacle we call reality. But suddenly, because I brought it up, you are thinking of Spain, and every time you think of Spain it brings to mind that bit in the *Aitareya* Upanishad, that bit about the bull. What is it? God pulls a bull out of the water, then a horse, then a man. There is God, going about creation messily, engaged in the hot, dark, slick, wet process by which life is dredged from the depths. You like this bit – God the diver and delver, slumping his finds onto the bank and giving them life with his breath.

You left before the end of the bullfight and sat outside the plaza in the street, chain-smoking some little pencil-thin cigarillos. By the time we found you there was a handful of spent ends piled up by your toes. 'How could you watch it?' you said. 'It was like watching Henry VIII slaying his wives. You two would have been the kind of people who went to public hangings.'

We thought then that you would be unbearable for the rest of the evening; Nicolas looked glad it was the last day. Forgive us for thinking that everything you had enjoyed about Spain had been undone in one afternoon in a bullring – we were wrong. You said something that evening as we were walking back through Almería in the dusk that I have maybe only recently interpreted fully. Teddy commented that there was no grass, or no green bumps, as he called it – hills, pasture, meadow. He was right, it was just coastal plain, mountain or desert canyon. And when, at the thought of English greenness, Nicolas began humming 'Jerusalem', you said something like, 'The Jesus who walked upon England's mountains green was a fop, that is the truth, a fop who got lynched.'

I remember it, because it was only half an hour or so after leaving the plaza, and if ever the green pleasantness of England was going to come into your favour it should have been then, in your recoil from the bullfight. But instead you opened up from your tall stoop and walked so as to maximise the evening air on your chest, and back at the villa you cut yourself a fringe with kitchen scissors so that your face was an open window and Spain could come flooding in, like fresh air into a sickroom. It was the emboldening a person gets when they see another behave more despicably than themselves; it was a final sealing of a friendship that you and Spain had been developing all week.

I have thought about this since. England has always seemed to you sort of jolly, neat, falsely gay. Unable to contend with the prospect of a God who gets his hands dirty. But Spain was another matter; from the moment you set foot in Spain you felt it was the kind of place that could worship a God who got down with the slick and seminal things. Maybe an irrational thought, but even so. Something about the way the land itself had seemed to sink through the hot air like a layer of sediment, and felt dense and warm to walk on, whereas in England the fields and hills sit pertly, like some nervous pre-pubescent girl.

Almería had scorched afternoons and clammy dark evenings, oversized insects and locals with oily overcooked skin, steep orange desert canyons, red dust that stuck to sweat, warm, slow-moving tides pulled by distended moons towards the unknownness of Africa, viscous bull blood, a lump of unfamiliar animal on a dinner plate. This overgrowth, this slight impure libidinous danger – it always makes you draw a connection with that hot messy passage in the Upanishads where God opened the suture of the skull and entered the first human. We are egg-born, it says: egg-born, womb-born, sweat-born, soil-born. God is passed on in the exchange of seed. England turns its head politely, either too pragmatic for God, or too squeamish for this God. But in Spain, where people were so much freer with their flesh, touched more, laughed more, were irrational and passionate and callous and more easily angered; in Spain you would not be laughed at if you tried to get to heaven by going downwards rather than upwards, if you tried to get there by passing through another's flesh.

This is what it says in the *Aitareya* Upanishad: a man is inside himself in the form of a seed. It is only when he ejects that seed into a woman that he is born. But he must be born again and again before he can break out of the body and be free. Your road to freedom passes through the bodies of others; it does not involve some levitation of your spirit or the quelling of the things that stir in your loins. God put that stirring in your loins so you could be born into another, and thus start your journey to immortality.

So now, flushed, I see you. You are thinking back to the Plaza de Toros, and even now you can feel the sweat between your thighs and see the crowd tossing cushions into the air, which is beginning to feel like boiled milk. In the noisy heat of the bullring you need something; not a cigarette, it is too hot for smoking, maybe a shot of something dissolved in water. Needle better, but no needles on this holiday. It is not that you need a lift, but that you feel lifted and want to celebrate it. You cannot even say why you feel this way in this heat, which is insufferable, at this bullfight, which is disgusting – but something has risen in you that feels like religious feeling, or divine licence, which is close to rage and hate and love all at once.

Something of that mood was with you from the moment you set foot on Spanish tarmac, heightening at the sight of the desert badlands and in the markets of La Chanca and in the orange spears of the bird of paradise that grew in the garden. And oh, I know, I know – you will be finding my memory of it all a little too stagey and false. The blood and the heat and the flora and the sex; the *lust in the dust*. True enough, Spain has become a filmset to me, the whole of it barely more real than Fort Bravo itself. It has become a piece of strange theatre in the otherwise prosaic run of my life, and maybe this is the only way I can understand it. But all the same there are the facts, whereby on the last night, after the bullfight, with the moon hanging between the villa and the sea, you, feeling irrepressible, lay naked on the grass when you thought everyone else was in bed, and might have been surprised – though maybe not all that surprised – when Nicolas came to you.

Do you not think I know how many times you have wished this letter had not arrived, since all it does is remind you of things you are no longer interested in. You think I don't know how uninterested you are, but I know. You are not interested in the recriminations that so tediously follow what you and Nicolas did that night; it is like recriminating a woman for slingshotting a dove, without acknowledging that she did so to feed her starving child. Sometimes the ends justify the means, and you are tired with this banal preoccupation with the means only. But the very mention of Spain from a third party, from a source outside your own mind, is one of the more interesting turns the letter has taken. You read the section from the Upanishads again and your heart swells. *Sage Wāmadewa,* broke out of the body, did all that he desired, attained the Kingdom of Heaven, became immortal; yes, became immortal.

Suddenly the geese on the screen look no more substantial or significant than puddles that have evaporated. It is their sound you now notice, that rough feverish call to adventure, calling you back to the realm of things that exert themselves with living. If you are ashamed at all of what you did, it is because you now know better; Nicolas, or any other man or woman or living or non-living thing, was never going to save you. But you are not ashamed of adultery, which is, as the name suggests, adults being as such. So when I got out of bed and came out to the garden to see where Nicolas had gone, and saw you no more than fifteen feet away, astride him on the grass facing the villa, you did not freeze with guilt, but looked at me and shook your head, left, then right: a firm, complicit no.

One of your hands was resting on his chest, trying to feel for the banging, longing muscle of heart inside. Spain has shown you a tunnel out of yourself, into the world of action. As Nicolas joins you in the tunnel you think of that very passage in the Upanishads that starts with God dredging a bull from the depths and culminates in Sage Wāmadewa's immortality. And now sex feels like a religious act; the whole holiday feels like a religious act, and England and marriages and pastures and cool summers are a blasphemy.

Sage Wāmadewa did all that he desired; why not you? More fool those who do not. Life is short. Life shoots you a lethal dose of time. Time is a drug that wears off. You seem to stare at me from under that crooked fringe as if to say, *You* brought this up. Or worse, as if to say: Put your pen down, my friend, forget it; I will never be sorry. I was trying to save myself; I failed, but at least I had the dignity to want to be saved. More fool you, if you don't want to save yourself too.

B ut really, is that what you call saving yourself?

When I last saw you, you did not look like a person who was saving herself. I always see that platform empty of trains, and you at the far end. When I see this I have to wonder if you are even alive, and I tell myself you must be, simply because death has a strangely efficient grapevine and we would have heard if you weren't; this is my only consolation, and maybe an empty one at that. You left us in the winter with a little bit of Spanish tan still on your arms, and you came back pale and thin as paper. A little under two years without sight or word of you, and there you were all of a sudden with your weight off one foot, an animal that has been shot in the flank, not the heart. Like I said before, a wounded wolf. The flank slack; head hung, shoulders dropped, eyes half closed. Sore is the word that comes. You were always quite solemn and meek in profile, something that surprised me every time I caught you from the side; this day you were especially meek and harmless – maybe it was the dip of your head, or the way your head looked too heavy for your shoulders. But when I walked nearer you looked up, flashing pure irony, and you smiled ruefully in the way people do when they think something morbid is funny.

I wonder if not being able to see ourselves is one of the great paradoxes of being alive – knowing oneself intimately and also not at all. You turn to look at your own profile in the mirror and it is gone. It means we can harbour all kinds of illusions about ourselves that others can see through as clear as day. What I mean is that if you had been able to see yourself objectively that afternoon you might have realised that the game was lost, but instead I think you fancied yourself in some little role in some little story in which you were the heroic returner, the one much waited for, the one who would be forgiven by some obscure law of justice that grants immunity to the tragic.

It was late October, and I suppose there is something heroic and melancholy about autumn and these monolithic trees unable to keep for themselves a single leaf, and things coming home and coming in and coming back and preparing to shelter again. And the world is going down onto its knees. You show up on a station platform in October of 1986, after almost two years without word. One train after another pulling in and out of the station while you stood watching and waiting for nothing. You had been there for hours before you called us to pick you up. To your mind's eye you might have been positively operatic, a woman in her late thirties alone at a station in an ankle-length out-of-fashion dress and a shawl and her hair wrapped up in a green scarf, standing beneath the transom of the waiting-room window where she holds defiantly to the burden of her beauty. Leaves gathering at her suitcase and feet, like the children she never had. Tell me you did not think like this.

You think like this because it is difficult to accept that when we find ourselves most operatic we are usually just farcical. I could cry to think of you now, the way you turned to smile at me when I walked up to you. You had the Devil dull and black in your eye. You were too thin and you were not old enough to look as old as you did, which is not to say you were no longer beautiful – for an overwhelming minority of people, beauty is an affliction they have to bear regardless of what they do to themselves, and which prompts other people to expect too much from them. Fools others, I mean, into thinking that the beautiful always have cause for hope. I expect you had already fooled fifty people that day. Maybe you could have fooled me too, had it not been for one thing, your shawl, the tear at its left shoulder. Or maybe that is overstating it. But it was the torn shawl that I remember most. How can one ripped piece of fabric call up such loss, somehow, of dignity, or of eligibility in this world, of care for oneself? And it was a cold windy day, but your shoulder through the hole was bare. Because of this blind spot we find ourselves in, you won't have known how scandalous that shoulder looked, sharp and white, with its little collection of thrusting bones. You exposed yourself on that chilly platform like a degenerate in a city park. Scandalous; a strong word, but I mean it. Even the trains hurried their passengers in, with a sort of motherly protectiveness, and rattled away.

*

Our conversation in the car at the station went something like, 'What happened to you?', to which you replied, 'What happened to me? *I* happened to me. That's always my problem.'

'You look terrible.'

'It's kind of you to notice.'

'Where have you been?'

'Somewhere north of your opinion, where it's cold.' You might be interested to know that I since realised this was a vague and spliced bit of *Twelfth Night* (which I happened to see with Ruth last year). You might have also said something like, 'I've been walking through the blizzards of your disapproval. I have been in the Arctic of your disgust.' I don't know; whatever it was you said while we sat in the car at the station, it was oblique and facetious and aloof, purposefully insincere. I turned the ignition key.

'So you haven't come back to say you're sorry, then,' I said. 'Or to see if I'll forgive you. Just to stretch out like a cat on your old territory.'

I have a feeling you didn't answer, but watched me all the way home out of the corner of your eye.

This music we hear now is vocalese; it is not your favourite. You would call it mewling or warbling. You would say, Why are you listening to a record played backwards?

Well, it is not my favourite either, but when you hear somebody do it well, the singing voice sounds just like the instrument, not so that you can't tell them apart, but so that the voice takes on the instrument's qualities in the way that a Cézanne painting finds the qualities of a given landscape, without slavishly reproducing it. It just looks, and picks out what it considers true. I like this about it. I have had the window open all evening and let the music from Jimmie's drift in while dusk comes and the buildings disintegrate. The best song I've heard (which isn't to say I have heard them all) was a woman's rendition of 'Goodbye Pork Pie Hat', her voice had the saxophone's hollow depth that most other singers never manage. Climbing up and down the scales to a background of percussion.

This evening Yannis called by for a short time, and two things are strange about this. Today is Friday and the only evening Yannis has away from his shop is Tuesday, which is his day off. Also, although he knows which building is mine, he has never been to my flat before and he had to ring all four buzzers. So when I heard him on the intercom and when I opened my front door and called merrily hello as I watched him come up the stairs, I knew more or less that either his shop had burnt down or his wife had asked for a divorce; and there had been no fire engines that I had noticed going past, so I said, 'Is she going back to Crete?' He nodded.

Inside, I poured us each a vodka and water and offered him some cashew nuts and dried apricots, which was all I had. You must offer Yannis food; to not offer him food is akin to not offering somebody else a seat. (Yannis would not mind if you forgot to offer him a seat, he likes to stand, which is why he has only two small tables in his café.) He took a clump of apricots and read from the packet. 'Stoned and ready to eat,' he said sadly. 'This sounds like my son in his early twenties.' He went to the window and leant out as if trying to see the sound. 'When is she going?' I asked, and without turning he slashed his throat with his hand. This is something he does, which is how I recognised the gesture even with his back turned. 'Already gone?' I asked, and again he nodded.

'Can you believe that she came to me on Tuesday,' he said, 'to tell me that by Thursday she would be gone? You can't believe this, can you? She has her ticket, she is going. Akis is meeting her at the airport, her witch of a sister is coming to me sometime soon to pack the things she wants to ship home, and I may visit any time from June, if I want to talk about a reconciliation. This is what she said, and then she was gone.'

'A reconciliation, though,' I said. 'That's good news?' To which he replied, 'No no no no, because you don't know my wife. By reconciliation she means surrender. We may stay married if I surrender. Do you know what I think of that?' I said, Yes, I did; he told me anyway. 'What I think of that is she can put it in her spare hole and sit on it.' I said, Yes, that's what I thought he thought. Although I have no idea where he got this phrase from, or which, in his view, is her spare hole. For a moment I felt happy for her that she had left. 'Do you want to play cards?' he said. He stood by the rocking chair then and finished his drink, so I poured him another, which he finished, and I poured him another.

I did not want to play cards, you have to be in the mood, you have to feel alright about losing or otherwise feel invincible; I told him I was sorry. 'She treats me as if I am a monster,' he said. 'What have I done? You're a woman – tell me what did I do?' It was here that the music at the club started up, or that I noticed it had started up, so I stood with my arms open and beckoned him with a quick flick of the fingers of one hand, like I used to with Teddy when he knocked his knee and was about to cry. We held each other loosely and danced in slow steps around the room to these drifting sounds of bebop. Yannis put his big head on my shoulder. How dare she do this to him? I thought suddenly. This wife, whose name I don't think I have even imparted to you and which I now don't think I will, in case she is not deserving of it. How dare she simply escape like this, as if she has no responsibilities?

I have always felt a kind of solidarity with Yannis, maybe in part because we both have just one child, a son, from whom we are far too estranged. Sometimes I feel we are both like disused sea ports, no longer harbouring anything. But this is self-pitying and ridiculous, I see it; we made our children, we were not made *for* them, we are not nothing without them. This is a coward's view of life. And then I felt that his wife, Stefania – perhaps she does deserve a name after all – was precisely not a coward because she was doing what she wanted without giving quarter. Why should we give quarter? It is so hard in life to know what we want that surely, when we do know, we must act. She and Yannis had been together since they were teenagers; she had been a mother since the age of eighteen or nineteen. She had earnt herself some autonomy. This is when I heard your voice: The tyranny of possession! it said. The greatest tyranny of all is men's possession of women and women's possession of men. We want to own one another so that the other cannot outgrow us. You know how Chinese women bind their feet until the feet are deformed? This is what we do to one another's hearts.

I want you to know that I had these thoughts quickly, and that although I heard you say all those words, I heard those quickly too, so that the song we were dancing to – it might have been 'Cotton Tail', I don't remember – was not even a third of the way through by this point. I found I was humming into Yannis' ear, and that my shoulder, which was bare because of it being a warm night, was moist with his tears.

Then, just as I had made peace with Yannis' wife, I became angry with Lara. I thought, how can Lara escape her religion? I remembered her phrase, about carrying a sack of stones. A sack of stones that can be picked up and put down, dipped into as and when. But religion is not like this; the weight of God is upon those who believe, a burden from above, and love is the shouldering of this burden, the glad acceptance of it. Lara wants to think there is nothing higher than her head, and that she can orchestrate her own salvation through her acts. Next she will become a humanist, without realising that humanism is to a Christian what methadone is to a heroin addict, a way of weaning off. She will begin to believe in humans instead of God because it is hard to give up believing all at once. And then, when humans fail her, she will become a spiritualist and decide she can flee this illusory world like a bird sliding obliquely off the screen, slip through its gauze, as if religion's sole purpose is to make escape artists of us.

Of course, I was not angry with Lara. It is strange how unwilling anger is to alight directly on its object. Yannis' hand slipped to my lower back and then down a little further still, and I let him because it did no harm. I said to him: 'Yannis, the student asks the master why Japanese teacups are so delicate and easy to break. The master says that the teacups aren't too delicate, it's just that the person who drinks from them is too heavy-handed.' He drew his head back and looked at me with the same slightly hostile incomprehension he had shown over the word *humus*. I concluded: 'It's not for teacups to change, but for us to adapt to what is.'

It was the wrong thing to say, I know, because he raised his hand to my waist again in disapproval. And it was not really even all that relevant to him, but I said it because I was pressed upon by a feeling of – what can I say? – stringency, or obedience. It is not for us to try to change the world to something that suits us better, but for us to change, to bend to a greater weight. When he left ten or fifteen minutes later, at the end of the next song, which was 'Goodbye Pork Pie Hat', which we danced to in thoughtless silence, I stood at the window and watched him lope down the street towards his shop. He was going to get ready for the others who were coming at ten-thirty to play Poker. All I could think of was how I had used to dance with Nicolas and how unexpectedly gifted he was at finding a coherent stream of movement in a piece of music and how he would thread us both along it. We danced, you know, a lot, never formally but around the house, especially the big, decrepit house we rented in London just after we were married and before Teddy came. He was not a good dancer as such, he was just good at finding what others could not beneath the surface – mining, I suppose, mining the music for its rhythm. He had a way of holding my waist as if it were a piece of machinery he had undergone five years of training to use.

We lived in that house for eight months. It didn't have a single useable surface that he had not danced me towards and laid me on and entered me at. There was no surface that both my back and front had not become intimately familiar with, and no view of the floorboards or ceiling's coving I had not had through the blind or ecstatic or gentle vision of being made love to by him, and no part of the bathroom mirror that had not reflected our daily selves doing their daily things, our white teeth bared for the brush, our bodies lowered into the bath, no spring in the bed that had not known the weight of our deepest of sleeps, no knot of the hallway rug that had not known the precise indent of our four feet, no inch of brass on the doorhandles that had not been dulled with our palms.

Shall I tell you what I think? I think Yannis should go after his wife. I think he should rush after his wife and bind his feet in front of her.

H ere we are, you and I, just back from Spain. We oppose each other across a table with a fan of thumbed cards. Twist, you say. Twist again. Like we did last summer, I reply. Your cards pressed onto the table add up to twenty, mine to eighteen, there is a flurry of dealing in which fingers fly and a twist and a twist and a stick; maybe I win. The games are quick and thoughtless and fill a post-supper lull while Teddy sleeps and the cottage becomes a dark missable shape in the lane. The cards are dealt, the pack settled, the trivial risks taken; if you are going to twist you flare your nostrils, if you are going to stick you suck in your cheeks: this is how I know your next move and how I have the card ready when you ask for it.

In the two or more years you've been staying with us you have been trimming your hair by increments and oiling it, so that it is thick and dark and seems to flesh out your features, and the fringe you cut for yourself in Spain makes your eyes look startled. There is none of that flaming orange grease on your lids, and without that your eyes are freer and wider and the space between them more emptily purposeless. You have taken to looking at me squarely while your pupils expand and shrink with the movement of candle flame. You ask me if you should leave. Where would you go? I reply, and you shrug one shoulder as if this is irrelevant. I don't give you a yes or no, and so you stay.

I deal you four low cards, which leave you on something like sixteen. Deal me a queen or a king, you say, with a jut of chin and a short laugh. *Bust* me. Your face is surprisingly tender with its Spanish tan. When you make this invitation for me to bust you (half teasing, half morbidly serious), I know you know that there have been poisonous words hissed in your name in a marble-floored room at the back of the villa; you seem to know that I pummelled my fist uselessly into the side of Nicolas' neck, how I saw that new light you put in his eyes and flailed my hands at it. You look at my hands holding the spread of cards as if they are something quick and savage that has, by mercy, gone temporarily still. Your moist bright eyes seem to say, Did you feel like strangling him, like strangling me? – then maybe you should have. You should kill me or leave him, your expression suggests. Or both, do both. And so, asserting my only power, I do neither. It is like we have turned a corner with one another. You have wronged me, and you dare me to care.

I deal you a nine. Not a theatrical bust, but bust all the same. You say we should pray, just in case. Pray for what? In case of what? In case God exists and praying makes a difference, you say. So we pray separate silent prayers while we bend cards from pack to hand and we agree not to tell the other what was asked for. Whoever wins, you decree, will have their prayer answered. It comes down to the next game. I win again. You gather our cards in a small, neat heap and say that in this case I shall have my prayer. But I prayed I would lose, I say.

You dip your hands into the gloom beneath the reach of the two wall lights, re-deal and remind me with a smile and a sigh, and with no words, that the victorious never pray to lose. Without discussion, we switch to Poker and gamble with a stack of coppers, undisturbed by the universe until two in the morning when Nicolas arrives home from a show in London and almost wordlessly shifts away upstairs to sleep, like an animal that has been ousted from the pack and is too tired to fight its way back in.

Without him we go on in this sweet, smoky, murmured combat of yours, which is the only way of loving you know, just like a dog loves a bone. With its teeth and also its tongue. I win a hand, you win a hand; we play so long we start to read one another's cards with our minds.

A fight broke out at work today. One of the residents commented that in Australia there was a ban on smoking in restaurants. His daughter had been there and had reported this news back; I bet England will soon be doing the same, he said. You watch.

I couldn't have anticipated the reaction to this. These are people who receive news of fatal heart disease or nephritis or the death of a spouse or child with a certain aged poise, yet rumour of a smoking ban in restaurants inflames them to violence. One of the more dispassionate residents, Claudia, pointed out that they didn't go to restaurants anyway, so what did it matter? This was where Frances, who has been made bent and quiet by months of pleurisy, found her verve again for a minute. Nothing in life stays where it is, she said; it starts in a restaurant in Australia and suddenly it's everywhere – not just restaurants but every last place, including their smoking room at the back of the lounge and their summer house in the garden. Everything spreads like a joke, and suddenly you're eighty-seven and you can't smoke in your own summer house. Then you have to stand out in the rain, and life's bad enough without that.

Claudia replied that they shouldn't smoke anyway. Uproar

ensued. Frank, sitting next to her in the lounge, reached across and grasped her wrist with a fervour I cannot say I have ever seen in him before, and Claudia's response was fast and majestic – an arcing slap to the face, her pink-nailed hand flying so elegantly towards the nice flat mottled surface of his cheek. I intervened. Please, I said, be calm. But by then there was shouting and rebellion against Frank for his violence towards Claudia, which lasted only so long. As soon as Frank reminded them of what Claudia had said, the judgement she had made about them, opinion swung. Who was she to say they shouldn't smoke? Who were the Australians to say they shouldn't smoke? When you've fought in a war in the East African mountains or driven an infantry tank into a destroyed Normandy village and put your own neck on the line for your country, why not smoke your lungs down to prunes? They're your own lungs, that's the thing, why not?

And suddenly somebody took off his shoe and threw it at the wall, and so more shoes flew, and magazines, and cups were overturned, and even non-smokers became incensed. I am not sure anybody really knew what they were incensed about – but then I have always been amazed and amused by how quickly causes crumble and general childishness and petulance begin. Part of me wanted to applaud them. It is good to get angry, to throw your shoe! I wanted to throw mine. Instead I had to calm them down, which I did by standing in their firing line with my eyes closed and arms open. The shouting died down and the last of the flung things hit the wall or floor with apologetic thuds.

Then I collected and reallocated possessions. In all of this, Gene had been sitting at the table in the corner taking apart the TV remote control, which has broken. He had laid out its component pieces and started putting them together again with only an occasional glance up at the furore. I made tea in two large stainless-steel pots, took one pot out to the summer house for the smokers who had made an emergency congregation there, and the other to the lounge. They all drank with those glassy fevered eyes that you only see in the elderly; even Claudia joined their larger cause and drank with them. Frank stroked her wrist and muttered warmly, *Bastards!* A swearword thrown back at the things that deny us, I suppose. Anger at the brutality of getting old. Later I found a teaspoon wedged in the bars of the gas fire, now bent because I had to prise it out. When I found it, there was a pool of tea in its belly still, held down by some centripetal force while the thing spun across the room. I stole it. Because it reminds me of your hurled fork I will enclose this little trinket of rebellion with the letter.

W here are the younger selves in these people? Did we see them just then? Was that a thirty-year-old Claudia who unleashed a slap across Frank's face? Was it a teenage Frank who muttered, *Bastards?* Did the eighty-year-old man throw the shoe, or did some stubborn child inside him do it? Some child who doesn't understand the concept of eighty, let alone the practicality of getting there. A strange thing happened at The Willows during that fight, a truly strange thing: ghosts appeared. For a few minutes our number was doubled and we had the company of ghosts of selves past. I saw them at everyone's backs, I felt them. Young, lean rebels; I felt them, Butterfly. And then what? When we settled back down into our chairs, where did they go? When will they come back? Do they mind our betrayal of them?

I am not only talking about getting older, no, I am talking about splintering. We hit certain points, we splinter, and bits of ourselves are left behind. I don't know why this should be, only that time isn't a slick medium that we slide through into old age, it is lumpy and irregular and breaks us into pieces. I see Nicolas dancing in the house in London or I see the man with leaves in his hair, who walked tall and was happy one autumn morning, or I see myself somewhat vaguely (it is always vague with myself) taking bones out of the sedge at the shore or standing with my arms crossed in the kitchen doorway watching Teddy immerse his hands in puddles on the patio. There is freedom there; there is always freedom in the past. The self you left behind lives in endless possibility. The older you get, the bigger and wilder the past becomes, a place that can never again be tended and which is therefore prone to that loveliness that happens on wastelands and wildernesses, where grass has grown over scrap metal and wheat has sprung up in cracks between concrete and there is no regular shape for the light to fall flat on, so it vaults and multiplies and you want to go there. You want to go there like you want to go to a lover.

Have I stumbled on an answer to Nicolas' proposal, is that why I'm telling you this? Doesn't this amount to the conclusion that we cannot remarry? We will not be faithful to each other, I will have to tell him, and then he'll frown as if I want to invent problems, just as he thinks I always do. Then I will have to tell him that as we get older – if we are honest – there are no longer only two people in a relationship, there is who you are now and also the person each of you used to be, or the one you always wanted to be, the one you split from at some point in the past, and try as you might you cannot get rid of these others. Just as you try to start again and let the past go, they wander into the house and hell breaks loose.

They point out all the things you should be dissatisfied with and suddenly you fall in love with them. Their courage, their unwillingness to compromise, their passion! They went off and saw the world, they took risks, they played the high cards for big money while you dabbled with the low ones, and they have come back strong and empty-handed to show that your own clinging is pointless. They are commendable in every way you are not – they haven't gone back on their principles or put out their fire or need forgiving for the unforgivable, that is, for becoming unattractive, frightened, despicable, for falling in on themselves like a mountain in an avalanche. How can a person be forgiven that? It is such hard work to love you now, they say. Who will love you now? It used to be so easy, back when. But now, so much has to be made out of so little, more effort than Christ had to make with the fish and the bread. They like to remind you of all these battles you have lost. They haven't lost any! You become besotted with them, hungry for them, like an old man for a schoolgirl who makes him forget he is ineligible, had it, finished.

This is what I think I want to explain to Nicolas when he comes back, that we are all more than one person and we all conduct love affairs with the selves that we were – it is a sort of lurid duplicity in which we creep off back into our own pasts and try to make ourselves whole by becoming jealously infatuated with the self that got away. Any marriage we had now would have to be bigger and more generous than we could make it, because I bring into it another woman, he another man. I want to warn him: if we lived together again as husband and wife neither of us could be faithful, we would sneak down-stairs every night to that other person.

June 2002

You see? Time has passed, another week, gone with the snap of a twig. This is exactly what I mean, about time. Where and how it goes is unfathomable to me. I make my way back and forth across the city half watching out for you, until everybody looks like you. I know the futility of this, but the eyes look, don't they, without the involvement of reason. Meanwhile June has come as you can see, the start of the gracious season, the season for forgetting that one's windows need cleaning because the light is too high and full to glare off the glass. You would think that living is a kind of scholarship in time, and that the longer we live the more expert we become at coping with it, in the way that, if you play tennis enough, you get used to coping with faster and faster serves. Instead I find that the longer I live the more bemused I become, and the more impenetrable the subject shows itself to be. I sit on a heap of days. My feet no longer touch the ground. The day after Teddy's fifth birthday he asked if it was his birthday still and we had to tell him no. He began sobbing inconsolably and he didn't stop, nothing we could say would make him stop.

Is this a trick played on us? I remember stroking Teddy's hair then and feeling that, as a mother, there ought to be something I could do, somewhere I could lodge a complaint.

A dog is barking. Something small like a terrier or a – I don't know. I don't know a thing about dogs. Making a chopping sound through the forest, which is driving you spare. After two days of this you bash about the hut singing, you clank pans with sticks, you shout out: This is perfect, this is perfect! This is perfect, perfect, perfect, perfect! You turn up the squawking of the geese – honk, bark, honk, bark, an animal orchestra; if only you had not caught the mouse that thrived in the one food cupboard on bags of oats and barley, then there would have been vocals to the percussion and that would have been perfect, perfect, perfect, *perfect*. Outside the hut you stand and bark with it. It, you, it, you. It hesitates at first because it doesn't recognise your language – dog, but not dog. You are some big dog, a mastiff maybe; you howl. It barks. You growl, it barks. You bark, it barks. Please! you shout, and it barks.

You pull up a log outside the hut and sit; if you close your eyes and do that thing whereby you gather the outside world inwards, you can put the dog in your head. If the dog is in your head it is not a dog any more but a passing perception. What is it they say? A cloud, moving across the clean sky of your mind. A dog-shaped cloud, bounding through your mind; a dog, barking in your mind, a dog up against your skull, a dog-bark gnawing through your skull.

Why is there no peace! The dog must be shot, or pelted with stones. You march down to the lake where the mosquitoes swarm and you go in up to your ankles. If you were a different sort of a person you would swim, it being the right day for it – warm and still. The water sits motionless against the shore like a spread blanket. If cold water did not make you feel instantly hostile, you would take off your tired old cotton dress and get in and get your head under, into the dogless silence. If you were one of those women who love to bake and to swim, you would. You know the ones I mean – women with curves and a boisterous brood and recipe books from their grandmothers, women with wild-flower arrangements and menstrual cycles that work with the moon, women whose milk flows, whose cheeks are ruddy in the cold, whose long thick hair lightens in the sun, who can improvise something interesting with rhubarb or even turnip, who reread the classics, who rub almond oil into their nice thick middles, whose skirts give to a full easy stride, whose calves are strong and ankles fine, women with small dignified noses amid wide compassionate faces, women who are trusted by birds and lambs.

You stand ankle-deep in the water and let a mosquito settle on the vein on the back of your hand, before squashing it quick as a flash. It gave so easily; it is hard to take any pleasure out of this retaliation. You flick its corpse off your hand, angry at its weakness. Angry with everything today because of that dog, angry with this forest and this country. The spruce-pine-spruce-pine, the violent swinging of the seasons, the brackish lifeless sea, the food that sits like clay in your stomach; everybody is melancholic and drunk. They all drink too much. The national disease. You shouldn't say it but there it is, the truth. Your ancestors, coming to Scotland, must have been relieved to find a similar picture there, and no wonder they failed to prosper on the whole. It was only your grandmother who slipped through the eye of that needle.

Evening falls, but not darkness. The dog is still hacking away at the calm. You lie for a while on the charpoy but more of the ropes have broken and your weight is unsupported on the left side; using an old winter scarf you lace it up again like a shoe and contemplate your exile. Why has she put me here? you ask. Why has she locked me here in a forest inside a letter? On one piece of evidence that is extremely scant: a postcard to Teddy with a Lithuanian stamp and a comment, rashly made, about deserts. From which she fashions a life. Does she not consider that I sent that postcard on a visit to see Petras' grave, perhaps? A four-day visit, nothing more? No, instead she fashions a sad and absurd life.

I have considered that, of course. You made it clear that day on the windowsill, when you showed me the photograph of your great-grandmother scowling drably from the roadside, that you did not want a heritage. There is a type of person who does not want back, but wants out. Out! Out of the confines of yourself. You are not the type to have a sentimental relationship with your past, or to feel, like Gene, drawn back towards the valley of songs. The Jew in you is indifferent. She is sorry that the past has been one long fight, she is sorry for the suffering; sorry, but not that interested.

Heaven is for those that are masters of themselves. They can move anywhere in this world at their pleasure. Anywhere in the world, you say aloud. So why here? You take out from under the mattress the short letter Petras wrote you before he died, a letter that, in reality, might not even be in your possession. But I am giving it to you, herewith. It arrived at our house a few months after you left in January 1985, and I opened it, because you had left no forwarding address and because I owed you no discretion. Whether it ever ended up in your hands depends, I suppose, on Nicolas, whether he passed it on to you when he saw you next, or else sent it to you later, and this is for only you and him to know. But here, I have stashed it under your mattress and given you the will to look at it again.

As you see, it describes great happiness at the prospect of a free country now that Gorbachev has come. He is so young, Petras enthuses. So progressive! Attached to the letter is a newspaper clipping with a picture of Gorbachev; the clipping is seventeen years old now, and looks it. You inspect his square, strong face, fascinated by the violent wound of a birthmark and the downturned mouth that appears so kind. So unassailable, yet avuncular, so trustworthy; he is the sort of man you have to assimilate all at once, because the separate parts of him don't add up.

Meanwhile Petras and his scientist friends are planning to test the eutrophication of Lake Drūkšiai to see if the nuclear-power station has warmed the water, and this all sounds hopeful and noble indeed, and with Gorbachev and his reforms on the scene they might even be able to publish their results. You let the letter drop to the floor. Five months later Petras will over-indulge his love of a drink and will spread himself face-down on the roof of a car that is hurtling along a dark lane and will die laughing, as will his friend who is driving. Weeks away from forty and he dies the death of a teenager.

Why have you put me here? you say. Punishment? To teach me a lesson? You were always the coward in a family of heroes; it was the others who fought the fight, and that they only some-times won is testament to their courage. This is what you think I am trying to tell you now by trapping you here, still alive, in a country the rest of your people have left, either by accident or

design. That you are a coward. I have consigned you to pining
for those who were bolder than you. I have you craning your
neck backwards. I know you feel you have tolerated me enough,
my insinuations and implications. *I am a coward*, you say. *So what?*
I never claimed to be anything else. You lie flat. All this with Petras;
why must you be forced to rub up against terrible loss that cannot
be undone when all you want is to be free, and when I know that
this is all you want, and take it from you out of cruelty.

I have contemplated, between this paragraph and the last, a
peace offering. How about if you put on your shawl, take some
oatcakes and a bit of leftover chicken in some newspaper from
the pile by the stove, and walk out along the track towards the
only building in the vicinity, where the barking dog must be tied
up. I have given you this building, and this sudden compassion
for the dog, out of sheer love and friendship. It seems wrong for
you to be so alone. But I think, when I approach you with this
idea about the chicken and oatcakes, you shake your head. I see
you sit up on the charpoy and look intently ahead as if I were
sitting opposite; you are wearing that look, the one you reserve
for arguments you don't intend to lose. You straighten your back
a little for dignity. Do you think you have punished me? you say.
You will have to try harder than that; let the thing bark.

So, deep into the night, it does.

A s I say, I am not a gentle person. I have not succeeded in becoming one, despite my efforts.

At work I was called in and asked how I had allowed that fight to happen, and at first I said the usual things, like there being nothing I could do, and that I had stopped it as soon as I was able, but we all knew that if it had been another member of staff on duty the fight would not have happened.

Why? Because I suppose I liked it happening. Of course I could have stopped it, but I enjoyed the flare of energy ripping through that room, and I wanted heartrates up. I wanted them to be angry again, instead of lost. We find ourselves in anger, we shout and there we are. I appreciated the bit of pink on Claudia's wrist where Frank had grabbed her. I thought: She flushes still! Her body is alive enough to object to violence against it. She feels pain. Good. They want to smoke their lungs down to burnt prunes: encourage them. If their lungs can wither, that means they are living things, since only living things wither. We let elderly people smoke forty a day because we think it no longer matters, they are as good as dead anyway so we let them do what they like. But I say do more than let them, it matters more than ever that they smoke, because only living things can smoke, wither, go pink in the wrist, reel out a slap, spit the word Bastard, hurl a teaspoon, a shoe, a cup, be angry about what happens in Australia, feel pain, protest.

There is that little bit of savagery in me that my grandmother did try, to her credit, to smooth away. She would say that it was always better to be peaceful and non-reactive and I don't think she would agree that we find ourselves in anger. On the contrary, we lose ourselves. But she didn't manage to take the last few thorns out of my side. Eventually I admitted at work that I had probably not done enough to keep control, and they talked to me at length about insurance, health-and-safety, legal responsibility, moral responsibility, *in loco parentis*. *In loco parentis*. At the age of their children we are asked to act as their parents.

And so I spent my breaktime watching over Gene's sleeping body, trying to glue together a porcelain statuette of a boxer puppy that had lived on the mantelpiece and been broken by something like a slipper, trying without success to imagine myself as Gene's parent. I can tell you I felt indignant on Gene's behalf that I should be asked to make him half a man like this, while I somehow, in this little shuffle of roles, became twice a woman. But I tried it, to feel that protective care I mean, to want to dandle his aged, frightened spirit while it creeps towards the next world; to let him be done for. To let him have nothing left to be angry about.

Since telling me about M that day he hardly speaks, to me or anybody. He keeps some interest in the things of life (like the remote control, which he obsessively dismantles and rebuilds), but he seems to have lost much investment in what happens to himself. I get the feeling he has come here to do one thing only, and that is to die with as little trouble to others as possible. Some days he barely gets out of bed and barely even wakes up, and he sleeps on top of the covers completely naked and with the window wide open. This made it all the more surprising when he said to me the other day, with sudden force, 'I should have chased her.' It was just after the fight, when everybody else went out into the garden and he was still at the table reassembling the remote control. He raised his head as I walked towards him and inspected the mess in the room. 'I should have chased her,' he stated as a fact. 'Who?' I asked. Because he said nothing I asked, eventually, 'M?' He nodded. 'Do you regret it?' I asked. 'Yes!' he said, pressing the side of his fist into the table.

I put my hand on his shoulder and said something consoling like, Don't regret it, or You did all you could, or simply, Well. I don't know which words slipped out and I don't suppose they made any difference to him anyway, but when I was tidying the room after that I found I was comparing myself to him again, in the sense of being passive I mean, passive to the point of losing somebody, and I enjoyed this fantasy. I bought deeply into it for a few minutes, thinking about those few months after Spain, before you suddenly disappeared, and seeing myself as docile, tolerant, self-possessed and, at last, gentle, in the way Gene is, and Yannis too. When I pictured you and I playing 21 just after we got back from Spain I was, in my imagination anyway, tending expertly and quietly to my cards in the way Gene had tended to the remote control, while the rest of the place went to pieces.

Went to pieces? I hear you say. Who or what went to pieces? – we were a house of calm. Weren't we happier in a way? I hear you ask it almost sweetly. After all, you might have slept with Nicolas, but you were never going to expect him to leave his family or give himself in any way to you; devotion was not a quality you asked of people, commitment neither; you did not give these things and did not ask for them. If you could give and receive moments of happiness and self-escape, that was enough, that was, in fact, everything. Didn't Nicolas become a different man after that, one who went from investing endless hope in a world that rarely delivered to one who had had a hope met? After a month or so of bitter exclusion he found himself gradually allowed back into the fold and he did not come back in regret and self-loathing, but with a certain muted victory over life and over the forces of loss. He had done what he liked and got away with it; his incredulity was plain to see, his new faith in the ability to be happy, to have what one wants. To have all the things one wants, at once, without conflict or reproach or guilt, to be allowed such a thing.

Didn't we live in a kind of new communal harmony? Didn't our household take on a new unity and balance? Everybody was someone and had a role to play. By that point you had been with us for two years as an outsider and then all at once you were part of our number. You developed a perverse obsession with cooking, mainly single-pan maverick meals of meat and foraged greens. You were going through a phase of eating liver and kidneys that the butcher gave you for next to nothing, so you dealt up fortified pans of iron and blood, and the zincy phosphorus of greens, thick glossy chard cooked down to a mulch, limp chickweed and sweet nettles that were, pre-massacre, probably emerald and springy; a plateful of soft metals that Teddy would not have eaten if anybody but you had put it in front of him.

I remember one meal in particular, one I'm sure you will not remember at all (or which did not even sink in far enough to become a memory), when you put one of these plates of chickweed and liver in front of us, and Nicolas, staring at it expressionless for a few moments, said, 'I am not going to eat this.' There was no anger in that or even impatience or frustration, he just put it to you as a fact, and you smiled from somewhere remote and said thickly, 'You don't like the look of it?' 'Starvation would be preferable.' You patted his knuckle lightly with your knife: 'Starve then.'

Once, you see, before Spain, he would have been too polite to refuse your food because you were a house guest and his wife's friend; even after two years of you living with us he managed to maintain that courtesy. Now you and he had a relationship of your own, whatever that was, and that meant he could be critical of you in the way people can when they know a cord is not so fragile as to snap under a little pressure. You, who would once have hated to offend him, your friend's husband, treated him with the confidence of somebody who has earnt the right to offend a thousand times.

And as for me, I sat without a word, docile and unruffled; I did not get up to make Nicolas something else, as I probably would have before, instead he got up and made us all something else, a quick thing like a fry-up, I expect. After dinner he went to put Teddy to bed and you washed up while I dried; it took you over half an hour. You were slow and heavy-lidded and moved your arms like a swimmer, and broke a plate by smashing it against the tap in a misjudged movement. Afterwards when you had sunk down into the sofa in a drowsy ebb and flow of consciousness and I went for a bath and Nicolas spread his paperwork on the bed and Teddy slept, I remember feeling almost content, a feeling I relate to being a child when my family was all together, one of knowing everything is in its place.

Everybody has a sudden power. Nicolas can say, I am not going to eat this. You can say, Starve then. I can refuse to get up and help. Nobody bears any responsibility to please, everybody is tongue-and-groove with everybody else. Nicolas takes on a new intensity in bed, which is to say, You are my *wife*. It is not gratitude that makes him passionate but a zealous kind of – what can I say? – revelry, revelry in the unbreakable bond, so that somehow the two of us have become closer, our marriage more magnificent, I think, in his eyes. You and I too, closer – in a de facto way more than a practical one, but all the same closer; because we are always closer when one has taken too much from the other. Always closer when ousting and threatening, because a meaningful relationship thrives on reasserting yourself against the other; that is what it is to relate rather than to be alone – which makes me realise now, as I write, how I never for a moment felt alone in that period between Spain and you leaving.

Neither could you have; you were busy turning your attention to the most intimate, faithful relationship of your life, one you practised in the privacy of your room. You affixed a lock to the inside of the door so that Teddy couldn't amble in, and when you came out sometime in the early evening your face and neck were flushed and you would move languidly about the house in uninterruptible peace, and at times go about a period of prolonged, ecstatic cleaning, and then curl up in the armchair and sleep. Once a fortnight, you told me. One needed a strict limit with a drug like heroin, and one had to know where the tipping point was. For you it was once a fortnight, this and no more. If you could keep it this way you could manage the addiction and it was better, when you had it, it was all the better for the wait.

I suppose there is no more loyal and private a relationship than that between a user and her drug, it leaves no room for anybody else. Either you were locked with it in your own world or you were weathering out the time until you could have it again. At first this seemed workable, and certainly on that October morning in the mist, when you spoke about the gauze of life and you and Nicolas danced through your conversation about the deities of the morning, jubilant and quick-witted, certainly then you seemed lifted. But by Christmas of that year you would spend your fortnight in such anguish; you might not know how agitated you became then, irritable and barbed even towards Teddy, and restless, messy, withdrawn, more and more unkempt, a nightmare, a slow-occuring natural disaster. We went to the coast of mid-Wales one afternoon in early December and while we walked the coastal path you sat on a short promontory watching a wave smashing at a rock; I tell you this because I doubt very much you remember. We had to go back for you at the end of the walk and pull you to your feet. Your fists were clenched. This was what day thirteen began to look like, and then day twelve looked like it, and eleven.

And so I have told you, and I will tell you again, that I am not good, or lenient, or gentle. What kind of a friend will watch this happen and nod, and allow the idea that heroin only once every two weeks constitutes some sort of healthy, moderate regime? I was no kind of a friend to you, a thing we both know. It was not Gene's docile passivity that made me accept our triangle. You had looked, shaken your head at me, shaken your head! No, you had said, do not intervene, and I had stood there in the humid Spanish night as if drugged, convinced that what was happening was somehow an inevitability of your fate, to which we were all silent witnesses and secondary players. But then you were always so convincing, and your fate was always the most pressing.

No, let me make it clear. I was not docile, or passive. I dressed myself up as the forgiving sort, but there is forgiving, and there is also tolerating, which is forgiveness in rags. And then there is something else, which is nothing short of a heartless fascination with somebody's downfall. On our journey back from Spain, looking at you as you slept, I began to realise that if it was your fate you wanted, you could have it – your sad, sordid, wretched fate of self-annihilation. In my defence, Butterfly, you made it so easy, I never once had to lift a finger.

I would never have chosen that path for you, I hope you know it. I have loved you, but you have not at any point made this the obvious or logical choice, and when I went into your room that January morning in 1985 I was not even sorry to find your bed stripped and your things gone.

Maybe if this letter is a form of defence it is only to object that I may be unkind but I am not weak, as I know you think I am. I am unkind because I didn't want to forgive you or Nicolas, but I am not weak, because forgiveness of you was never my choice. You cannot forgive somebody who doesn't ask to be forgiven. There is no point leaving somebody who agrees that you should leave. We can argue with a piece of bad reasoning in another, but we cannot argue with somebody who acts under the influence of love, as Nicolas did. I might almost have felt sorry for him after you left, if he had invited even a moment's pity. In my ignorance and my hardness I hadn't realised what effect you'd had on him, what you had given him, which I see now as the gift of risk and loss. Finally he stopped believing that you would come back, or that he would find the cow shin or the other half of his peacock figurine; he lost his foolishness and he broadened and aged like a tree.

Even weeks after you left he would comment that he could smell you on things, that sharp smell of saplings, of bitter green wood on the cushion on the armchair where you had taken to resting your head.

Yannis' place is as clean as a child's conscience. Together we spent today scrubbing it from top to bottom so he can try to sell it as a going concern rather than fold the business and give up the lease. This is after almost two weeks of deliberation and long phone calls to his wife in Crete, who is unbending. Have you ever tried to wield a cloth with a broken heart? I can tell you it cleans at half the rate. It was as if Yannis were trying to put back the grease the cloth was taking off, which was after all *his* grease, his footprints on the lino by the fryers, his fingerprints on the till.

'A year,' he said, 'I will give it a year. And if my wife and Crete are giving me a headache I will come back.'

I told him this was a fair plan, but I know he will not come back because certain moves are irrevocable. I don't know why this should be, only that we know in our hearts when they are, and the more we tell others how easy a thing is to undo, the more we know we never will undo it. I will miss him. Not only him, but the others here we sometimes play cards with – Christos, a Greek man Yannis knows from the cash-and-carry; Tam, a gentle Jamaican English teacher in his fifties who discovered Yannis' shop through a love of baklava and who recently lost his wife;

then there is the Nigerian, Muyi, whose suits are from House of Fraser, if you remember, and his friend Winnie. And others, but it is too late in the letter to tell you about them now.

Not that I know any of them well, except Yannis, but sometimes it is the little rituals you miss most when they end. The scrape of coppers across the metal table top, Winnie using her thighs and the table as percussion to the traditional Ugandan songs she sometimes breaks into, olive-oil fingerprints blooming on the top left back of the nine of spades and just left of centre on the two of diamonds, and everybody noticing and noting and pretending they hadn't noticed or noted; Muyi's gifts of salted caramel truffles from some improbably priced place on Madison Avenue (he has brothers in New York and crosses the Atlantic probably more often than I cross the Thames), his enthusiasm for New York speakeasies, his intolerance of conservative white men, his vehement refutation when Yannis calls himself a conservative white man, despite that Yannis wants more than anything to be one. Muyi tells him he cannot be because he is an immigrant and self-made. Yannis visibly heats with frustration at this basic right being removed from him.

These speakeasies that Muyi goes to – he was telling us about them last night when we got together for a kind of pre-emptive send-off for Yannis, who might not leave for weeks, but these people have a great sense of ceremony. Apparently you have to access speakeasies with passwords and winks and membership fees that buy you a particular table and a waitress who knows how you like your gin. Muyi goes to ones in London, though there are hardly any, but the best are in New York. You push against a door that looks boarded up, he says, and you go past a doorman who pretends to be Mafia or a 1920s Chicago detective, you go up some stairs or down some stairs and through a second door, which might have been pulled off a shed or a phone booth or might be an old headboard for a bed or might be a bullet-proof bunker door writ with invective from the Old Testament about how God hates a drinker. Then you step into a low-lit secret temple, a gin den or vodka joint and a menu with fifty-plus cocktails and discreet barmen and beautiful black waitresses and live bands, as if it is still Prohibition.

I could see you in such a place. While Muyi was speaking, and pouring American gin with his lovely hands, I pictured you with him or somebody like him in a place like that. As everybody argued about the point of speakeasies in an age of legal alcohol (and Tam was calling them theme parks and telling Muyi he demeaned himself and black people by going to places that were invented, in part, to keep black people down) I was giving some of my attention, as I have come to do, to the street outside Yannis' shop. I used to look for you only in the way people look out for dead loved-ones, not because they expect to see them or even hope to, but just as a reflex, or maybe through curiosity. *I wonder what it would be like if so-and-so walked around the corner now?* Lately, do I look with something more like expectation? I don't know if it could be called that, but I have at least run out of reasons why you couldn't walk past. Something both sinks and rises in me, Butterfly, when I think like this.

At night most of what I can see in the glass is a group of people huddled round a high circular table with fans of cards. And last night the conversation continued about the revival of obsolete things, times, people and places, gangsters stabbing black men in back alleys without anybody so much as lifting a brow, beautiful black waitresses growing old with oppression. I was listening and not listening. I was looking out of the window at myself looking out of the window; I couldn't peer around my own reflection, which was – pensive. (It has taken me a few minutes to land on that word, having gone through sad, defeated, nondescript, shadowy, wary, weary, confused, suspicious, anxious, wiry, concerned, murderous, lonely, defensive, dark, old, refined, narrow, superstitious – none of which were right, some of which were ridiculous and make me sound more like a piece of furniture than a human.) I looked pensive, or more specifically like someone who has been drawn down too many pathways of thought and is no longer able to double-back. Contrast this with Muyi, who must be in his forties and glows like a stone that gathers no moss. Or even Yannis, who is solid and guileless and fends off complexity like a cow. It is a crime to think too much. Yet I think too much. The thinking buries my sense of joy, which I know is there; and I am jealous of those like Muyi and Winnie who have not buried themselves like this.

But you did not bury yourself, either; you would get so far into your troubles and then break out irritably, impatiently, would throw your head back in raucous laughter and shrug the world off. Last night when Muyi was talking about New York speakeasies, I could see you with him and I could no longer justify, even to myself, my solitary confinement of you in a forest. I am sorry for this, sorry for the geese, whose concept I knowingly abused.

One stiff frosty evening not long before you left I brought coffee to your room and sat on the floor while you told me how the flight of the goose is the symbol for escaping continual rebirth, getting out of this agitated world. The goose flies, we break free at last without needing to come back and do this life again. Do you remember saying this? You pulled back the plunger and I saw a swirl of blood rise up in the needle, and then you closed your eyes and said that you could taste it in your mouth, and then that you were washed with warmth, and then you stood by the condensated window with your fingertips touching the pane until droplets ran down.

'Anything is possible,' you said, spreading your hand against the glass. 'Ask me to do anything and I will be satisfied doing it.' You regarded me with wide eyes and such deep stretching peace. Your hand slid down the pane and lay on the sill. You told me there was not one grain of fear or discomfort in you and nothing you could not or would not do, and do again, and love. You were made of light, were part of everything. Every beautiful detail of your childhood was right here to be lived again, you were burying Petras in the sand, you could feel the air on your back teeth. A most lovely sensation, the air there. Whatever you needed to do or be you could do or be. Nothing impeded. You had hit the ceiling and ripped through it, ripped through the gauze, there was light everywhere and you were it. Total acceptance of the way things were, gone any trace of desire to harm or bear a grudge, you were saying the word harm but it was a sound, the concept meant nothing to you any more. Instead of it you had the most visionary focus and patience, your beliefs came in colours and smells that overwhelmed the world with sense, logic and beauty, because there was nothing wrong, nothing to put right, no barriers, no emptiness. You were the goose in flight from the anxiousness and suffering of the world. I am the goose, you said with a shallow, euphoric smile as you rested your head against the wet pane. I am the goose!

I know you did not even notice when I left the room and went downstairs. There is nothing worse than witnessing somebody else's salvation, Butterfly, when all you want is your own – when you were promised your own, when you grew up to believe there would be a great reward. And now, well, how easy it is to start living out one's own reveries about the other, or worse still to project the future one thinks the other deserves, rather than the one she probably gets.

I have kept you lonely and baffled by the Upanishads. Your

vegetables grow and their abundance reminds you of all the people you cannot share them with. I have given you a lake and not let you swim in it. Your video collection is very poor, even by your own standards; the geese fly but they are trapped in the screen and will never be free. Your beauty is for nobody to see. Your forest is nondescript when it comes down to it, just trees, all of them straight and none of them perfectly straight. I have given you food that makes you thinner. I have been untying the ropes on your charpoy one by one so that your sleep gets ever more uncomfortable, until you cannot sleep at all. I have given you one pen, and soon I will take it away. Then you will not even be able to keep a record of your life, and so you will be undone, my friend, you will be undone.

They have it that jealousy is the most corrosive of emotions and I have felt it corrode me and whittle me down to something dishonourable, this is the truth. I have looked at – not even taken from its box, just looked at – the lock of your hair and have been filled with heat that is as close to panic as to any other emotion I can name, the kind of panic one feels when one's place is threatened. A survival response perhaps, one that comes from seeing that one's position in the world is not central or has been usurped.

I generally dislike this tendency in us to try to boil down everything we think, do and feel to a base instinct for survival, as if we are not responsible for our reactions, or as if we have no choice. But in this case perhaps it is true; we realise that somebody we love has loved someone else more, and we feel swiped aside like a skittle. Nothing essential holds me in place, all that I am is swiped aside and scuttled out of sight. For good or bad this is how I feel when I look at that lock of hair. I can't touch it; I can only take out one of the ten-pack of cigarettes that I buy after the life-class, light up, stand back and inspect it from a cautious distance. Why did she? I think. Why did they? How did they? Was it worth it?

This is not something I very readily admit, and I will never tell Nicolas, but I went to stay at Mrs Ellis' guest-house once. It wasn't run by Mrs Ellis any more, but a man called John or Simon or Peter Ellis, who I assume was her son. I knew that Nicolas used always to rent the back room on the first floor because he mentioned once its view of the garden, which Mrs Ellis stocked with bird food. The roof of the portico, which was just below his window, was harangued (his word; this is the only time I ever remember him using it) with birds that landed on his sill. He kept his window shut. How could he complain? If he resented Mrs Ellis' kindness towards birds he would have to resent it towards himself too.

I booked in advance and asked for this room. It was big and light. There was an iron-framed double bed against the left wall, badly made with sheets and blankets that pined for a hospital corner – an old pink, patchily bare woollen blanket, and pastel-striped pillows, a thick towel on the end of the bed that smelt of packaging. Nets at the window with worn lace, a tasselled lamp on a cheap, modern bedside table of plasticky pine, what would once have been a handsome wardrobe with broken fretwork above the doors, a light-blue carpet, a floral border on the woodchipped walls, a discoloured landscape print above the bed, a travel kettle with a limescaled spout, instant coffee, no teabags, no milk, three ashtrays (on the kettle tray, on the bedside table and on the windowsill), a dressing gown hanging on the back of the door as if somebody had left it there in error, a clean but not fresh smell.

I arrived in time for bed. I did nothing there but go to bed, not even wash. I used the toilet in the bathroom across the corridor, that was all. Because I always sleep naked I made myself, but I didn't want to. For an hour I lay in bed with only the light from the lamp and with my arms by my side on top of the covers; I suppose this was about nine years ago, I was forty-three or forty-four, although I don't know why this is relevant to mention. Just that I saw myself then as I was writing and my hair was long and my skin holding on to a last sheen of youth. The cheap pine bedside table looked like a new thing, otherwise I expect the room was exactly as it had been when you were there. I doubt if the son had done anything to the guest-house since his mother, presumably, passed away, he was just running it down – it had that feel in any case.

One of those nights passed, when you don't know if you really ever slept. The hours slip away somehow. There was an uncanny quiet stillness for a long time of the sort you would never expect in London, but then Nicolas did always remark on how quiet it was there. I will tell you what I imagined: he is agitated and belligerent, a mood you have not seen in him before, and he stands by the window with his hands in his pocket. You have had a long train journey together and although it was spent largely in silence, there is anyhow nothing left to say and you wish he would snap out of this mood. He brought you here, bundled you on a train so unceremoniously, you did not ask him to come with you, you did not ask him to bring you to this place. He is cross because you left, cross because you have come back; you simply can't win. You take your clothes off, sit on the end of the bed and shrug: This? If not this, then what?

He stands there as if in terror. There are aspects of this imagined night that I felt I was not making up, and this is one of them. I lay in the lamplight and I could see him at the window, unblinking and paralysed by the inevitability of the scene he has set up and which now overwhelms him. I know this feeling, I have had it thigh-deep in the sea as a nine-foot wave rears and thunders in. You lean down into your bag and take out a tin, which contains pre-rolled cigarettes, light one, light another off yours and hold it out to him. You tell him what it is; you have injected your last, now you just have these two left to smoke and that will be that. No more. After tonight you are getting out of this *disagreeable* habit.

Nicolas has never done such a thing. He extends his arm to say you will have to bring it to him. An attempt at asserting some power over you. You do. At the window you rest your weight on one leg and look out as you smoke, perfectly unbothered by your visibility in a lit room on a dark night. He goes to where you sit on the bed and makes his first inhalation deep and reckless, and expects something. When there is nothing left to smoke and he still feels normal – if stricken with anguish, longing and anger can be considered normal – he lies back on the bed and counts the flower, leaf, flower, leaf that alternate around the ceiling rose.

If my decision to stay at Mrs Ellis' seems perverse to you, I should say that one of the main reasons was to establish whether Nicolas did or did not use heroin that night. If he did it would have been the first and last time, I have no doubt about that – and all the more transformative for it. This was always a question that bothered me and one I could never decide on, or ask him. When he came back home two days later, to pack his bags, something in him had changed, this is all I can say. As if a chemical change, not only in his demeanour but in his brain, as if a crucially nervous, searching part of his brain had been unplugged and had left him relieved of the kind of peripheral anxiety and unease we pray God to remove, if religious – or simply live with, if not.

Of course, the room had no answers in itself. All the same, an answer came. I don't know if it was right, it didn't need to be right, it only needed to be an answer. Of course he used the drug; he sat there on the end of the bed, leant forward, elbow on knee, and cast you nervous, accusatory glances as he smoked. At some point it started raining and I got up to close the window when the rain began clattering down in poles.

From the room opposite mine sounds came through the rain, that violent gratification that is incapable of censoring itself, the woman finally shrieking, which was so subtly but profoundly unlike a shriek of pain, and carried a kind of song.

One day I suppose I will be able to laugh at the unfortunate twist of that soundtrack; without it maybe I would have imagined a cooler, more indifferent night in the lavendery chintz of Mrs Ellis' room, maybe I would have decided you had not offered him anything to smoke or that the night had been sullen, resentful and regrettable and only briefly pleasurable. I might not have imagined the blood slowly warming and the immense light and euphoria you described, Nicolas taking off your one remaining item of clothing, the green headscarf that had made you look so defiant and inappropriately proud at the station earlier that day. His hands on your waist, your breasts, your face, your hair.

In the night I got up to make a drink and had to settle for black coffee from one of the sachets – this is how I know there was no tea, or milk. Do you know, when Nicolas grabbed your wrist in the garden and pushed you into the car and drove you to the station, I had no idea if he was going to hurt you and I was worried. I was good enough to be worried. I wondered if I should have protected you, but then protecting you from Nicolas seemed preposterous as things go, so then I worried about myself. I waited something like three hours before going to the station to see what had happened to him, and I expected to see you both in the car, as you and I had been only a few hours before, or to see Nicolas holding the steering wheel quietly, trying to rid himself of you finally before turning round and coming home. What I found was the car with the keys in the ignition, and both of you gone. I drove home. It was two days before I saw him again and even then he came only to apologise and to tell me you had disappeared once more, and to pack.

There was something about you that made Nicolas animated and angry. Do you remember that same day how he stormed indoors when you said all that about Laurence Olivier. 'I've been in an elevator, looking for love,' you said when we asked you once again where you had been for almost two years. 'Did you find it?' 'No.' 'You look unwell, what do you need?' 'Nothing.' 'There must be something, you don't look well.' 'I wanted to find Laurence Olivier, it turns out he doesn't exist. Now that the one thing I needed is gone, I don't need anything.' And he stood from the wrought-iron table in the garden, and he must have been making a windbreak of sorts because the leaves on the table flew upwards when he went; I remember this so distinctly because it looked like they were fleeing his anger, and you winced. It was a theatrical wince and I was glad he had not seen it.

The wind blew, the leaves flew, the sky was as big and grey as a road to nowhere with no one on it, your hair wafted smoke and evergreen, the pipistrelles came out in the dusk, rain stirred, flakes of enamel paint from the table stuck to our thumb pads, Nicolas came outside again and clutched your wrist and yanked you to your feet and took your bag and pushed you into the car. 'I am getting out,' you said to me as you left, with flat reassurance. 'I just want you to know that I am getting out.' This is what I kept thinking of as I sat in the dark, drinking watery coffee; did you get out? Here, in this room, did you begin to? Did you and Nicolas pass through each other's flesh into something else, did you find something, were you rewarded, was it happiness?

What is the injury? What is the extra *injury*, Butterfly? The two of you had done this before, after all. What takes the thorn from the side to the heart, what decides if the heart is punctured? I know the answer, and yet it is never quite a complete one. Spain – Spain is lustful and heady, full of grand but futile gestures, Spain hosts the bullfight and the things that seem glorious but are not, and these things come to nothing, to no good. These things begin to sicken us when the music and colour are gone. What happens there happens in a degenerative heat that we have to forgive or else simply accept, just as we would the beautiful vulgar flowers and the moths as big as bats.

But England is cool-headed and premeditated. Mrs Ellis has put out a little vase of first snowdrops that are greener than they are white, she has put pouches of lavender under the pillows and the cotton is clean and cold. The radiators struggle against the draughts through the old windows. She has left a hot-water bottle in the bed in its own little island of warmth. Passion has a thousand places to leak from, but still it comes, and it comes so heavily that it crushes a marriage, which I picture, despite myself, as a train crushing a deer.

Nicolas gathers your hair in his fist and cuts, or – and this is something I have not ever been able to decide – he gathers it and asks you to cut, so that it is you who makes the offering. He always had a certain prescience, or at least a long range in his thoughts, and I am sure that when he went to get scissors he knew he was unlikely to wake up in the morning and find you there. He was a gracious man fundamentally, and I say this without irony. He is the kind of man who would hear you get up and leave before dawn and pretend to be asleep. Then get up a couple of hours later and go down to a breakfast with the lock of hair wound around his fist, to a solitary breakfast of perfect eggs and tea brewed amber and Mrs Ellis' motherly hands fussy over warm pots.

He gave the lock of hair to me out of solidarity. This is the only reason I can think of. It was years later, at my father's funeral in 1993, and he turned up unexpectedly having learnt about the death from Teddy, sat at the back of the church in a strange woollen brown suit, on his own, and appeared to have been crying when he came up to me afterwards to offer sympathy. I understand about tears, they fall clear but they come from a murky collection of emotions all at once – he was not crying only for my father (whom he did like) but for everything that had caught up with him at the back of the church. I think the gift of the hair – if I can call it a gift – was not a form of apology but a sharing of a loss, for which a funeral seemed to him the right occasion.

I contemplated fury. To be truthful, I was too limp with grief on that particular day. I suppose going to stay in Mrs Ellis' back room was a form of fury, which I justified as curiosity; it was only a month after my father's death when I went there and, when I think back to it, I probably wasn't in a good state for such things. After a night of no sleep, of listening to the animal moans from the couple opposite, it was the breakfast that finally did make me furious. Bread as thin and cheap as the blankets, and a toaster. Some margarine, no jam, certainly no eggs. I had never in my life been further away from buttery comfort, from solace. I think Mr Ellis did not inherit his mother's care for the human soul through a soft honeyed yolk. I took, with chilly shaking hands, a piece of bread from the mean array on the dresser and said aloud to the empty room, Is this it? And then louder, screwing the bread up in my palm like an old love-letter: Can this really be it?

L ara came to The Willows yesterday evening, but I was on a late shift so there was no point in her waiting. Instead I invited her in for a cup of tea. It was a quiet time anyway, dinner, and most people were eating, so we went into the kitchen and made a drink.

She commented on the other nursing home up the road; she meant The Lodge, a thing of magnificence and luxury with en-suite rooms in the eaves, and with crescent-shaped grounds and working fountain and joyful cherub. 'We don't speak of it,' I told her. 'They have afternoon calligraphy classes and a spa bath. You must never speak of it again.'

She smiled and pinched her lips closed with her fingers. I saw she was looking at me with something new, which might have been pity, but perhaps not as strong as pity. Sympathy? In any case, a greater interest than before, one that made me think she was sorry that I worked in this care home and not that one, and that also made me think she might ask me about myself. So I said quickly, 'That's a beautiful necklace, where did you get it?' It was a piece of light-blue topaz laid into silver, and looked like it might have been naturally blue and, if so, relatively rare.

'Eighteenth-birthday present from my parents,' she said. I got a Bechstein for my eighteenth, I was going to tell her, because I like to point out how spoilt I'd been, how smeared with love like a basted bird, in case it forgave me something. I don't know what: a selfishness or blindness. But this seemed an unnecessary aside, so I said, 'It suits you well' and she held the topaz away from her neck, peered down at it and thanked me. We sat at the tiny table in the kitchen, me moving my chair back a little so I had some view of the dining area in case my colleague, Peter, needed me for anything, and I waited for her to speak. (I haven't said anything about Peter and I won't, he isn't the kind of person you would be interested in.) She seemed to waver between possible starting points, and then she rested her hands loosely on the table.

'I seemed really childish when I spoke to you last time, about giving up God.'

'I don't think so.'

'I did mean it though. I've done what you said, which is to walk away, and see if God calls me back. He hasn't, you know.'

She broke this as news; I wanted to say, Of course he hasn't, he was never going to. God is not like this, he is an egotist, he fires himself all over the skies, he rocks the seas, he shakes the earth. It will be years before he notices your defection. In any case she sat with her shoulders tilted forward and her neck long and everything pale and soft, like a Roman bust. 'Is life different without him?' I said.

'Without him?' She pouted in thought and her dimple became deep enough to house a raisin; this is exactly what I thought, and I imagined a raisin there, and wondered if it would stay, or fall out when she smiled. 'Paul in Corinthians: *Let all your things be done with charity*. I embroidered this onto a piece of cloth when I was about twelve and I have it on my bedroom wall.'

'My grandmother had that on her wall too,' I said, suddenly remembering it.

246

'And I thought that was the whole point of being religious. But actually you don't have to believe in God to do all things with charity, so what is the point? Why would life be any different without him?'

I swilled what was left of my tea around the bottom of the cup and told her, 'Come with me.' We went out of the kitchen. Peter was in the dining room seeing after everyone at dinner; when Lara and I walked through there was a chorus of greetings. You drop youth amidst old age and it is like showing food to the starved; we used to eat, you can hear them thinking, we used to know the taste of that! I took her into the corridor that led to the bedrooms, and I went into one of the rooms and asked Lara to wait outside. There was Gene on the bed, like that bull dropped on sand. He goes off to sleep in the way you used to, abruptly and completely. I covered his nudity with a sheet and whispered into his ear, 'We have to get you ready for the nurses. I have a friend with me, do you mind if she helps?'

There was no response for a few moments, and then he murmured from somewhere near sleep, 'I don't mind.' He was lying naked on top of the covers, as I said he tends to, with the window wide. I couldn't blame him, it's filthily hot in those rooms. Still, we have to go in, put his pyjamas on, cover him, pull the window to. We're told we have a duty of care to do these things, and that to leave him naked with a window flung wide amounts to neglect.

There are six permanent care staff here and we are all unanimous in agreement that this is nonsense; we do it only when the nurses come in for their morning and evening rounds, as they were about to do. So I called Lara in and asked her to put cushions behind his back while I lifted him, and we propped him up. If we disturbed his sleep further it wasn't enough for him to open his eyes. I filled a bowl of warm water and sponged the sweat off him, and went through the drawers to find a clean T-shirt, since he has made his hatred of pyjamas clear.

Lara perched on the edge of the chair by the bed, looking quite openly at the eighty-five-year-old in front of her. You would like Lara, there is something of the warrior in her – she is not one of those 'all flower and no fruit' girls that you used to scorn, but somehow brave and direct, a thing I noticed as she sat there with her eyes on Gene. 'Here,' I said, and handed her the T-shirt. 'I'll lift him forward and you put it on.'

She did this skilfully; let her commit her acts of charity against Gene and not me, I thought. I had the distinct impression that Ruth had said something about me to her since we last met and that she was commiserating silently over my reported losses. How, oh how (she would be thinking, because Ruth would have said) did this woman come to be working in a care home? She lives alone in that flat, she plays cards with strangers. She hardly sees her only son, then there is her breakdown and the loss of her marriage. She used to be beautiful once, before – before it all. I wanted to comfort Lara by telling her that I did not lose my so-called beauty but squandered it, and that there can be no pity for somebody who squanders what they never deserved anyway. I was left with my due, I wanted to say, and tried to say it by organising Gene's covers and pillows in that efficient, matronly way women do when they have become their role completely, forgotten all they were once as a girl, when somebody used to do it for them.

From late spring the evening light comes straight into Gene's room, and now that it is mid-June the light is beginning to flood the bed. I want to tell you something about this: seeing his old, brightly lit body, I had a small revelation, because he appeared almost completely abstract and not a body at all. He was a collection of shapes and colours, and surfaces that were reflective to differing degrees, and angles that went all the way through the compass, from the steep pyramid of his ankle bone, which looked like it had been broken at some point, to the flat plane of his earlobe, to the cratered bullet wound in his left shoulder.

I will surprise you with the fact that I remember exactly what the exhibition was at the Serpentine when Nicolas and I went twenty-six years ago – it was a retrospective of a painter called Jeremy Moon, who made abstract canvases of blocks of colour that were supposed to represent nothing. He wanted us to see a canvas painted yellow and not think of the sun or of cornfields in childhood or of golden beaches or of happiness and optimism, but to see only yellow paint. I did not like his paintings much, but I have always held onto their noble cause – to keep working away from the seduction of memory and metaphors, towards the honest, simple truth. This is green, this is blue, this is yellow, this is a slope, this is a curve, this is bright or dark. I have failed abysmally in this. And yet at work, seeing Gene, at last! Twenty-six years too late, but suddenly I have looked at the body of an old man and managed, with some success, that most difficult of things.

I told Lara that charity isn't about being kind and humane. It is about seeing without interpretation, as a lens sees. What Teddy called 'the neutral lens'. I'd completely forgotten about that phrase of his until just then. The neutral lens. Possibly a phrase you gave him. The eye looks on others and itself with motives, games and tricks, and makes things what they are not, but the neutral lens leaves a thing to be what it is.

Lara nodded and turned her pale face on Gene with the kind of cool attention the moon gives the Earth. I admit, though I have never been the meddling type, that I hoped against hope suddenly, watching her, that she and Teddy would meet and fall in love. I married them off with one thought, and with the next there were grandchildren. Four or five, actually. So easy is life! And death too – the way it slinks in. Gene died this morning in the T-shirt Lara and I put him in, a few minutes before I arrived for work at seven a.m. It was just a breath in and no breath out, as simple as that. Like that bit in the tenth Upanishad that you used to enjoy, when Yādnyawalkya says to his wife: 'Dear! I am going to renounce the world.' And so renounced, the world – this world, much slaved after and cried over and so full of vulgar triumphs and impressive defeats – is gone.

Part drunk after a few glasses of wine with Yannis, I have been hurriedly preparing for Nicolas' arrival by taking clothes up from the bedroom floor and vacuuming down the side of the sofa and throwing away the turning milk and hiding the cigarettes and bundling our letter into order. The wine has reduced me to a teenagery sense of misbehaviour. When I was gathering the letter together I reread what I wrote at the beginning, about the gauze and so on – which I hadn't read since – and I found it childish and defensive, that I should have felt the need to insist like that on having had the kind of experience that could be called 'metaphysical' or 'transcendental'. I am not at all sure it really was, when I come to think of it. It was just the coming together of unusual things: the collecting of the bones, my grandmother sitting dead downstairs, meeting Nicolas on the flood wall and knowing in some acute way that it was a significant meeting. And then you appeared to be hovering by my bed on Boxing Day as the first flake of snow fell (I wrote then that you were hovering expectantly, but I was just being kind, because I was trying then to be kind. In fact you were not hovering expectantly, but *accusingly*) and I felt put upon to account for myself, so I stammered something out, and so we began.

Once, it must have been 1979 because I was pregnant with

Teddy, I went with Nicolas to the Kent marshes where he had grown up, to his old clapboard bungalow, which was unlived in by that point, and while there I at once understood and accepted who he was – a searcher. Who could be born there and not be, when every point of anchorage slips away into an odd unending blend of water, shingle, scrub and sky. There was nothing else around the bungalow, it was empty as far as the eye went. And yet there was a low brick wall marking off a garden, which seemed such an arbitrary boundary that I could see their lives as one continual striving for perspective, or perhaps just for the comfort of scale. A wall, a raised bed, a wheelbarrow of heathers, a rockery piled with driftwood, a rusted metal stake holding a wind chime made of stones and anything small that clanked or tinkled. Everything owned had been searched for. And I saw him in this setting, a giant against the bungalow's front door, but a dwarf against the confusing run-in of land and sky. He was tapping the chimes with his fingers, and I thought with victory and tenderness that I had him all worked out. But as soon as we decide someone is a searcher we dismiss the idea of what it is they want to find; they search, that is what they do, so it will always be.

Then you see something in that person's eyes that is yearning and you dismiss it. They are always yearning! This is one of the things you fell in love with and also, over time, one of the things that is irritating; when they pull a pearl from acres of rushing water you are full of perplexed love at their tenacity, and when they speak again of going back to the Thames to find the lost cow shin or the tail of a peacock you feel compelled to pick a fight with them: You're grasping and obsessive. Well, you're impetuous. Why can't you let things go? Why are you always telling me what to do? Because you're like a mole-rat, ridiculous, that's what I think you are, ridiculous. At least I'm not like the Stasi.

A door slams, a book drops, dust flies, a head falls into hands. It is nothing new between couples. But either way, love or hate, the one thing you do not do when you see that yearning is wonder how you can fill it. This never strikes us as possible. Sometimes those closest to us are the most neglectful, I believe this to be true. Another person comes along who sees that yearning and knows instantly what to do with it; it is not a fact to be accepted but a call to arms: Let me take this burden of longing from you. Yes, this is what they say: Let me take this burden from you! And they do, even if only for a few moments and even if replacing it with a longing that is greater still: the longing to have the longing taken again. They do take it. Then streams break out in the desert, as it says in Isaiah. Is it Isaiah, or is it Psalms? Or Jeremiah. My Bible knowledge is terrible these days. But streams and rivers spring up and surge in the desert.

I sometimes put pen to paper and wonder what more I can say, and then I find myself saying what I had never intended. There is always more. And yet now perhaps there is not. Nicolas arrives back in London tonight, or in fact in the small hours of the morning, and is coming straight here from the airport. He should arrive at about five a.m., which happens to be just before I leave for work, though I haven't told him that. He won't mind, since it means he can spend the day here sleeping it off. (This plan to arrive at five a.m. was conveyed to me by postcard a week or two ago, in a message that said nothing more than that – a garish postcard with a picture of Fifth Avenue mostly obliterated by the slogan *Howdy from New York!* He is not the kind of man to invite himself; I read this move – of course I might be wrong – as his final advance, his last act of courtship, to see if I retreat.)

I won't write any more, Butterfly, once he is back. The pen seems to fall dead at the idea of going on. The nib has split further and it has developed a creak; every time I pick it up nowadays I feel like I am sending an old man back to war.

*

But then there is always one more thing.

Do you remember the game we used to play, called Chair? It's strange how I thought of it only tonight, and not back when I wrote about the chair in the Pinter play; it hadn't occurred to me then at all, perhaps because I had been thinking more of your absence than your presence back then. In any case, we would put a chair in the middle of the room, the big red room at my parents' house, and one of us would stand five paces in front of it with our eyes closed, then wait silently for a minute. The room was often very dark. The object of the game was to judge whether the other was sitting in the chair at the end of the minute. It was a question of honour that the one with her eyes closed should be able to sense the movement of the other, should be able to know when the chair was available to sit in. We did not make it easy for the other, we learnt to move silently and misleadingly.

I don't know how you remember this game, but for me it is always with some excitement and apprehension, and also fear. To know there is another person in the room and to not know where they are, but to try to sense them, as subterranean animals must. If we felt that the other person was not in the chair we would take five paces and sit in it ourselves, but to get it wrong, to sit when the other was already there, was a kind of transgression – we would not screech or collapse in laughter, but would flinch as if burgled. It was a betrayal to share space, to blunder into the other's space; if we really knew one another, loved and understood one another, we would not. It is only when I think of it now that I can see the peculiar premise of that game, that intimacy is a form of distance, that you become sharply aware of the other's existence only in order to avoid it.

Maybe it has given me a kind of paranoia to not know, for so many years, where you are. That and a sense of failure, yes – paranoia and failure. If I don't know where you are, perhaps I will never see you again, or perhaps I will turn round and you will be there, and I am never quite sure which is worse. Sometimes I have felt you near, or have mistakenly thought you were there, as I did that day clearing the snow. Other times you leave me so clueless and empty of instinct that I have to resort to random imaginings that I know are wild and far-fetched. And then for a moment or two they do not feel even remotely far-fetched enough.

Teddy did send me a photograph from Lithuania, in case it interests you. It was back in February, in fact I think a few days before the Pinter play, a few days or a week, but I didn't want to tell you because I didn't want to share Teddy with you if I am giving you the truth. It was not a photograph he had taken himself but one found in a shop of old Lithuanian ephemera – a black-and-white aerial picture of men, women and children standing in a line of joined hands along an empty road flanked by woods. The 1989 Baltic Chain, as you will know. It made me cry with some old reserve of hope. I counted them. They were twenty-one of two million people joined hand-to-hand through three countries to protest against their occupation, twenty-one of two million; four million hands, joined. I became overwhelmed by the thought for a little while. We are joined. 'Naima' sounds to my ears like 'Ruby, My Dear', then (in the way a silver fish jumps out of the water and flashes purple) I hear something of 'Sinnerman', then the voices of worried praise, then of gospel. There is no way the things of this world can isolate themselves or be isolated. We encroach on one another, be it painfully or pleasurably, we encroach and run into each other, and this is what we know fondly or otherwise as life. It is not life to think that to love somebody is never to be where they are and never to intrude upon them.

I am really not sure now which of us invented the game of Chair, I always assumed you, but I have been led to wonder. In any event it was you who proved later in life its complete unworkability as a strategy. I took five paces and found you in my seat, and I could not dislodge you, you would not go. But maybe I have learnt, or I am learning through writing this, to be glad of your many trespasses. Even theft is a form of connection after all, and I do not mean this flippantly; to be encroached upon is in itself to be reminded of your own position amongst things. To be touched by the hand that stole from you or pushed you aside. I have tried lately not to isolate myself, to strike up friendships however loose, random or mismatched, odd little bonds formed over sardines or religion or cards or regret, and these bonds for the most part, to my own amazement, have outlived their starting points.

It is half past three in the morning now and Nicolas will be here soon, and I have to be at work in two hours. *A woman is not born to toil*, I have been thinking, somewhat repetitively. While making tea and worrying about lack of sleep I suddenly remembered this absurd notion of Kierkegaard's, passed on to me once by my grandmother: A woman is not born to toil; if she wants to move towards infinity, she has to travel along the gentle path of the heart and imagination.

I really do not know what kind of blessed lives my grandmother and Kierkegaard had, to make them think the path of the heart and imagination is *gentle*. It is like walking on nails. It is like walking on nails having first been set on fire. With your hands tied up your back in forced prayer. And a stake through your throat. A dagger in your back. What I mean to say is that this path we are trying to chart is not an easy one and I forgive you simply because I hope to be forgiven; I know it is not your way, but if I were you I would take forgiveness, even if it is only mine, and even if it belittles you.

The fact being – though I was not going to write it – that I think I saw you. I don't know if it was you, but until I can verify it I will have to assume it was. I saw the back of you walk down the street past Jimmie's and up towards Guilford Street, the way I would go if I were dropping in on Yannis, walking quickly in the rain with your head down, in a long raincoat and high heels, your feet not so much touching down on the pavement as piercing it and pushing it back behind you. Your familiar purposeful, long-legged walk.

But let me go back a moment so you know why I thought it was you, as opposed to any number of other women in this enormous town. It was lateish last night, around eleven, and I was in the living room, sorting through the pile of mail that had accumulated downstairs in the hall; post is one of the problems with living communally, there is so much of it and most of it is junk. But if you throw the lot away you might throw out something important, that was missed, something from Teddy, for example. This was part of my tidying frenzy before Nicolas coming back, and a strange and irrelevant one because it isn't even the kind of thing he would notice. I had the post in a pile on the floor and was sifting through, trying I suppose to wind myself down to sleep so that I could get up at five-thirty a.m. for an early shift.

So I was sifting through. I was tired. I'd had a few glasses of wine at Yannis' just before that, as you know. The window was open and it was raining, but not much. Then I heard voices on the street below my window, voices of a man and woman standing there, not walking past – nothing unusual in this, at night there is always the routine emptying-out of bars and the talk and the singing, which I go to sleep to – ever the lover of people, I sleep badly when they are not there. I think you never did understand that. People were to you a kind of beautiful problem. You needed their approval, and you disapproved of yourself when you did not get it, and disapproved of yourself even more when you did, as if you had done nothing to earn it.

The man said, somewhat desperately, 'You are love of my life.' This might have been the first thing said between them while standing outside or it might just have been the first thing I noticed them say. His voice was deep, not English, maybe Hispanic, I don't know. And the woman replied, in an exaggeratedly deep, soft voice that might have been done to mimic his, 'You are *the* love of my life. You must use *the* in front of *love*, it's the rules.'

Maybe the poor man was embarrassed; I could imagine him stooping his shoulders and almost curtseying away from the mistake. 'However you say it. I am sorry.'

'Don't be sorry, I just wanted you to know, for when you need to use it in the future.'

He must have missed the playful insinuation there because he just said, 'I don't understand. All this *the* and *a*, you think it will be simple, it is never simple.'

'Yes, it's simple, amigo, it's just a little word. Don't be a child, come on.'

And she laughed, and maybe she ruffled his hair or tugged lightly at his collar.

I think I had stopped breathing at this point; I had certainly stopped moving. It was not only that her voice was just like yours, but that I remembered you having almost exactly the same conversation once with a man in Embankment Gardens. Do you remember? A stranger came up and declared his love for you, and you kindly corrected his grammar. You saw his embarrassment and you took his hand so that you could draw him down to the grass, with the care of someone handling an animal that is dependent on them – and you gave him an impromptu lesson on the definite article and abstract nouns.

I don't know if this memory can possibly be true; it seems too much of a coincidence. I thought perhaps it was just that the woman's voice reminded me so much of you that I had suffered déjà vu. And yet the memory feels to exist independently of that moment last night, so much so that I can remember what you said to the stranger on the grass: 'The narrows down big things, there is ocean and there is the Pacific Ocean, air and the air in one's lungs, love and the love of one's life. Beware of the, it has a tacit manifesto to bound and restrain.'

Your words: *tacit manifesto to bound and restrain*. You said this and then you both stood from the crouch and he went on his way. Whereas the couple outside said nothing of this sort. I thought – but I could be wrong – that the woman said something about being too old to start being the love of someone's life; at her age it was too long a race to start running. She had come here to see old friends, that was all. Am I right about this? That she said she had come to see friends, whom she believed lived here. And the man muttered or swore in a foreign language, or at least in an accent I couldn't recognise. But this was murmured and a floor below, and though I was by then right by the open window I hadn't wanted to stand in front of it or lean through; perhaps I am mad or deluded and overheard wrongly – and yet.

After this they either didn't speak at all or what they said was now more whispered than murmured. It made me wonder if they were holding one another, or whether he had hunched his shoulders in pain or anger and was jabbing his foot at the pavement, or was staring past her at the wall.

I only looked out of the window when I heard the click of the woman's heels along the street, left towards Jimmie's. I put my head out and I saw the man on the other side of the road, standing with his hands in his pockets as if trying to decide which way to go. He looked up at me, then he walked away to the right. Mine is a long street, which you will know if the woman was you, and so when I turned I could see you partway along it, going, like I said, towards the main road with your head down and hands in the pockets of your raincoat. It was one of those elegant raincoats that are belted at the waist. You would be in your early fifties now, but you looked no older than when I last saw you, in any case from behind and at a distance and in the dark. It was your walk and yours alone, the long, loose stride that is nonetheless not flowing but forging. People tend to either flow or forge when they walk, and if they forge they are never loose. They map out their destination, set their stride, and brace and aim. But you – never content, I suppose, to practise convention – you forge loosely. Which is not to say you have a great inbuilt sense of purpose, more that you proceed like a sailing boat pushed forward by a tailwind. The boat is a meanderer, it is the force at its back that makes it look purposeful. The thing chasing it.

I ran downstairs in jeans and T-shirt and whatever shoes were to hand. No, let me pause one more time to tell you what happened before I ran. I took my keys from the chest of drawers in the bedroom and I looked at the pillow and projected a day forward, when Nicolas' face might be half buried there, swampy with jetlag – and a thought occurred to me that seemed to be the first truly religious thought I have ever had. It went: If she is here and he wants her still. It was not, as you see, much of a thought, not even complete. This is how I recognised it as religious – one of those enormous broken offerings we make, someone stammering in front of the Lord. It was a thought that was braver than the person who had it, which is why cowardice stopped the sentence halfway through. If she is here and he wants her still. The rest of the thought had to be had unconsciously, and directed at me as if it had come from a better mind than my own. If she is here and he wants her still – it told me – then you will stand aside and be good enough to let them both go.

Then I picked up the keys and thought, as I went back through the living room, past the escritoire where this letter is kept, that this must be grace, to be defeated by one's better nature. I thought there must be nothing beyond this left to say on the subject, that defeat had come in one passing moment of imagining Nicolas' head so conspiratorial on my pillow – and how sweet it was, and uneventful, and how it shocked me.

I ran downstairs in jeans and T-shirt and whatever shoes. By the time I was out on the pavement there was no sign of you; I ran all the way along until my street met Guilford Street, but by that point you could have gone in any direction – left towards Russell Square, north towards Euston, right towards Gray's Inn Road, which led on to a hundred streets I didn't know at all, and so I stood in the rain for what I suppose was much less than a minute, but felt like ten, peering almost aggressively into the darkness before I gave up. I called out: *Nina?* Your name rushed to my lips like that, and left them warm. And just for a moment the years slipped back to times when it was only us, and you were in that chair in the dark. I thought I would go back and find that man you had left in the rain. I went back, and not only was he not there, but the whole street was empty. I think I have never seen it empty before; it was as if I had imagined not just you, but humankind as a whole, as if I were the last person on Earth.